A THOUSAND MILES OUT OF MY MIND

A THOUSAND MILES OUT OF MY MIND

Grant Sisk

LITERARY PRESS
LAMAR UNIVERSITY

ISBN: 978-1-942956-92-1
Library of Congress Control Number: 2021946244

Lamar University Literary Press
Beaumont, Texas

Acknowledgments

I owe a huge debt to novelist Clay Reynolds, poet Nick Norwood, and Bob, Shawn, Sallie, Jean, Laurie, Wade, Todd, and Kurt, all members of the Denton Alcohol and Tobacco Exchange, a grad-school-era writer's group where this work first began to take shape.

Other fiction from Lamar University Literary Press includes:

Robert Bonazzi, *Awakened by Surprise*
Kevin K. Casey, *Four-Peace*
Jeffrey DeLotto, *A Caddo's Way*
Gerald Duff, *Legends of Lost Man Marsh*
Gerald Duff, *Memphis Mojo*
Dede Fox, *On Wings of Silence: Mexico '68*
Phillip Gardner, *where they come from where they hide*
Andrew Geyer, *Lesser Mountains*
Britt Haraway, *Early Men*
Michael Howarth, *Fair Weather Ninjas*
Gretchen Johnson, *The Joy of Deception and Other Stories*
Dave Kuhne, *Maintaining Texas Pride*
Moumin Quazi, *Migratory Words*
Harold Raley, *Lost River Anthology*
Jim Sanderson, *Trashy Behavior*
Jan Seale, *Appearances*
Melvin Sterne, *Redemption*
Melvin Sterne, *The Shoeshine Boy*

For information on these and other
Lamar University Literary Press books, go to
www.lamar.edu/literarypress

This novel is dedicated to my parents, Bill and Sharon Sisk, who provided my sister Elaine and me with a loving home, an extensive library, a parrot named Alex who flew freely and cageless around the house, dogs, cats, and a host of other unconventional opportunities that encouraged inquisitiveness and allowed the imagination to soar. It is also dedicated to my wife, Heejung, who puts up with me for reasons I will never understand.

Chapter 1

Hurtling west like a madman in a '65 Corvette, with no clue why I stole it and no clue about anything else I'd done, is how this story begins. Motive . . . maybe nothing more than the lure of screaming down a two-lane blacktop, stereo up, top down, while eight massive pistons pounded the refined remnants of prehistoric plants and animals into raw power and an open-throated roar I controlled, and the center stripe melting into a never-ending, golden ribbon. Maybe it was my short and dismal return to the university where my advisor suggested I seek a trade, something that didn't require critical thinking, planning, and impulse control. Mostly, though, I think it was rebellion against my stepfather, who kept insisting that I and everyone else call him "Gianfranco" instead of Ralph like his parents intended.

Over the years, the car's ignition switch had worn down, and as the car surged over a low bump in the road, the key slipped out, hit my knee, and bounced to the floor. Absently fishing around the footwell, I found the key and reinserted it. The car ran without it, but that key belonged where it belonged. Everything has a place in this world, no exceptions. I cast an uneasy sideways glance at the leggy brunette I'd acquired, or more accurately, who'd acquired me, and my thoughts drifted back over the past hours, to north Dallas—home—to Ralph, and to how exactly I'd come to be in possession of this Corvette. And her. Or her of me. Or . . . shit. Whatever.

Chapter 2

So, the backstory is that things had been normal enough: Ralph and I were having one of our typical explosions, and, per usual, I wasn't helping de-escalate, largely because Ralph's tantrums relating to moi always have to do with his image and because I didn't enable it. In brief, the man's whole raison d'être revolves around a single theme: himself. He was with my mom because a couple of years before, right after breakfast, my dad glanced out the window, said "Oh," and died.

Nowhere near long enough after that, she met Ralph and traded down, traded Dad for a larger-than-life ego with motor skills. Old news, I guess. Anyway, the day of the latest fight, he and I were in his new car, a huge land-yacht from Germany that probably cost enough to keep a moderate-sized third world country fed for a year, and he was whining at me about my continued use of his name (Ralph) instead of his adopted alias (Gianfranco). My argument—specifically, that I called him by his name because it was, you know, his name—was, as usual, summarily dismissed. I thought then and still think now that he honestly believes that eventually everyone will know and love him by the name Gianfranco. I also think he's living in denial.

At the time of our exchange, I was riding with him to his office because Mom's car was down and mine had been totaled, all of which had been accomplished in the space of three alcohol-fueled-and-inspired hours the previous week. My plans during this orgy of mechanical violence had included his car also, but I was unable to find it, owing partly to the condition of my faculties, a problem aggravated by my being at the wrong house, on the wrong street, and—in all candor, I must confess—the wrong city. An honorable attempt was made all the same, using a surrogate Mercedes that resembled Ralph's car, and if you'll hang with me, I'll tell you all about it. Maybe. As it fell out, though, the Sun of Fortune had been shining favorably on me all along, or I wouldn't have been driving Ralph to work at his company, Transcontinental Conglomerate, LLP, Inc., which really is just a nationwide chain of DVD and gaming rental stores that, even with all the new video streaming technology, was far from circling the drain.

On the way to his office, we passed Classic Cars of North Dallas, and there, sitting in a pool of light, I saw God in one of His billion manifestations, this one being candy-apple red. I tuned Ralph out as he explained for the umpteenth time why it was unthinkable to undermine the cultivation of his "brand," vitality, and importance by answering to a name as plebeian as Ralph, particularly in public. I craned my neck around to stare at the car and absently muttered "Uh-huh," as the words "PURE SEX" and "YOU BE HAPPY!" flashed in my mind like an opiate billboard in front of a strip joint in Juarez.

Ralph dropped his tirade quicker than usual, mainly because I think he mistook my silent, materialistically-induced contemplation for acquiescence. Regardless, an idea had begun to form in my id, and boy was she a doozy.

Chapter 3

At Ralph's office, I got behind the wheel of $160,000 worth of my stepfather's facade and assured him I'd go straight home. I never spoke a truer word.

Fifteen minutes later, I wheeled into the parking lot of Classic Cars of North Dallas. I parked, walked in, and was pleased to see the floor salesman jump to his feet a little too quickly as he met me at the door. My dad once told me that if you are going to sell something, anything, and want your price, act like you couldn't care less how things turn out. The salesman, though, didn't subscribe to that philosophy. But I do and found that the same rule applies to Grand Theft Auto. Writ Large.

I put on my best "spoiled college kid" act (not too hard after seven years of on-the-job training) and lied to the salesman, i.e., that I'd been driving this boat around for the past six weeks and wanted to trade it in on something a little more practical, safe, and low key, like that bright red convertible Corvette with the enormous 327 V-8, leather interior, and every other option known to God and man in the Year of Our Lord, 1965. He said he understood, but that ordinarily they didn't take trade-ins that were worth more than the vehicle they were selling and wouldn't pay out the difference. I said that, from where I was standing, the Corvette and the Mercedes looked to be about equal in value, if one took into account such variables as top speed, wind resistance, ease of parking, and the overall historical context, sex appeal, and divinity, all of which were heavily weighted in the Corvette's favor. The salesman nodded, and I was about to throw in the Holocaust as more evidence against the Mercedes, but before he could say anything, the opening bars to the theme song of *The Good, the Bad and the Ugly* filled the room. My cell phone. I excused myself, got in the car, rolled up the window, and answered.

"Hello?"

"Colin?" Ralph asked.

"Ralph?" Riposte mine, missing nary a beat.

"You home yet?"

"Just hit the last stretch. There's Mrs. Wilson's cat still stretched out on the street. I figured Animal Control would have been out by—"

"Yeah, okay, Colin, stop. Please. Look and see if my billfold is in the glovebox."

I looked in the center console first, more on principle than any expectation of finding it. I hate following his orders. It wasn't there, so I checked the glovebox and, sure enough, there was the object in question, a three-inch-by-five-inch piece of Ralph's wardrobe that had cost him 300 bucks but cost the alligator its entire life.

"Yeah, it's here," I answered.

Ralph sighed. "Good. Can you run it back up here? I have a lunch meeting and no casholine. It's got all my credit cards in it."

This was an interesting new development.

"Sure thing, Gianfranco."

"Excuse me?"

"On it!"

Just as I heard "Thanks, son—" I hung up.

A brief perusal of the wallet's contents yielded an inventory of one key to the locker Ralph kept at the airport, six Visa and/or Mastercards, two ATM cards, and one American Express card, Black. Definitely an interesting new development. I got out of the car and addressed the salesman.

"That was my old man. He wants me to quit screwing around up here and bring the car to his office. He said, if you don't mind, I'll just leave the Benzo as collateral, and, if you do mind, blow it off and he'd talk to a friend of his down in Houston."

"Well, ordinarily, our company policy dictates that the salesman accompanies the prospective customer on the test drive to, ah, answer any questions he might have, but I, ah, don't see why we can't accommodate your father." He looked very happy.

"Stepfather."

"Pardon me?"

I shrugged. "Nevermind. Key?" I asked.

"Of course. A minute," he said brightly.

He came back with the key, and I explained that my stepdad was paranoid about buying cars because he didn't know the first thing about them, so if it was okay, we would keep it overnight and have our mechanic look it over. He seemed a little hesitant until I suggested that he call the police and have them verify that the Mercedes was ours. About that time, a manager wandered over, asked what was going on, and when I told him what I wanted, I could see the wheels turning. He figured he was about to make 20k on top of the Vette's asking price and said calling the police wouldn't be necessary. I got back into the Mercedes, got the wallet, and snagged a pair of Maui Jim sunglasses and an unopened envelope from Valero. On closer inspection, it proved to contain a Valero Platinum card. I figured it might come in handy, especially since Ralph probably didn't know he had it. Then I called Ralph to explain that I'd be a little late because I'd had a flat and the guy at AAA auto club said it'd be at least an hour or so before he could get to me.

Ralph was put out, but I apologized profusely and hung up. I got out of the car, hopped in the Vette, and asked one of the floor guys to clean the windshield. I wanted it bright and clear; I didn't adjust the rearview mirror.

And just like that, God and I hit the hot top.

Chapter 4

My first official act after committing Grand Theft Auto was to add larceny to my ever-growing resume of felonies. I stopped at the first ATM machine I saw and punched in the access code that Ralph had thoughtfully penciled on the card's slip cover. "Access denied." I thought about it for a minute and reversed the sequence. Bingo. Sneaky boy. Good thing the card didn't fall into the wrong hands. They'd probably have gotten it right the first time. I took a peek at Ralph's checking account and was delighted to see that he had a little over $27,000 available for immediate gratification, though according to the machine, I could only withdraw $1100 per transaction. I thought about going into to the bank and trying to get it all at once, but figured there was no way in hell that'd work without them calling Ralph, so I resigned myself to frenetic driving all over town and acquiring a callous on my index finger.

After hitting about ninety-seven machines, I had all of it in twenties, fifties, and Benjies, and a healthy dose of paranoia. The only thing I hadn't done was raid his locker at the airport. That had to count for something. I thought about returning the car and giving Ralph his money back, and probably should have, which in retrospect would have been a simple fix, though at the time it didn't seem so simple, and anyway, a voice in the back of my mind kept saying, "I want!" Beyond that, I'd had to call the bank and impersonate Ralph to make them release the money, as the flurry of activity had made them lock the account a couple of times. I explained that, as I had earned the money and chosen to deposit it in their bank, I felt what I did with it and how I chose to do whatever I did with it was my concern and not theirs. The clerk told me she thought it was irresponsible, before she hung up, though not before I made her transfer me to her manager, who promised to approve any and all upcoming withdrawals.

While hitting this ATM and then that one, I had occasion to be glad that Ralph had underestimated my involvement with his company. I didn't have a regular position because, though he wanted me to work so that I wouldn't be spoiled, his ego couldn't bear the weight of having a stepson who worked side by side with his employees. So mostly I just sort of hung around and talked to everybody, except for twice a month when I had to conduct Cognizant Enlightenment Trainings, which were canned Power Point slide presentations that Ralph bought from some online consulting firm. On the surface, it looked like a good idea. According to the training manual, it was an "integrated training course designed to help stakeholders perform better by reinforcing good skills, value additive techniques, and best practices . . . to help while servicing clients." Unfortunately, they were long on promises and buzz words and short in terms of anything useful. Unless, of course, one needed buzz words, although I thought "servicing" meant something pretty specific, which wasn't our line of business. But who cares? The result was that the employees hated sitting through the courses as much I hated delivering them, as most people really don't want or need a 5-hour Power Point refresher course on things they should have learned in the second grade. Add the fact that obviously the same person or persons (read Team) were responsible for inflicting this on the general public, and you were left with a series of largely redundant presentations that covered the most obvious topics and used the same photos and images again and again, albeit to highlight different points. One that I swear I must have seen a thousand times was this picture of three men and three women—a team—earnest and well-groomed, huddled around a table. Sometimes the caption informed us that this was "A Team in Crisis," other times, "Performing! A Team in Sync!" One was a group of mountain climbers, all roped together and trudging through knee-deep snow. The caption had the required "TEAM EFFORT!" but underneath was, "The team on top of the mountain didn't fall there!" and had always led me to think uncomfortably about the Andes flight disaster and the fact that falling, coupled with bad choices, was exactly how that team wound up on top of the mountain.

When we weren't looking at duplicate slides over and over, desperately trying to figure out what the Power Point "team" was up to, we'd likely be looking at an unfamiliar slide that made no sense at all: a dilapidated barn in a weed-choked field with the caption "Teamwork! Teamwork!" What? The barn was full of hay, and a team put it there?

16

Maybe a team needed to get together and mow the pasture, repair the barn, and then paint it red? Who knows? I won't even go into the sound effects except to ask this: Why use a machine gun noise to accompany words popping up on the screen? Hopefully, you get the point. Thus, in an effort to blunt the pain caused by all of this—and because I wanted to be liked—I decided that my real function at the company was as a sort of goodwill ambassador between Ralph and everyone else. As liaison between the two entities, I felt it was my duty to receive and disseminate information, as well as do what I could to help ease tensions at the office, make it a better place to work. That sort of thing.

One of my ideas in that area was "Memorandum 13," which I dreamed up, wrote up, and loaded up from Ralph's computer in his office. As with many policies that are generated in offices, it didn't really mean anything, but in this instance, that is what made it a stroke of genius.

Memorandum 13 was a form memo that read:

Until further notice, all operations in _____ will continue as before, utilizing the same processes and procedures, but must be approved by this office.
Gianfranco, President

Naturally, this caused no end of confusion and slowed down whatever project it was thrown into, by a good six days. Let's say that Betty, Ralph's secretary, suddenly needed to go somewhere for the weekend, but she also had a big job to complete. Instead of having to rearrange her plans or beg for a last-minute vacation approval, all she had to do was type the name of her department into the Memo 13 form, print it up, drop it in her "To Do" box, then go ask Ralph what the deal was. When questioned, Ralph, ever reluctant to admit he had no idea, always took credit for putting the memo in there. Then Betty would bring everything she was working on and give it to Ralph for approval, who would keep it on average about three days before "approving" it. It was a nice set-up, and to be honest, wasn't really abused. Well, not much anyway.

Unexpectedly, useful information began to trickle back to me in the form of questions about goings on at the office, though for the most part, gossipy in nature. But one day, a question hit my inbox: "Why does your stepfather keep so much dollars in a locker at Dallas-Fort Worth airport?" That one came from Ernesto de la Paz in Accounting and seemed good, so I emailed him back, saying I had no idea but would make sure nothing fraudulent was going on. He agreed and coordinated with Jagger Alfson in Facilities, got me the padlock key, and in less than three hours, I was at DFW airport, key in hand, standing in front of a locker Ralph had leased. So I checked it out.

The answer, like so many that deal with Ralph, was simple: he'd watched some gangster flick in his office when he should've been working, and the hero's survival depended on getting money he'd stashed in an airport. To Ralph, it looked like a good idea. Made sense to me too, especially now.

I put all the cash I'd taken from the bank accounts into a grocery sack, but decided to leave the money at the airport alone. Afterwards, I went to NorthPark Mall where I walked around for a little while, trying to figure out what to do next. I went into Dillard's and put twenty-dollar bills in the pockets of ten or fifteen dresses. I bought everybody's breakfast at La Madeleine. I checked the bridal registry at Neiman Marcus and sent Durian-scented (what fool would even think of that?) candles to everyone listed. Instead of perking up, though, I was blue and getting bluer. When Vanna, the manager at La Madeleine, refused to give me forty dollars' worth of dimes for the wishing well, I decided it was time to leave town for a day or two.

On my way out, I passed a hipster store named Bone and Wool, turned around, and walked in. Every piece of clothing, every gadget, and whatever else the urban adventurer who'd never adventured could ever possibly want was in there. A salesgirl walked up and asked if she could help.

"Sure," I said.

"What are you looking for today? We have a sale—"

I cut her off. "It's my birthday, and my parents are in New Zealand doing environmental work—"

"Neat!" she interrupted.

"Whatever. Anyway, they called to say that there was some problem with the gorillas being poached or some kind of rare eggs being stolen—I forget which—and they can't make it home for my birthday." I looked at her closely. She seemed to be buying all of this so far. I don't know why I lied. It just seemed like the right thing to do.

"I am so, so sorry," she said in a sort of whiny-aggressive voice. She wasn't a bad liar herself. I felt a connection.

"So, they told me to go and buy a bunch of stuff. Clothes. Stuff. And here I am, the dutiful son."

She laughed. "Well, we have all of our summer shirts on sale—"

"They expressly forbid me to buy anything on sale."

She cocked her head to the side and squinted for a moment, but recovered quickly. "No problem. What's your name?"

I told her.

"Okay, Colin. Right this way."

I don't know if she was a good salesperson, but I honestly thought I'd need all that stuff. By the time Ralph was, unknowingly, ready to pay up, a small crowd had gathered to watch. There were lumberjack-style shirts, skinny chinos, denim jeans, and pants and socks and boots and belts strewn all over the counter. A compass and some kind of steel and stone firestarter. There were things I don't remember picking out and things I knew no name for. It was cool. While she totaled it, I saw a pair of jeans that were $300.

She hit a button and the register showed $7517.59. Her eyes widened a bit, maybe in shock, maybe in pleasure. Before she said anything, I asked if the jeans really were $300, and after checking the tag, she said they were.

"Take them off?" she asked.

"Okay, but I'll need to put them on first," I said. Someone groaned behind me.

"Off the total?"

"Nah," I said. "It's only one-fifty per leg."

She grinned and asked if there would be anything else. I started to say no, but then I remembered the young fortune I had stowed in the grocery bag. I asked if they had any money belts, and some guy behind me said that was one thing I probably wouldn't need. Impulsively, I pulled most of the transaction slips I'd gotten from the teller machines out of my hip pocket and asked him to hold them; they looked like a small phone book. She said, yeah, they had money belts, but when she brought one, the tag said it'd only hold $500 in twenties. It wasn't big enough, so I bought two. Then I looked over the counter and saw a big, waxed-cotton duffle bag.

"Give me that," I said. I looked over my shoulder for the guy who had all my receipts, but he was gone. She totaled it again, and I gave her one of Ralph's credit cards. She ran it through the machine, and it cleared.

19

"Come again soon, Colin, or Ralph, or whoever" she called as I turned to leave. The store manager carried everything out to my car and told me I'd made his whole month. He was a very happy man.

I was happy too, because, you know, I aim to please.

Chapter 5

I cruised down the expressway, soaking up the sun and the envious stares from the young execs in their BMWs, Infiniti, Lexus, and other luxe brand cars . . . men, women, and undecided headed full-tilt into maximum credit extension, double mortgages, and lives of anxiety because, among other things, they really meant to make good on their commitments. Dead fish behind tinted glass. I wondered if those cars came with steering wheels. The roadside shops weren't a distraction until I noticed one named "Condoms to Go." Wondering what I'd missed, I imagined myself walking in, making my selections, and then being asked by the salesman or salesgirl, "Will that be to go?" Oh dear. The implications were, shall we say, enormous. After that, I spotted a billboard picturing some guy named "Father Amoco," who was peddling low-cost insurance and dressed like a clergyman. Then another billboard sporting an anorexic model, who was howling into the camera and obviously on methamphetamine; she was selling kids furniture. I sped up.

By now, my immediate destiny had taken shape—albeit an abstract one—in my mind. This led directly to my next stop at Bill's Record Store where—regardless of the fact that my smart phone had literally tens of thousands of songs on it—I charged a few hundred dollars' worth of CDs, from Otis Redding to The Gourds, The Clash, Gary Clark Jr., Turnpike Troubadours, Henry Thomas, Jason and the Scorchers, My Morning Jacket, Sonvolt, Johnny Cash, Bob Dylan, and a bunch of others I'd never heard of. Some random Japanese girl band called Babymetal. Richard O'Brien. I figured that would just about cover the whole emotional (and technological) spectrum in pursuit of what I decided was the only justification for breaking loose in such a stupid and clearly futile way.

Mission: A cross country drive towards my grandparent's house in Oregon, in search of the perfect road trip. Goal: Goal? I pointed my newly acquired modus mechanicus due west and floored it.

Chapter 6

As with many journeys that begin with that painful first step, mine was delayed and beset by obstacles from the start. About halfway between Dallas and Fort Worth, the Texas Department of Transportation decided to shut westbound I-30 down from four lanes to about three quarters of one lane, creating a traffic jam that looked as if it might stretch into the next century. I checked the navigation app on my phone, and the map just showed a line of red as far as I could scroll. The top speed was about twelve-and-a-half mph. This was going to take a long, long time, and though I had nowhere to be and no set time to be there, I didn't want to be behind schedule. I had paired the Bluetooth to the car stereo earlier, but even though I wasn't out of the metroplex, it was starting to get spotty. At first it was just a missing word or beat, but then whole sections of songs began to evaporate so I switched to Sirius satellite radio. The first station I chose had some senator or representative named Billy Stan Freeburgh howling about greed, immorality, indecency, and, as far as I could tell, everything else America stands for.

"The Devil's taken a seat in the Guvenment!" he cried. "It's time we jumped up and stamped him out! Stamp that Satan out!"

I agreed and changed the station.

His tirade continued. "Make a donation of the money the Lord's been givin' so I can send that old Devil back to the Pit where he belongs. Make him stop hasslin' decent folk!"

I looked at the radio to make sure I'd punched a different button, and yes, I had. I changed to another station and then another. Between station changes, the words I missed in his diatribe didn't amount to one short sentence. I switched back to AM radio, and Billy Stan Freeburgh's voice chased me there too and resumed the assault, seemingly unreduced by the narrower bandwidth and loss of high-fidelity stereo . . . though it was a tad flatter, like he was preaching from inside a tin can.

It turns out that he'd managed to coerce his congregants into donating enough money to buy simultaneous air time on every radio station, AM and FM, satellite, you name it, for a two-hour harangue, which might explain why streaming tunes wasn't working so well—lots of folks who ordinarily were listening to sports, talk radio, and news must have been fleeing BSF. Then again, I had to admire his style; that's a lot of money to get what you want.

I put in a CD, turned up the volume, and began enjoying the view. I crept past Six Flags amusement park and remembered all the fun I used to have when my dad took me there. I could tell already this trip was going to do me good . . . if TxDot would just open up about twelve more lanes.

I finally hit Fort Worth—"Cowtown"—in exactly five hours and twelve minutes. A little later, I was on the western edge of Weatherford and figured I'd traveled about seventy miles. The highway was still shut down to one lane, ostensibly for purposes of repair, but I never saw one work crew. Just eight million cones separating me and the other drivers from those other two lanes that were clean, free clear, and led to the promised land, or somewhere close.

Pointlessly obeying needless intrusions on my pleasure isn't a trait that describes me, so I sidled between two cones and onto open road. Just as the Vette had spooled up to cruising speed, passing cone-locked cars, trucks, RVs, etc., near disaster struck. A large square of highway-less highway was looming on the horizon. TxDOT had removed what looked to be about a thirty-foot-long chunk of road. Thoughtful. Jumping on the brakes, the car slid to a stop right on the absolute lip of the void, a massive rectangle of concrete gone, cut clean and straight, like a knife, a laser concrete-cutting knife, five or six car lengths long, two feet deep, and all the way across the lane I was in. The stream of cars to my right honked, people jeered, cell phones appeared and I was videoed, and presumably uploaded to YouTube, Facebook, Instagram, the NSA—no telling. Within seconds, my phone began blowing up with texts and Facebook pings from all my "friends"—many I couldn't have positively identified if they were in my living room—asking if I had a new car, what was up, why was I sitting on the side of the road, everything except, "Are you okay?" or "Do you need help?" I sat there feeling like a fool while the procession, well, you know, processed. After an hour, an old, gray-haired woman in a blown-out, thirty-year-old pickup stopped, looked at me hard, then motioned me to cut in while everyone behind her honked and revved their motors.

Chastened, I drove more slowly and noticed the landscape change. As the cars thinned out, so did the green vegetation of north Texas as it faded to the dry, brown-yellow of the west, and the soil bloomed gradually from black to red, while the variety of trees dwindled down to scrub cedar, Mesquite, and not much else, stunted, tough vegetation stretching as far as the eye could see. No more grassy, rolling fields, just flat, arid country. Gradually, all there was to see was sandy dirt, Mesquite trees, cacti, and the occasional tumbleweed as it rolled brazenly across the highway.

I kept driving, and eventually the Department of Transportation relinquished another lane, bringing the total count up to two. The Vette's exhaust smelled like varnish. It was running rough and getting terrible mileage, so I stopped for gas at a Valero, the versatility of which impressed me no end. I wandered around inside in a sort of daze. I'd never really paid that much attention to how far gas station technology had pushed the envelope, but one could literally live in one of these. Food, drinks, magazines, postcards, even clothes—of a sort—were all available and in quantity. A sign read: "Everything you need to customize your vehicle." And sure enough, it was true, or at least true enough to be true. They even sold gas and oil. At that moment, I vowed to stop at Valero early and often, and from thenceforth did, sometimes for nothing at all, just to look around. They all had signs on their gas pumps stating, "Anything in the store may be purchased with your Valero card," and I was eager to do so.

The hundred-mile-long traffic jam and the attendant problems it created had really slowed me down. But beside my newfound glee in discovering Valero, it was nada. One thing I was certain of: while I didn't know exactly where I was, I was way ahead of schedule.

Night fell, but there was no need to stop. I had a new old car, enough new clothes with me to stock a small store, and other necessities. Life was good. While driving along after dark, I was struck by how visually accurate some of the old movies are. My mom used to love old Cary Grant, James Stewart, Clark Gable, or old Anybody movies, and even though I loved watching them with her, I'd make a big deal about how when they were driving at night, you could tell it was phony because the road in the rear window looked fake, like some couple was sitting on a couch making clever conversation while all this blue-tinged scenery fell away behind them into the distance. Driving that first night, though, and glancing more than usual in the rearview mirror, it was there, just like the movies, blurred scenery being sucked from the car while the road weaved back and forth in the middle. I'd always thought the color was a dead giveaway too, but that night, driving from nothing to nowhere while the full moon howled down, it was the color of the movies: perfect. Then again, maybe it's always a full moon in the movies.

Later that night, as I came barreling up on another of the countless eighteen-wheelers, the idea of reaching out and touching one as I passed seemed worthwhile. I don't know why. As the next one hove into view, sudden, dark, and massive, I whipped over into the right lane, slowed down, eased the Vette close, and as we each drifted in our lanes, I reached out and just barely brushed the side of the trailer with my fingertips.

An electric shock arced through my arm and deep into my shoulder. At first, I thought I was injured. I swerved away, stretched my arm out, and looked as if I'd never seen it before. Static electricity made the hairs stand straight out, and sparks arced between my fingers. It was incredible; the truck had pulsed and throbbed beneath my touch, like a live animal.

Not the wisest—maybe not the dumbest—thing I've done, but for the rest of that night, it's how I occupied myself, driving, stalking truck after truck after truck—and one motorhome—counting coup on the highway.

About ten p.m., I stopped at a Valero truck stop in Ranger and filled up, got some coffee and a box of chocolate doughnuts, and, as the night was getting chilly, pulled a safari jacket out of the heap. I got back to the road and drove, letting my mind wander—why didn't I buy the pith helmet?—and jamming along on auto-pilot as the small hours crept past.

Chapter 7

I knew I was getting farther from civilization because the roadkill kept getting bigger and bigger. In the old days, when cartographers hit the end of their leash and inscribed "Here be Dragons," they weren't entirely mistaken. Having just swerved to miss an unidentifiable mass of grease and hair, The Vacationers got in front of me again. I'd first encountered them back in the traffic jam where, inexplicably, they'd managed to inch past me. For nearly 200 miles, they'd been my punishment, my gadflies, my harpies in a Winnebago, always drifting into the lane I wanted, slowing down for every corner, bush, bridge, tree, fence, you-name-it, and keeping me within a mile or two below the speed limit. As we came to towns or gas stations, anything, I'd floor it and get around them and still, within an hour or so, after gas, coffee, any short break, I'd look up in time to see them flummoxing down the road, ahead of me again. Some people spend their lives looking for truth or beauty—all noble pursuits—but for me, to find just one who knew how those who drive slower always end up ahead would leave me content. I'd stay to learn wisdom.

As it was, there was no one to unpack the mystery for me. In the night, I took a wrong turn, and after several hours of oblivious driving, wound up in Van Horn, Texas. There was a little Mexican restaurant just off the road, and though the lights were on and all looked normal, it was vacant. Maybe they were closed and didn't see a need to lock the place. Who knows? It seemed to be empty, but the margarita machine was whirring along, twisting up concoctions, and a neon Modelo beer sign flickered and buzzed sporadically. A mural on the wall depicted the outside of the restaurant and featured John Madden, a massive tour bus, and what would amount to about a 3500-foot-tall Jesus Christ with outstretched arms towering over all. Looking around, I spotted a large black cat looking through me from the counter, and I decided it was time to keep on keeping on.

Chapter 8

Outside of town a sign read:

El Paso

115 Miles

I pulled over and studied the sign. El Paso. The name sounded familiar, nostalgic. Maybe we'd taken a family trip years before that included doing time there. Thinking it over, and as El Paso and I were on the same road, it seemed logical to head that way. As I began to wheel back onto the road, a guy in a dune-beige Landcruiser with oversized tires and a loud radio blasted by, maybe six inches from the car, turned in his seat, and flipped me off. Nice. I guess he was in the Navy, because the spare tire cover sported a skull and crossbones with "Sub T-16" written underneath. I looked up and down the highway. Seeing no other traffic for about six hundred miles, I eased off the shoulder and headed the direction the sign pointed.

Soon there was no trace of anything except dirt and rocks, some more dirt and more rocks. And cacti. I guess. Regardless, all indications suggested that when the settlers rolled through, they kept moving.

Rounding a corner, I passed a fenced-in field that was lit up in brutal detail by huge klieg·lights. I slowed down to get a better look, then stopped entirely. There were twenty or thirty ostriches running, doing what looked like wind sprints. The giant birds would race to one end of the field, and when they could go no farther, would stop, turn, and tear en masse to the other end. Most perplexing. They seemed particularly intent on avoiding a bunch of bright orange scarecrows that were interspersed throughout the field. Scarecrows. It seemed more than a little bizarre to coop up a bunch of Volkswagen-sized birds with an apparatus used for centuries to terrorize, well, birds. I slammed the car back into gear and drove, intent on putting distance between myself and this sick alchemy. Scarecrows and ostriches are a dangerous mix, and I had no desire to be around when the last straw broke and a bunch of deeply disturbed, pointlessly provoked, and thoroughly badass beasts that clock in at four hundred pounds apiece came flapping and howling across the wire. Ask Johnny Cash.

Exhausted but determined to make it to El Paso, I kept driving. My head felt like it weighed a couple hundred pounds, and the muscles in my neck were cramped and burning. My eyelids had an agenda of their own, opening and closing involuntarily and, in short, refusing to behave. Still, El Paso was out there, and I tried to keep going by telling myself how good a hot shower and a big air-conditioned room was gonna feel. But my eyes wouldn't cooperate, so I compromised, shutting one for a moment, then the other, then drifted into sleep, off the road, and into a flat spin that jerked me suddenly into shrieking consciousness, out of control and without options. I pounded the brakes and gripped the steering wheel that was as useless as a rudder on a spaceship. The Corvette, bucking and pitching like a loco mustang, came to a stop. I looked around and saw nothing but stars and swirling dust sifting earthward. Then I lay sideways across the front seats and slowly faded into sleep.

Chapter 9

Funny thing about summer in the desert, "the rosy-finger'd dawn" doesn't creep from its bed gradually. It vaults into the sky with the fervor of a newly ordained Jesuit. One minute you're blissfully asleep, awash in the smell of vinyl and gasoline, then—*bam!*—the sun pops up from behind a clump of rocks like a bandito while your brain frantically seeks to twist your pupils shut before the inside of your head is sunburned. For the rest of the day, when you close your eyes for a moment, two black suns swim around the backside of your eyelids.

Of course, I don't sleep with my eyes open, so it wasn't a problem. I just thought I'd mention it. Anyway, I got out of the car and appraised the situation. All things considered, if choice had actually been in the mix, I couldn't have chosen a better place to run off the highway. The land was flat and dry as a silica pancake. The car was in good shape with no serious damage. As por moi, stiff from the previous night's drive, my hands stung when I flexed them, and closer inspection revealed that the little creases on the backs of my knuckles were actually sunburned.

I got in the Vette and she fired right up. A couple hundred yards of barbed wire fence pointed in a straight line from the front of the car back to the highway, and I had a bit of trouble but finally untangled the wire and back-followed the trail I'd blazed the night before.

On the road again, I looked the car over from stem to stern, and the only noticeable damage was a few scratches and the occasional tuft of vegetation protruding from the undercarriage. I drove for an hour, getting hotter and ever thirstier, with no recollection of the last Valero I'd passed. I saw a rest stop and pulled in.

It was made entirely of Portland cement and was a huge heat sink, but as some dimwit somewhere would doubtless observe, "It was a dry heat." Regardless, it offered shade and had a water hose and a bathroom, all of which I availed myself of. I drank some of the water and then stripped down to my boxers, hosed myself down, and scrubbed the grit off with my shirt. While I air dried, I rinsed off the car, then changed into a new pair of khaki pants, white linen shirt, and Jesus sandals. I felt clean, waterlogged, and benevolent, so I stretched out on one of the concrete tables for a nap that wound up lasting the whole day.

Around 5:00 p.m., fully rested and ready to get going, I pulled onto the highway, headed west.

Nightfall found me entering the small town of Alpine, and I stopped at a Valero, filled up, bought two or three packets of No-Doz, some mints, and a deep-fried burrito, and asked for a cheap motel.

And because of my sins, they told me where to find one.

Chapter 10

Walking into the lobby, the night manager eyed me suspiciously and asked why I was there. I looked at him for a moment and then stated the obvious: I wanted a room.

"Single or a double?"

"Oh, I'm single but I'm sleeping double," I chirped. It's true; I was feeling a bit giddy and couldn't wait to be between some sheets. He looked at me and curled his lip back over his front teeth, which were yellowed and tobacco stained. We seemed to be at a sudden impasse.

"Whatever you've got will be fine," I said.

"This is America, boy. Men fought and died so even no-count people like you could have a choice. Now, what you want?" he asked as if he doubted I knew, which wasn't entirely off the mark.

"Give me a single, then."

He looked at me coldly for a moment, but didn't make any move towards the key rack.

We looked at each other, and a few of those two-minute seconds passed.

"A double?"

"Man wants a double, the man gets a double." He went about the business of filling out various forms, waivers, and what have you, while I pretended to look over the assortment of postcards that were in a rack by the counter. Even though my attention was mostly on him, it was difficult not to pick up the general theme. They all said things like "Visit Historic Lubbock" or "I Left my Heart in San Antone" or, my personal favorite, "The sun has riz the sun has set, yet here we is, in Texas yet."

I kept looking but never saw anything that even remotely hinted at the existence of Alpine.

"How many of them postcards you want?"

"Oh, uh, two, I guess." This was met with disapproval. "Four." We stared at each other. A clock ticked thunderously from the wall. "Five?"

He nodded in agreement. I picked out five postcards. Two Austins, one San Antonio, an Amarillo, and a Lubbock rounding it out. On my way out the door, I was struck with a thought.

"You don't happen to own any ostriches, do you?" He looked at me as if I had just calmly walked in and suggested that we drive up to the capitol and kidnap the governor. I smiled and shrugged my shoulders. "Guess not."

As I turned to go, he said, "I might could rustle one up for the right price." Before I could say anything, he nodded and said, "You let me know."

Chapter 11

One thing the motel had going for it was a bar. Sort of. Despite the name, Brewster is a dry county, so all the bars are classified as "private clubs." At any rate, they did serve drinks, and for the small fee of four dollars and fifty cents, I became a lifetime "club member entitled to all the rights and privileges thereunto entitled." Exactly what the rights and privileges were or are was never fully explained to me. If I had to make a guess, though, I would think that, for me at least, the r.'s and p.'s basically were the right to sit in a strange town and enjoy the privilege of drinking with even stranger people that I would have crossed the street to avoid passing. All my life, if so desired. I got a table away from the other patients, and after the waitress had taken my order, I began a quick review of the last forty-eight or so hours. The tally: I'd stolen a car, either the Mercedes or the Corvette, depending on who you asked—actually both—drained my stepfather's bank account, and driven close to seven hundred miles on the first leg of a cross-country trip to nowhere for no reason.

I couldn't remember the last time I'd been to visit my grandparents and couldn't really remember anything concrete about either of them and had no idea how to find their old place when—if—I got there.

I called the waitress back and told her to bring me the "New Drink" that, according to a hand-lettered sign hanging at an angle behind the bar, they were "Prod to serve." The sign looked like one of those ransom notes that are cut out of all kinds of different magazines and pasted together: no two letters alike either in size or color. She brought it over, and I could feel the blood rising in my face from embarrassment. It was in a huge vase-shaped glass and was about fourteen different colors. An umbrella was stuck into the top of it for decoration or purposes of humiliation. Everyone was staring from me to the drink and back to me. Conversations ceased and an air of expectation settled over the crowd. I took a sip and everyone kept watching, waiting for my reaction. A baby—yep, in the bar—started to cry but was swiftly silenced. It really wasn't a bad cocktail at all, and taking another sip, I settled back into my chair. My waitress was still hanging around, so I asked what all the attention from the crowd was for.

"Oh, they just wanted to see what you'd do."

I didn't quite follow and conveyed this to her.

"Well, you're the first person to try one of those things."

"Uh-huh. Out of curiosity, who decided to offer it? Did they try it?"

She studied me for a moment, as if the question had never crossed her mind, then looked toward the kitchen. I followed her gaze. A man who looked to be in his mid-thirties and wearing a hairnet over his jet-black hair peered intently at us through an oblong window. She turned back to me and then jerked her head back toward the kitchen. "Him," she said. "Jesus. He's always looking up recipes and stuff on Google."

"Oh. Well, I hope no one was disappointed," I said. "Especially Jesus."

The waitress took me at my word and hurried to assure me that no feelings had been hurt.

"It's just that it's such a funny lookin' drink, and most a the reglars is callin' it the Fag Detector, on account a its bein' so . . ." She stopped abruptly when she realized the magnitude of her faux pas.

"Yeah, I don't think we're supposed to use that word," I replied.

"I didn't, uh, I shouldn't a said that, and I didn't mean that orderin' that makes you a queer or nothin' . . ."

"That one either."

Telling her it was okay and not the first time, I asked her when last call was, and she said midnight. I sat around drinking and calculating for a couple more hours. Around 11:30, I called her over and ordered Fag Detectors for everyone, extra umbrellas, and told her to tell everyone they were from a secret admirer. Then I paid in full—$135, even with an extra tithe for Jesus—and as I was leaving, the first few carafes were arriving at the tables, much to the horror of the occupants.

When I paid for my room the following morning, the desk clerk asked me if I had slept well and if anything had disturbed me. He seemed to already know the answer and acted surprised when I told him I'd gotten one of the best nights of sleep of my life.

"Nothing bothered you?"

"No."

"No sirens?"

"No sirens, no."

"No screaming?"

"Not that I recall."

"Gunshots, horns honking, police radios, and fire trucks?"

"Zippo. Why do you ask?"

"Hell of a brawl in the bar last night. Right around close."

"Really? Were there any ostriches?"

He just looked at me and turned away. "Nada" he said.

Chapter 12

Next to the motel was a little roadside trailer serving breakfast burritos and scalding black coffee. Eating in the car and dripping hot sauce all over the upholstery while looking at the map app on my phone revealed I was sort of—big time—going the wrong direction. No bueno. So, I got back on the road to the town of old El Paso—which, incidentally, is on Mountain Standard Time—and took Highway 85, headed for Las Cruces, New Mexico.

The sign in Texas correctly stated that Las Cruces was 35 miles from El Paso. Once in the Land of Enchantment, however, information as to one's whereabouts became increasingly rare and downright whimsical, until it was replaced by a weird form of state propagated disinformation. Though it's true that I had the vaguest of itineraries and my "methods" of following them even more so, knowing which towns lay ahead and how far could have been valuable intel. However, sadly, and invariably, just as a sign hove into view, shimmering through heatwaves and the incoherent medium of untraveled space and time, hope always sprang to the fore. Speeding ahead, I'd lean into the front glass to decipher the letters, but that hope was inevitably dashed. Yet on I drove, past ancient hamlets, through dusty and dangerous crossroads and the New Mexico Highway Department road signs that informed myself and others of upcoming rest stops or historical markers, the former an erection of cinder blocks and cement, the latter almost always a pile of rocks, an arroyo, a mesa . . . sometimes a cross.

After seven hours of expecting this but getting that, I reached the conclusion that New Mexico should be fenced off from the rest of the United States and renamed "The Land of Disenchantment." New Mexico seems to be possessed of the philosophy that if you're not local, you don't belong . . . not necessarily a bad philosophy. Or maybe they just don't buy into the "Good Samaritan" mode of thinking. Then again, just maybe, they know that some folks get tired of wandering around in the wasteland like the Children of Israel, so they give up and stay, keeping the population up.

A dull orange glow to the west indicated that the end of the world was at hand, or maybe nightfall. Magdalena was a few miles out and seemed as good a place as any to face either, but watching the sun tuck soft behind the horizon, it seemed no immediate Apocalypse was at hand. Tired, hungry, a little let down, I pulled into the first diner, ate something, I guess, and then checked into a motel. The hot shower was nice and the bed soft, but I was coiled up like a new spring and sleep wouldn't, couldn't, come. After a couple hours of tossing and turning, I dressed and went outside to the car. I slipped behind the steering wheel, switched the radio on, and after fumbling the dial around, found XERF 1570, broadcasting way down in Mexico, across the border from Del Rio, wherever the hell that is. It was a mixed bag, but I did hear a ZZ Top song or two and some other country blues like my mom likes. Later, the program changed to a low and steady monologue in Spanish that was soothing, though I couldn't understand more than the occasional word.

It didn't seem like it, though, but time did pass while I listened to the voice from the wilderness, and the moon was considerably lower in the sky as the station reduced power to obey whatever rules they must and eventually faded to static. I thought about it for a moment, maybe longer, then started the Vette and pulled out onto Highway 60, headed west for Quemado. There was really nothing else to do.

Chapter 13

The country was vast and silent, and I imagined stars heaped like white-hot slag against the flanks of the buttes that pushed up from the red rock and sand, hard edges and angles diffused and softened by a ground fog. But the sun rose, that other star, and its pale light was robbed of all power by clouds that clung to the land and a cloak-thick mist which yielded only briefly as I passed through, only to close again seamlessly behind me.

I had been lost for hours while the fog beaded in huge droplets on the windshield and soaked my hair. The desert possessed an unreal quality, tranquility alongside menace in a way I'd never felt before but hoped to feel again.

The phone was fully charged, filled with apps for everything, but with no signal it was utterly useless. I stopped at a crossroads and noticed for the first time railroad tracks running parallel to the highway. I yanked out a road atlas that I'd bought for the hell of it and tried to figure out where I was. The map showed Quemado to be about 70 or 80 miles from Magdalena, a place I should have reached long ago. Of course, the lack of road signs pointing the way was nothing to worry about; there were no signs pointing to anywhere. A dull, metallic creak and out of the mist a rail car then another began to emerge. Finally, after at least 70 had passed—most of which had been tagged with what looked for the world to be petroglyphs and ancient script—came the massive engine, coated in ice through which its orange and black paint was visible. I don't know why the train was in reverse, but I guess they had their reasons.

A soft, scuffling noise caused me to turn from the train to find a woman in a black dress and black cape or shawl that dragged the ground standing less than a foot from the passenger side door. She looked impossibly old, and her face, ruined by exposure to the sun and wind, was framed by long gray hair hanging down to her waist. She held a clawlike hand out to me, and in her open palm, I saw a shiny, brand new key.

I didn't know what to say or do.

She smiled at me and nodded her head. "Found this," she said.

I nodded back. "It's real nice." I waited a moment and then asked, "Are you okay?"

She stood there smiling.

"Do you need some help?"

She smiled. "Nah, but I could use a ride."

"I have a ride."

She smiled and got in.

We drove along for a little while, and though I tried, I could find nothing to say. The old woman made no effort to speak, but watched me intently at times, other times looking off to the side, smiling and patting the dashboard, and I had a strange, oceanic feeling whenever we made eye contact, as if she herself was eternity, gazing in speculative ambivalence through time.

For that matter, the fog was heavy as earned guilt, and staying focused on the road ahead rather than the one behind seemed the better choice. Just when I was getting used to her, though, she told me to stop. We were deep in the badlands, and though her command surprised me, I stopped anyway.

She got out of the car and looked me over once more. "Thank you for the ride. You're not what I expected."

I had already abandoned all hope of making any sense of her, so I smiled. "I hope you weren't too disappointed."

"Not at all, young man. You be careful. Forget Oregon," she said. "What you want isn't there."

Then, without another word, she turned on her heel and the mist swallowed her. Gone.

It seemed odd enough at the time as I stared after her, but much later it would occur to me that maybe New Mexico is truly a place where some gods walk undisguised.

Chapter 14

The first clue that I was in Arizona was a sign that gradually solidified through the cloud as I approached it then faded into nothingness as it receded from me.

The sign read:

Wide Ruin 73 Miles

I pulled over and got out the road atlas to see what part of New Mexico I was in, but no luck. Putting two and two together took longer than it should have, but I flipped the atlas over to Arizona and there it was: Wide Ruin, AZ. I looked vacantly at the desiccated landscape, and just as I decided it only looked like more of New Mexico, my smart phone vibrated and a woman's voice sang out, "Welcome to Arizona!"

I looked around, half expecting to see the old woman again, but she didn't appear. The phone said it was 7:01, so I took a selfie. Afterwards, and because I was hungry, I tried to find a restaurant or something similar, using an app on the phone, but navigation was taking forever to load and a few minutes spent staring at the progress wheel convinced me to just keep driving towards Wide Ruin. And in the town of Wide Ruin in the state of Arizona, I found—and stopped at—Rosie's Roadside Grill, thereby changing my life. Forever.

To many passersby, Rosie's might be just another tourist trap/gas station a little west of nowhere and a whole lot east of Eden. I pulled up in front of the café, shut the car off, and sat there looking in as the engine ticked under the hood. It was easy to imagine that most people never notice Rosie's at all, but the ones who do might describe it as "quaint" or "rustic" or maybe "cute." To me, though, Rosie's Roadside Grill has another, more descriptive name: Casa del Hades.

A little bell announced my entrance. A nice-looking girl—or more accurately, woman—was sitting at the counter, dressed in a perfectly tailored black blazer, fitted matching skirt, with a Louis Vuitton clutch; when she turned at the sound of the door, I could see tears comingling with her makeup, causing the mascara to run down her face. I didn't notice her shoes at the time, but I'm sure they were nice. That aside, she was the picture of dejection. My heart went out to her, even if the two black trenches caused by her mascara did make her look a trifle deranged or maybe like a young Alice Cooper. But, being young and having failed theology, metaphysics, and Music Appreciation, I went and sat down a couple of stools away from her and ordered a coffee from the portly man behind the counter. His name tag said "JOE," under which was inscribed *"Service Technician."*

"Where's Rose?" I asked lightly, then took a sip from the cup he brought me.

"Who?" Joe asked suspiciously.

"You know. Roseanne? Rose? Rosie? The owner?"

He stared at me.

"I'm the owner, kid," he said finally.

"Oh, you're the owner."

"What do you want with the owner? Somethin' wrong with your coffee?" he asked, not unkindly.

"No, um, no." I looked at Joe. "No."

"Hey, kid."

"Yeah?"

"You okay?" Joe asked.

"He's okay," the girl said in a husky voice. Then she turned to me. "I'm Julie. Julie Smith. You are okay?"

I looked up at her. During the short exchange between myself and Joe, she had wiped the mascara off her face, reapplied it, and maybe some lipstick, more in a quick, effective makeover. It was like magic.

"I'm okay."

"He's just tired," she said. "Where are you headed?"

"Uh, Oregon." It sounded like something made up on the spot.

"Oregon is just lovely this time of year. At least, that's what I've heard." Julie looked down into her coffee. "I've never been out of Arizona," she finished wistfully.

"Yeah, but you've been around the world," Joe snickered.

Julie seemed on the verge of crying again, gulping air in great, exaggerated sobs, and Joe started laughing. I felt vaguely responsible, but didn't know why.

"What are you doing up here?" I asked.

"Waiting," she said, drying her eyes.

"What for?"

"Oh, opportunity."

"What opportunity?" I asked.

"The best kind of opportunity. The opportunity to do something I've never done before," she said.

"Do you need a ride?" I blurted out.

"No," she said. She glanced outside. "No."

"You want to stay here. Got it."

"I don't want to stay here."

"Well, uh, what?" I asked.

"I want to go to Oregon."

Joe started laughing again. I stared at Julie in horrified fascination. She began crying again.

"Oh," she wailed, "you don't want me to go. You think I'm ugly."

She pronounced "ugly" as if someone was squeezing all of the air out of her lungs, giving it the curious effect of being a four-syllable word. Joe kept laughing.

I sputtered, "I don't think you're ugly. I think you're totally hot."

At this, Joe doubled over as the bald spot on his head turned purple, and he wheezed, "Kid, there's somethin' you—"

"No." I cut him off, feeling very gallant. "The lady wants to go to Oregon," I stopped, taking a breath before my leap of stupidity, "and to Oregon she shall go," I finished.

Julie and Joe both looked at me in amazement and expressed themselves accordingly. Joe sat down behind the counter, laughing and screaming that he was ready to die, he'd seen it all, and Julie fixed a million-dollar grin on me and said, "You may regret this, but you're never going to forget me."

Joe got up off the floor. "Kid, listen at me. I'm tellin' ya—"

"Thanks, but no thanks for your, no doubt, excellent advice, Joe," I cut him off frostily. "Give my regards to Rose. Rosie. Roseanne. Whoever."

And with that, Julie and I stepped out of the café, me feeling very self-righteous and brave, and Julie feeling, no doubt, very much like a hungry cat in a roomful of hog-tied mice.

Not much later at all, I came rather abruptly to the realization that the age of chivalry, the age of knights errant running around all over the

42

countryside, depriving each other of life and limb while engaged in the pursuit of pointless quests at the behest of questionable women, died out for one simple, yet significant reason: It was an incredibly stupid and unsustainable idea.

Chapter 15

I stared at Julie as she walked to the car, partly because she had gone from screaming hysterics to whistling "Dixie," literally, in maybe forty-five seconds, but mostly because the girl was every inch of 6'3".

"Wow," she said, "nice car."

"Thanks. I mowed a lot of yards to get that car."

"By the way," Julie leaned toward me, her voice a hoarse whisper, "if you ever call me 'cute' again, I'll break your back."

I stared at her for a moment, realizing that not only was she making a promise, she was making a promise she could keep.

"Yes, ma'am," I said.

"Now back to this mo-chine," she said sweetly, and simultaneously getting in. "It's a '65, right? Thought so. Injected or normally aspirated?"

"What?"

"So does it have fuel injection or a carburetor?" she asked condescendingly.

"I didn't see, uh . . ."

"Injectors?"

"A carburetor."

"Injected then; not many of those. Nice paint and, oh my . . . leather seats." She made "leather" sound like an obscenity. I didn't know whether to shout for joy or push her out of the car. Didn't matter. One was futile and the other impossible.

We drove and talked for about fifteen minutes when suddenly Julie stopped talking. She was looking down the blacktop toward a dirt road that led off the highway. She told me to stop, but I only slowed down.

"Stop the car. I said stop! Now, I wonder what's down that road?" I had a feeling that she knew exactly what was down that road.

"Nothing," I said.

"We should go look."

"We should keep going," I said.

44

"Oh? When exactly is it that you're expected in Oregon?" she asked innocently. I'd already told her I was making a surprise visit.

"You know that I'm not 'expected,' which still doesn't mean that I want to drive down every dirt road we come across just to prove to myself that it leads to the town dump and not something wonderful."

"It doesn't lead to the dump, but I want to show you something," she said. "We're going to spend a lot of time together for the next few days, and it's imperative that we be honest with each other. Right?"

She had a point, of sorts, and momentary honesty might not have been all bad, so I gave it a try. "Not really."

"Yes, it is," she said.

"You said you didn't know what was down this road," I protested.

"I said no such thing. I said I wondered. Now let's go."

I sighed and steered the car down the road, which wound along for a couple of miles, past a ditch full of trash, and ended abruptly in a large clearing. Some marriages in Wide Ruin may be made in heaven, but I suspected that most got started right here.

"Give me the key," Julie said.

I yanked the key out of the ignition and handed it to her. The motor purred gently.

"Runs with the key out? That's good to know." She looked at me pointedly, inserted the key, and killed the engine. My throat suddenly felt tight and dry. Julie stepped out of the car and, with a mischievous smile, began to back away, slowly inching her skirt up at the same time, showing off her large, muscular legs and singing this weirdass song that was something like, "Don't get strung out . . . by the way I look. Don't judge a book by its cover . . ." She rolled her skirt up until it was at the bottom hem of her panties, and then, telling me to watch closely, yanked her skirt all the way up with one hand and with the other simultaneously pulled her underwear open and dangled the car key as if she were going to drop it inside. And lo, what my eyes beheld bulging against her flimsy underwear filled me with horror, and if I had to be candid, a twinge of envy.

Julie Smith, the goddess of love, the angel from heaven, had transmogrified into J. Smith, transvestite par excellence, demon from the pit.

Mom always said that if I didn't straighten up, my past would catch up with me. She never suggested the possibility of someone else's past catching up with me.

Now reason returned.

"I see you're thinking about the key," he/she said laconically, pulling down her skirt, and it was true enough, but that was about the last thing on my mind.

"Yes," I said, trying to sound calm and failing.

"You want it?"

Swallowing hard, I just jerked my head.

"I'm sure we can work something out. Any suggestions?"

I looked at her long and hard and tried to figure out where this was headed.

"Not really."

"Huh," she said petulantly. "A smart college boy like you can't think of any way to make me want to give back your key?"

Besides being completely intimidated, I was starting to get pissed off. "How about I take a golf club, beat you to death, leave you here for your gayass friends to find, and we call it even?"

J. looked thoughtful for a moment, then countered, "What an ugly thing to say. You really should be ashamed of yourself. Regardless, your, um, suggestion," she paused dramatically, "well, that won't work for three reasons. First, you don't have a golf club. Second, I'm considerably bigger than you, and if you had a golf club, I'd take it away and might beat your homophobic ass to death with it. And last, though certainly not least, while I have some friends who don't really conform to the status quo, so to speak, some because they're homosexual and others for other reasons, I don't have any—to use your hideous phrase—'gayass friends.' On top of that, I'm straight."

Though the first two reasons she gave were undeniable, I had a little trouble with the third.

"You? Gay? Whatever was I thinking? Somehow it slipped my mind that in Arizona, straight men routinely go around dressed like whores—"

"You seemed to like my outfit well enough at the café. Way you were looking me over, I thought you were about to proposition me on the spot."

"—and hang out in coffee shops," I finished.

"Well, I wouldn't exactly call it routine . . ." J. said thoughtfully, tapping perfectly manicured nails against the side of her leg, "but I'm certainly not dressed like a whore."

"No," I said quietly, after a moment, "I think my mom has that outfit."

"You don't say."

"Saks?"

"Yep," she said.

"Mmhmm," I said.

"Well, she sounds like a lovely woman!" J. exclaimed. She got back in, leaned over, started the car, and put the key in her purse.

To say that I felt all alone in a world turned suddenly hostile would be tantamount to saying that Napoleon probably thought Waterloo was a bad idea. I tried to keep a positive mental attitude, but the sight of a 6'3", 230-pound transvestite dressed like my mother didn't help. It seemed to only fire off those synapses typically reserved for visions of madness, confusion, paranoid delusions, and so forth. You know, the usual.

"What do you want?" I finally asked.

"I've told you."

"No. You haven't," I said slowly.

"Yes. I have." Pause. "I want. A. Ride."

"I'm not going to Oregon," I really thought I was lying.

"That's fine by me. I wouldn't go there if you paid me," she said.

"Well, where then?" I asked, feeling a little frantic.

"Graceland."

"Graceland," I repeated.

"You got it."

"Graceland?"

Paranoid delusions my ass.

Chapter 16

I put in a Robert Johnson disc, and at J.'s direction, turned the car around to head back the way we had come as the first plaintive notes of "Got a Hellhound on my Trail" found their way into the world again. If this wasn't a time for the blues, there never would be.

"You're out of your mind," I finally said.

J. seemed to think about this for a minute and then slowly said, "Maybe," dragging it out real slow like she was deep in thought. "That's been said. But who believes everything they hear? Besides, I want to go to Graceland, I need to go to Graceland, and I'm going to Graceland. There's something I have to do there. I'll go with you maybe, without you maybe, but definitely in this car. It's perfect." She finished her pronouncement just as we bumped off the gravel and back onto the blacktop, headed east on Highway 68 towards Gallup, New Mexico.

It was still early and the morning air was crisp. The sun hadn't burned the dew off the land yet, and it sparkling off the millions upon millions of cacti points, making the desert look like a new creation; every time I looked, it was different. I drove without saying a word. J., for her part, whistled along with vicious abandon and not much skill. I put in several different discs, hoping to find something that she wouldn't like, but evidently, her complete lack of musical ability included a complete lack of preference. She whistled the same tune, or perhaps, for the sake of accuracy, I should say non-tune, with equal enthusiasm and apparent satisfaction, maybe to annoy me, but looking back now, I kind of doubt that.

We stopped in Albuquerque for lunch about noon. J. killed the car and took the key into the diner with her. I could have run, I guess, but to where I didn't know, and I didn't want to leave the car with her. I'd just have to figure out some way to separate her from the key and the car before too much longer. We ate a quick lunch and kept on going.

Two hours later, in the middle of nowhere once again, a small cloud appeared off to the west but soon threatened to swallow the sky. J. didn't seem to notice at first, but then a sudden wind draft slammed into the car, accompanied by fat drops of rain pattering almost symmetrically across the windshield; the staccato slaps made her sit up straight. Smiling at J. wistfully, I fantasized about her, myself, and a baseball bat my father once gave me.

J. said, "I think you ought to put the top up."

I drove along for a while, thinking quietly and taking mental inventory of all that was jammed in the trunk. I didn't remember ever seeing the top for this car. J. turned the radio off, rolled her window up, and looked at me for a moment.

"Colin! I said I think you should put the top up."

I cut my eyes across at her real quick and kept driving. I was now positive that of all the options the car had, a convertible top was a conspicuous absence. "This car didn't, well . . . come with a top," I said.

J. looked at me incredulously and asked. "You mean you mowed lawns for God knows how long to buy a car and didn't get a top with it?"

"Ran out of yards," I said, staring straight down the road.

There was a long silence in which J., to all outward signs, appeared brain dead. As for myself, I followed my emerging philosophy of crisis control: drive, drive, and drive. It didn't solve the imminent problem, but it certainly did give the sensation of progress. The rain began to fall with purpose, and as we hurtled into it, every drop coalesced into a wall of water we slammed into and through, creating a vacuum of sorts that drew a fine, thick mist back into the Vette from the rear. I've heard that you never step into the same river twice, and that may be true, but I guarantee you never step—or, for that matter, drive—into the same rainfall even once.

Interestingly, the rain created a harmonious, if percussive, effect as it bombarded the vehicle and us. J. was trying to maintain a facade of imperturbable hauteur, but her hair—most of which I could now see was wig, plastered down on the side of her head near the window, while the other side bunched up like some small animal seeking shelter from the storm—undercut that a bit. It wasn't all that bad for me, due to the fact that here was something J. couldn't whistle to, and anyway, I have short hair. A bridge loomed up out of the rain, and more from instinct than intellect, I hit the brakes, skittering to a stop on the dry pavement beneath.

Water was falling straight and heavy now, so much so that the bridge appeared to have gray, translucent curtains on either side, into which the highway disappeared. I looked over at J., noting for the first time her heavy beard, poking as it was through what little of her makeup remained intact. What could I possibly have been thinking when I first saw her? I whistled a couple of bars from Paul Simon's "Graceland," got out of the car, and leaned against the front fender. I thought maybe a cigarette would do me some good, but then again, I don't smoke, so who knows? A sense of quiet, albeit humid, peace descended, and a feeling of timelessness stole over me.

As the desert opened itself to the rain, I could almost hear and feel it coming to life and wondered how long it'd been since a rain such as this had fallen here, to nurture and replenish this wilderness. My thoughts and senses began to expand, and it seemed I could now see a multicolored and magnificent star looming through the water curtain. I watched in anticipatory awe as an eighteen-wheeler, bedecked in amber, green, and red LED lights, hauling a trailer-load of wet, and understandably irate, very vocal chickens, suddenly hurtled through the waterfall and out the other side, missing me by mere inches. So much for earthbound cosmic phenoms. An atomized, barnyard-smelling mist, punctuated by chicken feathers, was all that was left to mark its passing. This was a touch too much. I yanked out my road atlas and tried to figure out where we were. I calculated, with very little accuracy, that the next town lay about ten to fifteen miles out there somewhere in the violent humidity. I expressed this miscalculation to J. and got back into the car. She just stared at me, but not in anticipatory awe. Nope.

I smoked the tires as we fishtailed in a long arc from under the sanctuary of the interstate grotto. For the next 70 miles, we hop-scotched between twelve bridges, three deserted gas stations, and one church, complete with steeple and, more importantly, an awning. Finally, cold, wet, and facing impending dismemberment by a 230-pound transvestite, I saw hope and swerved off of an exit ramp at 77 mph (according to my best calculations) into, across, and out the other side of the parking lot of what was misspelled—I promise—the "Ya'll Slide Inn Bar And Dance Hall" and sluiced to a stop in about a foot of mud. I looked over at J., who had done her best to stuff her less than petite frame into the footwell.

"Honey, we're home."

Chapter 17

Conversation stopped, heads turned, and mouths fell agape when we straggled into the bar. At last call we'd have been bad enough, but at 8:00 p.m. . . . well, we were a sight to make women run and grown men cry. Obviously, we were both drenched, though J., in particular, with the disarray of her synthetic locks and water streaming down her huge frame, looked like a creature from the deep. She clutched her purse like a talisman and went straight to the ladies' room, taking the car key with her. Lacking both a razor—and for that matter, the will—to slash my wrists or a need to make water, I sat down at a table close to the exit.

Everyone was still looking at me, and when the waitress came to the table, they looked at her too.

Before she could say anything, I asked where we were.

"Well, you're at the Y'all—"

"I don't mean that. I mean what town."

"Oh. You're 'tween Carrizozoandvaughn," all in a rush.

Tweencarrizozoandvaughn? I thought. What language is this? I had two bars on my phone, but I looked it up. Data was slow and nothing was happening fast. Still, I didn't remember that town from the atlas.

"Where again?"

"Carrizozoandvaughn"

"That's the name of this town? I—"

She cut me off. "No. There's nothing here, not exactly. We're between the towns of Carrizozo and Vaughn."

I looked around the room, almost expecting, I don't know what. She said there was nothing here, and I was becoming familiar with surprises. Still, it did seem that there was a fair amount of "here" here, so I tried something else. "Where's here in relation to Albuquerque?"

"Albuquerque?"

"Uh-huh."

"New Mexico?"

"That very one."

"Oh, 'bout a hundred fifty miles north and west a here."

I still didn't know where 'here' was supposed to be, but I did know it wasn't south of Albuquerque. Lost again.

"Where you tryin' ta get to, hon?"

"Well, we're headed for Tennessee," I said.

The waitress looked at me as if the situation vexed her and she wanted to help. "Ain't no Tennessee 'round here, but Tecolote ain't far. You sure it's Tennessee?"

"Pretty sure."

"Hon, you must be lost."

I looked up at her. "You don't know the half of it. Have you ever seen an old woman wandering around out in the middle of the desert?"

She shook her head. "Hon, you gonna want somethin' to eat or, uh," she smiled, "need more to drink?" She asked in that tone of voice people use when they're talking to someone's pit bull and wondering if it's one of the friendly ones.

"Got any Sterno?" I asked.

She didn't say anything at first, just looked at me and darted her eyes towards the bar as if she were judging the distance.

"No, baby doll, I don't think we do." She seemed to be choosing her words very carefully. "But I can sure run check . . ."

I didn't know what her problem was, but she was starting to make me jumpy, so I said, "Beer then. Bring me a Heineken."

She just stood there.

"Please?"

"Uh, honey, we don't have that kind of beer. I'm real sorry, but we, uh, just, you know, we . . ." her voice trailed off with a thin, high-pitched sound.

"Yeah, I know. Don't worry about bringing me anything you don't have. That just complicates the issues, right? Yeah, right. This is definitely one issue that doesn't need complicating. Bring me something you do have, okay?" I was starting to babble. I don't know why it is, but whenever I'm around someone who's nervous, I start getting nervous too. Probably genetic. She reeled off to fill my order, and I heard a murmur pass over the crowd, which was made up of about thirty-five cowboy and cowgirl types. They had turned their attention from me to J., emerging from the bathroom and looking, I must admit, like a million bucks. Like a million

52

and one bucks. Freshly made up, her confidence restored, showing just a touch of dampness around the edges, she was a sight. The young women looked at her with murder in their eyes, and the older ones with envy. And the men? Well, they had a look in their eyes, too, but appeared to have different intentions.

She came up and sat down with a flourish. "Where's my drink?"

"Still at the bar," I snapped at her.

"Look, you're going to have to deal with the fact that we'll be spending a lot of time together between now and Tennessee."

"Here," I said. "Here and Tennessee."

"Whatever, smartass. Now the way I see it, that time can be as painless as possible or it can be real bad. Real. Bad. Or you could just give me the car. Ever since I was a young," she stopped and kind of frowned, "well, ever since I was young, I've wanted a car like that." J. was feeling chatty. I wasn't.

"Don't they have yards where you're from? Go mow some . . . buy your own."

"Arizona isn't known for its lush lawns, and anyway, there's no need to."

The waitress came back, balancing a Milwaukee's Best a little shakily on a tray, set it down, and dashed off. I eyed the beer warily, but it was so cold that, even there in the high desert, condensation had formed into huge droplets that rolled down the glass. It looked like a commercial.

A very large, very drunk-looking cowboy approached our table to the accompaniment of varied catcalls and the other substitutes that pass for the spoken word.

"Ma'am, I couldn't help but notice," he started, looking at me, "well, noticin' that you're out with College Boy here, and I thought maybe I could convince you to take a turn or two out to the daince floor with a cowboy. I mean, of course, bein' if you don't mind, sir," he finished sarcastically, looking at me.

"I'd love to," J. started, "but as you noticed, I am with someone."

Cowboy Numero Uno looked at me and started laughing. Finally, he said, "Oh hell, honey, he don't care."

"How are you so—" she started, but I interrupted,

"He's right, I don't care. Dance to your little big heart's content."

J. frowned a little, but to my surprise she stood up. The Cowboy took a step back and the rest of the audience gasped. Evidently, they hadn't seen her in all her bulk. Or maybe they had, and some innate desire for proportion had overridden their collective senses. I don't know.

"My, you're a sturdy lil' ol' thing, aren't you?" The Cowboy, whose name, it turned out, was Red, blurted out as he stared up at her. There was nothing little or not-sturdy about her, I thought to myself. This bitch was built to last.

I sat back in my chair while J. and The Cowboy careened around the space between the tables and in front of the jukebox, in a sort of half-drunken, half-controlled pirouette. Half-drunken and half-controlled because he was drunk and she was definitely in control. No sooner had they finished reeling around the room a couple more times than two more of the cowboy variety were tapping Red on the shoulder and asking to cut in. Red brushed a tangle of black hair out of his eyes, bowed deeply, and said, "Sure, I guess." He stumbled back to his table.

J. was obviously no stranger to dancing, but she must have been used to taking the lead, which led to some awkwardness, to say the least. As the waiting list to have J.'s aggressive dance moves inflicted on them grew, I became increasingly aware of the fact that the entire crowd was looking in my direction and laughing, no doubt, at the paroxysms of humiliation they thought they saw on my face. It's true I was in anguish, but the exact cause of that had nothing to do with the fact that my dinner/traveling companion had danced with every man in the house at least twice. It had to do with the voice I kept hearing. Strangely enough, it was my mother's. She kept saying, "Any minute now, one of those guys is going to realize that they're dancing with a man, a man that you brought, and that means it's your fault!"

Thinking it over, I realized that, if that happened, trying to explain that taking J. for a woman was an understandable mistake to make would be received with very little tolerance. I was having a hard enough time with it, and I'm from Dallas, but out here?

A quick flutter at the bar caught my attention. It was a girl, maybe twenty years old, with long blonde hair and a slim build that made me think—I stopped suddenly. The thought of picking up two transvestites, both with a yen for travel and the infliction of psychic abuse, in one day, or hell, one lifetime, however slight the odds, made me dizzy. I clenched my eyes shut for a moment then looked back at where J. was struggling around the dance floor, locked up with some stupid redneck who was about 5'3". I grimaced. Seeing her towering over him and trying to look feminine and relaxed while his face was smashed into her nipples about made my hair stand on end. I wanted to run, but the car was stuck in the mud outside. And J. still had the key.

"Excuse me." A girlish voice. I looked up to see the blonde girl from the bar and tried not to whimper. I failed.

"I sit down?" she asked. I looked her over for a long minute in what must have appeared a most lascivious way. Everything seemed to have come standard at birth. "Can I sit down?" She was starting to turn a little red, and I took for this a good sign.

"Go ahead."

"Thanks. I'm Joette. You always this rude, or is it cuz of her?" She motioned towards my dancing transvestite and her rotating morons.

"It's not her. I was thinking of something else. I couldn't care less about her." While I was talking, it occurred to me that, yeah, I pretty much was usually that rude.

"Oh yeah, right. Why, if I was to go out with some great-lookin' guy and he left me stranded at the table while he danced with every girl in the place, I wouldn't mind neither."

"Well, you might or you might not, depending on the particular circumstances," I observed from my privileged vantage point.

"Oh, well, I guess you love 'em and leave 'em types are a little different than most," she laughed, sitting back in her chair and throwing an arm over the backrest, "but I guess most folks around here wouldn't take too kindly to it. And you ain't from around here."

"You're probably right about the first and definitely right about the second. Why are you here alone? You do this a lot?" I asked. I was thinking the bar looked pretty rough, but as so often happens, what I meant and how it landed were very far apart.

She sat up straight and fast. "I ain't 'up here by myself,'" she sputtered. "I ain't no bar-whore. I came up here with my boyfriend, Buck."

Great, I thought, just what I need to round out my evening: a nice thrashing from Buck. I looked around as I asked, "And just where is this Buck right now?" I didn't see anyone who looked like they were trying to locate a beautiful—and missing—woman. "Exactly?"

Joette made an effort for a moment, then just fell apart. Between sobs she gasped, "Heee's owwwwt there daincin'." I whirled around in my chair. The only couple on the floor was J. and a rather large fellow, who I strongly and accurately suspected would answer with an affirmative "Yo!" were one to yodel out "Buuuuuck!"

My distress factor had been at what I thought was the highest it could be, but boy was I wrong. While I watched J. and Buck, I noticed that she seemed to be paying an inordinate amount of attention to his backside. In fact, she was rubbing her hands all across it. I couldn't be sure, because she'd gone from wrestling for control for lead to the opposite, and they danced smooth and tight, braiding their steps together like an old couple. They turned and snaked their way down the far wall, and all I could see was Buck, eyes half-closed, with a look of kind contentment on his face. He did open them once to give the bar an empty glance, as if looking for something he couldn't quite remember. On their next pass, I was ready, but with the darkness providing cover and Joette's alternate cursing, sniffling, and one punch to my shoulder, for who the hell knows what, distracting me, I couldn't tell what was going on. It looked like J. was sort of rooting around behind Buck's back, when finally, and with horror, I realized what she was up to.

Son of a bitch—or whatever—was picking Buck's pocket.

About the time she got his wallet out, they turned sort of broadside, and Buck stiffened as he saw Joette sitting at my table. As for J., evidently recognizing the situation for what it was, she grabbed Buck by the hand and firmly led him over, seating him opposite me.

"My. Well, that was some dancing. How long have I been up?" she asked me innocently, fanning her face with her hand.

I looked at my watch and replied, "About forty-five minutes, by my timepiece."

Joette looked across at Buck, who seemed to be trying to figure out whether he could be mad at her for sitting with me, be mad at me for sitting with her, or if he had forfeited both by dancing with J. Joette's mascara was headed south, a sight which troubled me deeply, and for reasons that I know are obvious. She looked at J. with a mixture of awe and hatred. For her part, J. seemed perfectly at ease. No one at the table was her match in physical prowess, the girl's makeup was a mess, Buck was still weighing his options (or maybe trying to figure out if he had any), and I didn't have the key. We were hers to toy with. The waitress came, and J. ordered a round of drinks.

"I'll have a seven and seven. Buck here will have a Coors Light draft." She nodded at me. "He'll have another can of whatever swill they brew in Milwaukee, and give Polly Pureheart there a Shirley Temple." The waitress looked stunned.

"Oh, I forgot, we're out here in East Egypt. Give her some ginger ale. You do know what ginger ale is, don't yuh, honeee pie?" J. finished.

Why she was being so aggressive with the waitress I'll never know. But I was amazed that, in her short dance with Buck, she'd gathered so much from him as to know what he drank.

The waitress nodded unconvincingly and withdrew.

"Where were we? Oh yes. Buck, meet Colin. Colin, Buck."

"Hi, Buck. How's the libido?" I asked.

Buck snorted something that wasn't completely hostile and turned his attention to Joette, who was still staring at J. with an intensity that would have made a catatonic blush. J. was unfazed and looked right back, smiling sweetly, but truth be told, it looked like an act. I had a brief mental flash of the young J. in elementary school, wilting the teachers with that same look while he/she critiqued their outfits.

Buck finally broke the silence.

"Julie tells me y'all are on yer way to Graceland to see that Elvis Presley."

"That so?" I asked. "Did she mention that he's dead?" I cut my eyes at J. and added, "Or maybe just 'gone home,' as we say in the South?"

Buck squinted and, ignoring that, continued with, "M'self, I always thought he was kinda funny, if you know what I mean."

I indicated that I did, in fact, know exactly what he meant. J. kind of sucked her breath in through clenched teeth. Just as it seemed a bloodletting was imminent, the drinks arrived. Sadly, the waitress had indeed brought Joette a ginger ale, and this was, apparently, the end of her line. I feel obligated to say that while Joette had, up to this time, suffered in silence, when she did react, she was quick, decisive, and efficient. She held up her ginger ale in one hand and hissed, "I have been coming in here for three years now, Betty, and in that time I have never, not ever, drank anythin' but Pearl beer, and YOU KNOW THAT!" she finished in a shriek, at the same time throwing the contents of her glass on Buck and the glass itself at J., upon whom it bounced off to shatter across the floor. I would think that, ordinarily, a scene of this sort in a public place would have a fairly far-reaching impact, if for no other reason than the occasion it provides for everyone else to turn, stare, and snicker. In this particular case, however, that is what everyone had been doing since we arrived, so the repercussions were pretty much confined to our table. Buck, dripping beer and embarrassed, was livid but controlled himself, albeit with some difficulty. He resorted to the typical reaction of an ignoramus who knows he deserves every bad thing that is happening to him. He tried to shift the blame.

"Girl, I have tired of your jealous ways. I have been silent about you sitting here with this strange man." I cut my eyes at J., who just grinned at me. "But if you choose to pull another stunt such as this, you will leave me no recourse other than to take up with Miss Julie. I urge you to think upon your actions." He sounded like a bad soap opera from the 19th century, and it was, well, flat-out weird.

Joette became quiet, as if reviewing her options, or maybe she was just confused by Buck's sudden formality, but just as she opened her mouth, I said, "Buck, she's all yours. Take her."

Buck looked at me with shock and surprise, perhaps because the soon-to-be-jilted lover never says that in the westerns.

Joette's interpretation was altogether different, and looking at me for support, she took a deep breath and said, "Yeah, Buck, you do that. You need a woman around who looks like she ain't never done a honest day's work in her life. What's your idea of hard work, Julie, having to carry your shopping bags all the way across the mall parking lot?"

The cliché "You could cut the tension with a knife" was altogether inadequate. It was more like force building behind a failing dam or maybe when speeding across an ice-slicked bridge: the slightest pressure and devastating, irreversible consequences would be in motion.

Buck and Joette looked at J. to see what she would contribute to the present dilemma, and I knew for a fact that she would contribute a lot. I figured the odds that I'd leave in a rubber bag were pretty good.

"Well really, Buck, that is awfully sweet of you," J. drawled, batting her eyes at Buck.

He sat up straighter in his chair, flashing a malicious grin at Joette and me.

"But really, you're not my type." Buck sagged and Joette swooped in for the kill.

"Yeah, I think I actually agree with you about that, Julie," she said. "When you get the two of 'em together, ol' Buck there sorta comes up short, don't he?" she said lightly, but her eyes were flat and cold. "I mean, he's tall and all, but, you know," she dropped her eyes about belt buckle high, "not where it counts."

Every man, when faced with a crisis of this nature, will react in some, and almost always uncalled for, way. Buck was a man. And he looked at me with awful intent and tried to jump up, but couldn't because J. caught him by one arm and effortlessly held him in his seat. Joette started giggling and asked Buck if he needed any help "getting it up," and then she leaned over and kissed me on the cheek. The slightest pressure.

Something seemed to just give way in Buck, and wrenching himself free, he went wild and hit J. with a roundhouse to her jaw.

Then nothing for a moment that stretched into what seemed like hours in the elasticity that time possesses, a stunned silence broken only by Buck's ragged breathing. Someone in the crowd said, "Hold on there, Buck," as J. calmly stood to face him, spat some blood on the table, then grabbed him by the hair on the back of his head and slammed his face into the table, twice, breaking his nose and spraying blood across the plastic tablecloth. She let go of him, and he slid to the floor, the acrid blood-smell like sheared copper.

Joette wasn't laughing anymore. She sat rigid in her chair, holding the palms of her hands a couple of inches above the table, looking at the middle of J.'s chest, careful not to make eye contact; it was plain this wasn't the first time Joette had experienced violence like this—or worse—firsthand. She was terrified.

J. sighed deeply and leaned back, raised one hand slightly and said, "Go."

Joette slid soft and slow from her seat, eyes fixed on J.'s chest, and a couple of Buck's friends helped her drag him into the corner, where she began to clean him up. The crowd was silent, while a few, that I took to be particularly sympathetic to Buck or Joette, adopted a more serious attitude but sat down, still looking at us.

"What did you have to do that for?" I was appalled at the quick and efficient violence I'd just witnessed.

"Because the lowest form a man can take is one who hits women. I won't stand for it."

"But you're not a woman," I pointed out.

"He thinks I am. Besides. What do you care, he was about to tear you apart."

"Only because you wouldn't leave well enough alone. I saw you."

"Saw what?"

"I saw you take his wallet."

"I don't have his wallet."

"I saw you take it, which means someone else in here probably saw it too."

"I put it back. Besides, if anyone saw me take it, or anyone else's for that matter, they'd have called 'thief,' or whatever these hicks scream when faced with that circumstance," she said calmly. I doubted they'd ever been faced with that circumstance, but saw no point in arguing that.

"Why'd you take it if you were going to put it back?" I asked.

J. looked at me in exasperation. "Really?" she asked. "I didn't say I put it back in the same condition I found it. We need traveling money."

"Anyone else's?! That doesn't, I hope, mean that you took more than one wallet?"

"Took and replaced. Took and replaced. Big difference," she said, glancing around the room and then back to me. "Huge."

"Either way, when last call comes and everybody that danced with you figures out he doesn't have a dime to his name, we're dead."

"And that makes this a good time to leave."

"Sure," I said, "no problem. It's raining enough to make Noah say 'Shouldn't we be building a bigger boat, Lord?' My car is stuck up to the doors in mud, and you say, 'I know, let's leave.'" I looked away. "We're dead."

J. got up and asked if anyone had a truck that could pull her car out of the mud. About forty-seven hands shot up in the air. They were more than happy to help us leave.

"Good," she said. "It's the red Corvette outside. Come back and tell me when you're done. I'll gladly pay you for the trouble" About ninety-four pairs of legs ran out into the torrent. We had a couple more drinks.

Fifteen minutes later, a red-faced guy who looked to be in his thirties came back in and said, "It's out of the mud, ma'am. If he's the one that was drivin', maybe you oughta do it fer now on. I had a car like that, I sure wouldn't let jes' any idiot off the street tear it all up, no sir," he finished, glaring at me with resentment and envy.

"Why, thank you so much," J. said, sliding a twenty that she'd owned for less than an hour across the table to him. "Leave me your name and number so I can reward your kindness. I'll certainly think about your advice also," she finished, winking at me and making a face.

"We need to get out of here," I said under my breath.

"Can someone please recommend a good motel?" she asked.

The waitress blurted out, "There's one just up the road. You can't miss it."

If I ever get back to the Ya'll Slide Inn again, I'm going to strangle that waitress.

Chapter 18

We stepped out into the parking lot to see that the rain had let up. The moon was on the wane but still mostly full, and the blue-gray clouds in the night sky were shot through with its borrowed light. It was stunning.

J. told me to drive. She slid into the passenger's side, put the key in the ignition, started the car, then pulled the key out and stuck it in her purse. I really shouldn't have shown her that trick.

The motel the waitress suggested wasn't exactly "just up the road," but was more like twenty miles down the road and turned out to be a sort of home for wayward girls/den of iniquity. It was the only thing we passed, and in light of J.'s pocket-picking back at the bar, I thought we should keep on going. But she said she was tired, and the adrenaline had done a number on her. She insisted on stopping.

The waitress was right, though: anybody who drove past this place did so on purpose. Built to resemble the Alamo, it catered to the homeless, the shiftless, and, in our case, the witless. J. thought it was quaint.

I pulled into the parking lot, and J. inserted the key and killed the motor. Two or three girls in mini-skirts and spike heels lounged around in front of the building. They eyed J. with hostility.

We got out of the car and took in the scenery, in particular, the building itself.

"We are not staying here," I said.

"But I want to!" she exclaimed.

"Fine. Go ahead. I'm not staying here."

"Hope you brought your walking shoes," she said, dangling the key in front of me.

"Look. We can't stay here with any reasonable expectation of leaving in the same state of good repair we're in now. Anyway, we aren't that far from the bar, and everyone there knows which direction we're traveling."

"Don't care. I've never been to the Alamo."

"You can stay here till the Mexicans stage a second coming and still not have been to the Alamo. This is a whorehouse."

"So? It looks like the Alamo."

"Oh yeah, I forgot, for you looking like is as good as being like," I said.

Ignoring me, J. said, "They'll rent us a room. Besides, technically it's not a whorehouse. Yes, it may be a type of house and prostitutes may frequent it, but at heart and by definition, it is a motel." She looked down at me. "You're so judgmental."

Semantics.

"I'm not worried about them not renting us a room. I'm worried more about them giving us a disease."

J. looked at me and raised an eyebrow. I gave up, as had become my wont.

We walked into the lobby and glanced around, trying to look nonchalant. J. was openly impressed. The builder had not abandoned the Alamo motif on the inside either. Scorched and ragged Texas flags hung from fake roof timbers spanning the length of the ceiling. The walls had been made to look like limestone, replete with fake bullet holes. Or hell, maybe they *were* real bullet holes. Even the windows had those little stickers on them that made them look as if they had been shot a few times.

The manager came out from behind some curtains that had "Remember the Alamo" and "Remember San Jacinto" stenciled on them, walked around behind the counter, and stood in front of a life-sized velvet painting of John Wayne. He sized J. up in awe.

"Whaddayawant?" One word.

"We would like a room, please," J. said sweetly.

"Howlong?"

"Excuse me?"

"How many hours, lady? One? Two?" Then looking at me he said, "If I were you, I'd just take him out back. We don't never rent rooms for no ten minutes." He laughed a little at his joke.

I looked over his shoulder to where John Wayne hung on the wall, staring across the lobby, lost in silence.

"If you were me, you wouldn't be stuck out here," she said.

When he didn't say anything, J. went back to her original line of questioning.

"How much for all night?" J. asked.

"Well, like I awreadytol'you, we rent by the hour. Cost ya 30 dollars a hour, so however much that comes to, youfiggeritup," he growled. "Whenever you figger night ends."

I noticed that whoever had done the painting had forgotten—or declined—to paint the pupils in Mr. Wayne's eyes, giving him a strange, soulless look. I couldn't pull myself away, and I listened only vaguely to J. and the manager squabbling about the price of the room. I felt like I was at a place where what things seem to be and what they really are intersect. The fact that I had felt like that a few times already didn't blunt the oceanic sensation, a connection to this place, but also feeling as if I were standing with my back to an abyss that only John Wayne dared look out into.

"Well, it's midnight now, so assuming that we get out of here by 8:00 a.m., that comes to $240, which is outrageous," J. said.

"Stay till six and it'llcostless," he retorted.

I snapped out of my reverie and noticed that J. was getting a bit flustered, which did me a world of good. I liked seeing her upset. She tried to bargain with the manager, but he wouldn't come off his price, partly because he didn't want to and partly, I suspect, because he didn't know how to. I told J. later that she should have told him that thirty times ten was twenty-seven-fifty or something. She wouldn't have listened anyway. At any rate, she finally gave in and paid the $240 in advance, because he wouldn't give us the key otherwise. On the way out, J. asked him for a wake-up call.

"A which?" he asked.

That confused both of us. J. tried a different tack. "Call our room at eight. I can't afford to oversleep here," J. snapped petulantly.

"We don't give no wake-up calls here, lady."

"Never?"

"Ever." He looked at us for a second. "Lady," he said, gesturing expansively with his hands, "who would come here for sleep?"

As we walked to the parking lot, I looked around at nothing in particular. I decided that my life really wasn't turning out like I'd planned.

Chapter 19

From the look of the room, the decorator had been in touch with the whims of chaos. Magenta-colored walls struck a brutal contrast with a lime green shag carpet that lay on the floor like a geriatric punk rocker's hairpiece. A battered dressing table slouched crookedly against the wall to the right of the door and had a black and white television set from about 1996 chained to the top of it; this thing belonged in the Smithsonian.

Directly across from the electric artifact crouched a heart-shaped bed with orange tiger-stripe sheets and a red velvet comforter. Near the headboard, a coin-operated device was plugged into the right side of the bed and looked like it had braved some heavy weather. A sign above it read "BILL CHANGER IN PARKING LOT."

J. looked around the room with obvious disgust and threw her purse on the bed.

"What a pig sty!"

I didn't say anything. I was staring at a huge mirror on the ceiling above the bed. It was so badly smudged and tainted that I couldn't really see myself clearly. I sort of looked like John Wayne.

"I can't believe I paid $240 for this, this . . ." Words failed her, temporarily. "It's so tasteless, it even has a heart-shaped bed. Can you believe, a heart-shaped bed in a motel that looks like the Alamo? Sacrilege!"

"I guess the interior decorator didn't know what shape lust is," I said distractedly, still looking into the depths of the mirror.

J. looked at me for a minute and then said, "Bud, you have a lot to learn. Lust comes in all shapes and sizes."

Man, there was nothing to say to that. Something about being tutored by a transvestite in an Alamo-shaped whorehouse on the back side of nowhere seems to just shut me down.

I locked myself in the bathroom. I sat in the tub, for who knows why, and suddenly fell into a dream, only to find myself in a large room with no windows. There were no lights, but everything was illuminated with a strange blue glow, sort of like black light, but closer perhaps to the neon blue of a flat screen TV.

The room itself was split-level, with a rectangular area in the center, two or three feet lower than the rest, with steps on all sides that led down. There was a couch in it, off to the side, so I walked to it, sat down, and waited.

A faint dripping noise began to grow, faintly then louder, louder, and looking around I saw water beginning to trickle down the opposite wall. Within moments, water was streaming down the other walls and under the door as the lower level began to fill up. I looked for an exit and, pulling my feet up onto the couch, saw for the first time, on an adjacent wall, a large, framed painting of a guy walking out of a similar room, stepping into darkness and looking back over his shoulder. The profile of his face and one arm stood out in relief against the blackness of wherever he was going, illuminated by the light from the open door. A bronze plaque at the bottom of the wood frame was inscribed: "Departures."

In the same room, another man—maybe a corpse—lay on a marble slab; beyond him an older man and woman wearing a wimple sat with heads bowed, hands folded in their laps. Between them crouched a massive clown in red and yellow polka dots, fake orange hair, and plastic bald spot. Unlike the other two, the clown's face was top lit, casting his eyes in deep wells of shadow in contrast to his illuminated forehead and cheekbones. He stared straight out the door, smiling sardonically, with a look of malevolent speculation, pure and terrifying.

Realizing with a gut wrench that the body on the table was the same man in the foreground, I tried to shake myself awake, but no use.

Water was running down the wall and directly over the front of the painting now and was beginning to make the colors comprising the figures dissolve into one another, all but the demonic presence in the clown suit, stark and unscathed, who was watching me.

The water was to the top of the couch seat now, and wanting to run or scream for help, I couldn't . . . still trapped in sleep, and anyway, there was no one to call.

A loud pounding coming from the wall with the painting. It grew louder and louder yet, then I woke with a start.

I was disoriented, but the events of the last few hours began to coalesce. The heavy thudding against the door continued; J. was flailing away for all she was worth. I was sitting in six inches of ice-cold water and, reaching for the faucet, realized I'd never turned it on.

"Colin! Open up! We've got to get out of here!" J. yelled through the door.

I hesitated then opened the door, surprised to see J. standing there in a t-shirt and boxer shorts, sans makeup, and looking for all the world like a reasonably well-adjusted white male.

"What have you done with Julie?" I asked.

"Very few transvestites sleep in drag."

"That's comforting."

She looked almost scared.

"Shut up! Shut up now! We have to leave. The manager from the front desk just called and said some guys are in the lobby looking for us."

Chapter 20

It took a moment for the full weight of this little bombshell to sink in, but when it did, I became a man of words.

"They are going to come in here, take back their money, kill us, and bury us in a shallow grave."

I sat down on the edge of the bed, and as I put my head in my hands, inspiration fell on me like a benediction.

"You don't happen to have any men's clothes, do you?" I asked, looking at her, but I knew the answer.

J. shook her head absently. "No. Why?"

Now J. didn't look scared, but didn't seem interested in trying to fight her way out of the motel either. Regardless, she seemed to think I was trying to help her.

"I have an idea. Give me the car key. Then run into the lobby, screaming that a moose-sized prostitute and her pimp stole you blind. While you're ranting and raving, I'll climb out the window, get the car, pull around front, and when you see me, run and jump in."

J. looked at me and said, "If I give you the key, you'll leave me."

"No, I won't. Scout's Honor," I lied. "Look, you don't have a choice. You're too big to go out that window, and together or separate, we can't slip past them in the lobby. Try to walk out casually, they're going to think it a bit odd that you don't have any clothes on. If you get dressed and go out there without makeup, they'll likely shoot you on sight, and if not, at the very least, they'll hold us here for the police." I stopped and she still wasn't buying it. "Your dance card has been punched."

Tough logic to argue against. I was banking on her causing a big enough diversion for me get to the car. Then I was going to save my ass, but feed hers to the wolves.

J. thought about it for a minute and then tossed me the key.

"If you try to get away without me, I will hunt you down, find you, and kill you."

"Trust me." I smiled. J. took a deep breath, grabbed my duffle bag, and ran out the door screaming murder and mayhem.

I crawled out the window and ran around the edge of the building, but stopped short and jumped back into the shadows. A large bubba holding a baseball bat was sitting on the hood of my car. What is it with strange men and my car? It's the story of my life; that's what it is.

I'm firmly convinced that if the truth were known, for most of the great, heroic, and noteworthy feats that have been accomplished throughout the history of the world, desperation was probably the single most common motivating factor.

I took a couple of deep breaths and ran from my hiding place, yelling at the top of my lungs. I'd like to say that I was screaming a war cry calculated to strike fear and confusion into the hearts of brave men, but, as often happens when under duress, one's rational mind seems to step back, totally disconnected from one's body to say, "Yeah, I'm just gonna sit this one out."

Which is why, as I rounded the corner and closed in on the large farmer-type holding my car hostage, I was howling, "THE QUEEN IS DEAD!"

I never slowed down and never shut up. He slid off the hood of the car with the grace and elegance of a pregnant three-legged cow on a steep hill, while I closed the gap between us, chanting my unique little ditty from the backside of my subconscious and waving my arms around my head like I was fending off a swarm of hornets.

Approaching him, it became obvious that my stride needed to be modified a bit to fulfill my purpose, so I hopped straight into the air, skipped once, and hit him as hard as I could right between the eyes.

He slid to the ground with a groan, and I jumped into the car and fired it up, dumped the clutch, and fish-tailed around, headed for the gate.

As I rounded the side of the building, I saw J. staggering out with three or four guys beating on her, and probably the same synapses that fired off my "The queen is dead" thing hijacked my body again.

In any event, whatever it was prompted me to swing the Vette around and drive straight at the struggling mob. Cutting close, I swerved aside at the last instant and grazed two of them, sending them sprawling. I circled back, stopped the car, and watched.

The odds were more or less evened for J., and she threw one of the men still holding onto her down, then kicked him in the stomach. The remaining combatant tried to get loose, but J. grabbed him and started slamming his head against the front of the car.

I was honking the horn and screaming at her to stop, but she wouldn't. I jumped out and tried to drag her off, but she spun around and hit me in the chest with a flat, straight-armed punch that snapped the wind out of me. I sat down heavily, trying to catch my breath.

Then she just stopped. Gulping in huge ragged gasps of air, she looked around as if waking from a nightmare, looked at me, and as recognition fired in her eyes, pitched me into the car. Then I saw a blur out of the corner of my eye as something hit me in the side of the head.

I don't remember anything after that.

Chapter 21

I dreamed that J. and I were in a third world country gulag and had somehow gotten a laptop. It was imperative to communicate her message to the outside, and as she dictated, I typed furiously as the battery drained, lower and still lower. When she nodded an okay, I hit the "send" button, and moments later, an alarm sounded somewhere in the prison, followed almost immediately by another outside, deep in the dark city. Then others, farther and farther away, faint then fainter still, until once again there was only silence. We looked at each other, and she said, "Either it hit the internet and got loose or was flagged by the censors here." I nodded in agreement. "We'll see if they heard us," she said. I heard a faint cough somewhere close by. "They might be closing in."

I came to for a moment and then lights out again.

Wind in my hair, and she was stretched out on the beach, though what beach or who she was was a mystery. She was lithe and dark-haired, and as she turned to me, weird music played louder and louder, and then I woke up in the passenger seat next to J., who was smoking a cigarette and driving along in cat-eye sunglasses and a sundress that was about as old as the car. She had a scarf tied over her hair to keep it from blowing off. The only thing remaining from my dream was the music, and it definitely was stranger than fiction. Herb Alpert and the Tijuana Brass were driving straight into my brain while J. kept the beat by rapping her knuckles, some of which were conspicuously devoid of skin, on the dashboard.

There wasn't a cloud in the sky, and J. was all smiles too.

"What happened last night?" I asked her.

"Oh, guess we upset some people. Your plan didn't work too well."

"I'm going to Graceland with an alien," I said to the wind.

"How do you feel?"

"Okay, I guess. What time is it?"

"About 9:30. How's the noggin?"

"What?"

"Your noggin, your head? How is it?" J. repeated.

"Hurts. What happened?"

"Didn't see a thing. I put you in the car, hopped in, and drove like a girl possessed. When I noticed you, I thought you'd gone to sleep. Until I saw the blood, that is."

"Blood. I'm bleeding. Great."

"Well, you're not bleeding now. I looked you over. You'll live."

Herb was really starting to get to me.

"What is that crap you're listening to?" I yelled at J.

"Crap?" J. asked innocently, tapping herself on the forehead as if in thought. "Crap? Hmmm. I'm really not at all sure what you're talking about."

"On the radio."

"There is no crap on our radio," J. returned.

"There's no 'our' in radio either." We looked at each other. "Is there?"

"Well, that's fairly obvious, I think."

"The music then."

"Oh, you mean my new Herb Alpert CD. Isn't he divine?"

"Had something a little less complimentary in mind," I said, and then I looked down, saw the case and the price of Herb's latest crime against man.

"You paid $13.99 for—"

J. silenced me with a look.

"How silly of me. Of course you didn't pay $13.99 for Herb and the boys. Where'd you pick it up?"

"We filled up at a little Valero a ways back. I used your gas card. Hope you don't mind—" J. started.

"And Herb came with us," I finished for her. "So now I guess we can add the AAA Auto Club to the ever-growing list of people who have orders to shoot us on sight."

"Thanks for picking me up last night," J. said, changing the subject.

"A mistake I won't make twice. I meant to run over you."

"Oh, don't be silly. It was very nice. You did the right thing."

"Right? What's that? Don't answer. Don't say anything. Just leave me alone."

72

We drove along in silence for the better part of an hour until we saw a diner. The main part of the building was an old trolley car that was painted orange, black, and yellow. Fused to what would have been the back of the trolley was a cinder block structure that no one had bothered to paint. It was new looking, but then again, the desert was—obviously—dry, so it might have been forty years old. One lesson I was learning was that things sure aren't always what they seem. I told J. to stop, and she pulled up in front of the door. Two dogs trotted by, and I watched them until they disappeared behind an old truck abandoned--as opposed to parked—at the edge of the lot.

The cinder block store had a huge sign on top of it that read "MIKE'S BIKE EXTRAVAGANZA" in huge block letters, with "Bicycles for the Masses" in smaller letters directly underneath.

We walked in and sat down at a booth and waited. About five minutes passed, in which nothing was said, and then a short, stocky guy walked out of the back and up to our table. He was holding a bicycle rim in one hand and balancing two glasses of water in the other, which he placed in front of us.

J. and I took one look at him and I said, "You must be Mike."

"Yep, that'd be me!"

"Are you still serving breakfast?" J. asked.

"That's all we serve, morning, noon, and night."

We just stared.

"People break their fasts at all hours," he added.

Entirely too cheerful.

We didn't answer.

"What would you folks be needin' on this fine morning? No! Let me guess! Let me guess! Two of my famous Peddler's Breakfast Combos and a new, bright, shiny twelve-speed touring bicycle apiece!" He smiled wide and big. "I suggested the Peddler's Breakfast Combo because it's two eggs over easy with hash browns, toast, and choice of sausage or ham steak, and because it's morning—the traditional time to break fast—and you two look to be traditional!" He looked J. over once more, then asked brightly, "Want to make it three combos?"

Yep, that's us. Traditional.

J. got up from the table and stalked off to the ladies' room. Mike watched her go and then turned to me and said, "I surely do hope I've got a bike that is, uh, that can . . . what I mean to say is, that will accommodate a lady of her stature," he finished, beaming in satisfaction for having not put his foot entirely in his mouth.

"Well, I surely do hope so too," I said. "In case a lady of her stature does come in here with the intention of buying a bike, instead of, say, breakfast."

Mike took my hint.

"I'll get those combos on the stove."

As he turned to go, I stopped him. "What town are we in?"

He looked thoughtful, but I doubt he was. "Acomita," he said. As Mike went to the kitchen to fix breakfast, I stopped him again.

"Got wi-fi?"

"Sure," he said. "Password is on the bottom of the menu. Anything else? No? I'll make your food."

I looked at the bottom of the menu, and just as promised, there was the password: Pedalazzz!!! Jeez.

While J. was gone, I logged on with my phone, thinking I might check email. That seemed like a course of action bound to bring only pain, and figuring there'd be no shortage of dead spots between here and Graceland—or wherever this was going to end—I just downloaded and saved all the music in my account; luckily, the new phone had lots o' memory. J. returned from the bathroom, and I noticed for the first time that the left side of her face was swollen a little and that she was wearing extra makeup, which I hadn't thought possible, to compensate.

"The way I see it, we're about 500 miles from Memphis and . . ." she paused for effect, "Graceland." She breathed Graceland out like a benediction and looked at me solemnly for support or something, I don't know.

"Do you have a job? Who are you?" I yelled at her.

"Yes, I have a job. I work for the Arizona Department of Wildlife."

"Yes? And?" As per the norm, I was lost.

"I'm a game warden."

"A game warden."

The vision of four or five men being stopped by J. in the woods and asked to show their identification and hunting licenses got the drop on me. Four or five men, no doubt having saved their money and vacation time for the opportunity to get out in the woods, forget showers, nix shaving, and then here comes J., popping out from behind a tree, dressed in the height of game law enforcement fashion no doubt, to inquire. Four or five unsuspecting . . .

"Hello? Colin? Anybody home? I see that the lights—"

"What?" I snapped.

"Breakfast. My, aren't we touchy," she said. Mike was eyeing us from the counter, looking at what appeared to be a catalog.

"Why are you here? Shouldn't you be out making sure that the rights of ducks or rabbits or something aren't being infringed upon?"

"Oh, I'm on vacation. That's why I was in such a state when we met. The first couple of my vacation days are always like that, and then I get better, you know, stop hanging out at the café and such," she said nicely.

"So you've done this sort of thing before?"

"What sort of thing?"

"You know what I mean. This," I said, sweeping my hand around.

"I'm not sure I—"

"This!" I yelled. "Kidnapping! Extortion! Rape!"

"Don't be silly. No one's been raped." She narrowed her eyes. "No one's going to either."

"But you have done this sort of thing before. Used your feminine, well, your wiles, to lure some unsuspecting kid from safety, hijacked his Corvette, whatever, then forced him to drive you to Graceland."

"Kidnapped? You practically begged me to go with you. God knows what you had in mind."

I slapped the table with the flat of my hand. Her eyebrows rose in surprise.

"But you have!" I yelled. "You have done this sort of thing before?"

"No. I've never done this sort of thing before," J. said.

"But?"

"But I've often thought I should."

Up at the counter, Mike shook his head, muttered something to himself, flipped through some more pages, and absently swatted at a fly.

I glanced out the window and watched the heat waves rise off the asphalt, wondered if there is life after death and, if so, could my grandmother see me.

My reverie ended when Mike brought the food and the breakfast combos were not all that bad. I really hadn't had an opportunity to watch J. eat yet, but wasn't surprised to note that her table manners were good, even though she was obviously starving.

My head was pounding from whatever had hit me the night before, and every time I looked out into the parking lot, the exertion of squinting against the sunlight made it worse.

There wasn't a trace of the previous night's flood. In the distance, three or four vultures circled high up, wings spread against the blue sky that looked like eternity, lazily riding the thermals and watching, I imagined, me.

Chapter 22

The rigors of the previous day/night were taking their toll on J. The rain-drenched drive alone had been taxing enough, but the fight had left its damage too. Afternoon tilted into late afternoon, and her driving became more and more erratic as she nodded into one 70-miles-per-hour micronap after another.

We hadn't spoken since that morning, though she made a couple of half-hearted attempts every now and then to explain where we were, what roads we had taken or would take, and how long it'd take to get from here to there. As for me, I was in no mood for anything. The fact that this whole fiasco was the product of my botched attempt at God alone knew what really brought me down.

One lesson I'd homed in on was that you can try to run from your circumstances—real or otherwise—but the pound of flesh will always be collected.

About four, J. finally gave up and pulled over onto the shoulder. She looked at me for a long second.

"I'm worn out, but we can't stop this early. I'm going to nap and let you drive awhile. Stay on 66 and wake me when we get to Shamrock, Texas."

"Aw, hey that's great! You're going to let me drive my own car? Wow, thanks!" There might have been a touch of sarcasm in my voice, but no more than, you know . . . a touch?

J. let me know with a look that she didn't find it funny. I was thinking that maybe, when she got out of the car, I'd have a second to shove it into gear and leave her, but she nuked that plan by sliding toward me and making me crawl over her, like you do when you're driving and don't want to stop, even though, as I mentioned, we were stopped.

While we were struggling to achieve a maneuver that the engineers at General Motors probably hadn't taken into their calculations, several truckers and other passersby slowed down to stare and honk and, in general, make me feel most uncomfortable. The switch was finally completed, and we sat in our respective seats, gasping for air, arranging our clothes, and looking like two teenagers parked behind the stadium getting ready to head home after prom night.

"Which way is Shamrock?" I panted, all the while thinking about the weight of her pressing down on me.

Quick movement in the rearview mirror and I jumped, illogically thinking maybe the men from the Alamo had found us. Instead, it was the old woman who had given me directions out in the desert.

"You stay on the same road you started on," she said as she walked up to J.'s side of the car. "There are no turns between here and your destination."

"Hi!" J. said. "You need a ride?"

I wondered briefly where J. expected her to sit, but the old woman just smiled, shook her head, and began to walk back from wherever she had come from.

"You know her?" I asked. My eyes were opened as wide as my mouth.

"Oh sure," J said. "Doesn't everyone?"

"Well, I don't know her," I said. "I mean, not well. Not even her name. But I do know her. Sort of."

J. gave me a strange look.

"I've never seen that old woman before in my life, and neither have you. Now shut up and drive."

I started to say something, but a look in the mirror revealed that the old woman had disappeared. Again. I didn't see any point in arguing and didn't want to.

"Stay on this road, got it? She was right about that, even though there are definitely some turns between here and Memphis. Wake me up at nine or ten, and I'll be ready to relieve you," J. said, pulling the key out of the ignition switch.

And with that unfortunate choice of words, she went instantly to sleep. Relieve me. I sat behind the wheel and looked around. Car looked the same but felt different, like maybe it looked like a Corvette but had been assembled on another planet.

I eased the seat forward, put the car into first, and pulled back onto the highway. After a couple of minutes driving along and listening to the wind and J.'s snoring battling it out, I scrolled around on my phone for something to take my mind off the present. After a bit of vacillation trying to choose between Otis Redding or The Cure, I chose the latter, connected the aux cord, and turned the volume up. I listened along for a while and began to realize that most everything the lead singer had to say should be filed in the categories of "Depression" and/or "Weird," not that he had anything on me. I killed the tunes on the premise that listening to the pseudo-philosophical ramblings of someone who was more screwed up than me wasn't exactly what my condition called for.

Glancing to where J. sat slumped in slack-jawed oblivion, I wished there was some way to push her out of the car without killing her. There had to be some speed at which she'd sort of skid gently to a stop without sustaining permanent—ideally, any—injury (and maybe even remain sleeping!). But I was clueless how to figure out what it'd be. Obviously, I'd have to take into consideration speed, body weight, force of impact trajectory, and road surface, i.e., composition, texture, hardness, volume of broken glass, pebbles, metal shards, racoon shit, and other debris. And that was just the stuff that came to mind. I knew that, in addition to these, there would be other variables of which I was completely unaware. That's not exactly the kind of practical equations they teach in college physics.

One thing was certain: if I decided to shove that leviathan out of the Vette, I would definitely need speed on my side, but as the highway department is so fond of pointing out, "Speed Kills." Of course, lack of speed at the outset of, or any point in between, my exorcism of J. would probably have fatal consequences too, though not for her. So, it was her or me or her *and* me.

And just as I was about to give up, loomed the overpass.

Chapter 23

Massive, modern, smooth . . . it was grace personified in concrete and obviously designed by someone who, at one time or another, had needed to make a 180-degree turn without sacrificing velocity, or tipping anyone off. If only life had been designed with similar features.

The clock on the radio read "16:13," and figuring it was now or not at all, I hesitated then drew the steering wheel ever so lightly to the right and exited. Immediately, my unconscious burden and I were in a tight arc that curved to the left, and what had been eastbound was suddenly riding westward.

I tried to think of what to tell J., in the event that she suddenly woke to a sun setting in blazing jubilation east of Eden and Graceland, but gave up, deciding that, if she did wake, I'd just hope for the best. Maybe the shock would kill her. That possibility pleased me so much that I offered a silent prayer to any interested party or parties, that in the event of the untimely wake-up/demise on the part of J., I'd crank this sucker back, drive to Memphis, and leave her remains and the car at the gates of Graceland. Hell, I'd even leave the motor running.

The idea of depositing J.'s corpse at Graceland carried with it some obvious parallels to the commonly accepted destination of the soul that bordered on the mystical and that, at the time, seemed full of portent and power. Now, though, I just believed that my sanity was falling victim to the road and, uh, other things.

Evidently, my supplication found no takers, and so on we drove, enveloped in silence and trailing a shadow, which lengthened with the setting sun that marked, if only for a moment, our passing.

Chapter 24

It was almost 9:00 p.m. and the sun went down, as it so often does. I had settled down into a serious driving groove, and we had re-entered New Mexico, you know, "The Land of Enchantment," while J. was in the land of sleep. We were headed back to Arizona, with California looming on some horizon beyond.

The Vette needed gas, but J. was gone like the dead and didn't wake up, even when I made a pit stop a couple of hours past Milagro on Route 66, near Cline's Corners, then immediately made a wrong turn and didn't realize it until I stopped for gas again at the Flying C Ranch and discovered we were in some burgh named Encino. That said, it may be true that two wrongs don't make a right, but three lefts do, and pretty soon we were cruising north on 41, en route to Moriarity, where I took a left turn and pointed us back at Arizona.

Chapter 25

Around 3:00 a.m., J. woke up.

For the past several hours, I had begun to entertain the foolish hope that maybe she was so knocked out that she'd sleep straight through to Wide Ruin, where I could roll to a gentle stop, open her door like a gentleman, and then drag her ass out of the car, hop back in, haul ass, and continue on to somewhere near that Pacific Ocean. Oregon, maybe. Japan?

Didn't happen.

"Uuuummm . . ." Silence for a few seconds. "Where are we?"

"Beats me. I'm just a victim of circumstance. You're the pilot."

"What time is it?"

I looked at my watch. "Midnight," I lied.

"You've been driving for nine hours? You must be exhausted." She looked around and rubbed her forehead. "Pull over."

The truth of the matter was that I wasn't tired at all; I was wired to the gills, wondering what J. was going to do to me when she woke to see those saguaro cacti leering at us from the side of the road. Vacation was about to end on an ugly note. If only she'd go back to sleep for a couple of minutes, and I could find another one of those overpasses like the one that started all of this trouble . . .

"Colin!"

"What?"

"I said pull over and stop. I'll drive for a while."

A request this wasn't, so I reluctantly complied. J. put the key in the ignition and turned the car off. Then, taking the key, she got out and walked to the back of the car to relieve herself. Standing up. When she finished, she stretched and looked around, then walked to the driver's side.

I slid over, noting that it was much easier this way. J. assumed the driving chores, and I settled back into my seat. My teeth may have been chattering.

We drove for a couple of hours, talking about this and that but not really saying anything, when off in the distance a dull smudge, less dark than the rest, gradually coalesced into a pool of light that began to form, and J. said she would kill or die for a cup of coffee.

We weren't near any towns, and it was probably just some isolated truck outpost in the wilderness. I figured that when we stopped, if J. did tell someone where she thought we were headed, they wouldn't know from which direction we'd come.

We got closer and a feeling of deja vu settled over me, which wasn't too strange since I had been there before. In horror and amazement, I saw a sign that could not have freaked me out any more than if God Himself had suddenly reared up to straddle the foothills in a cloud of brimstone and ash, with lightening arcing and crackling across his body, to point down at me shouting, "THERE'S THE SON OF A BITCH NOW!" The sign read, "Mike's Bike Extravaganza"; you can figure the rest.

J. slammed on the brakes and stopped under the sign, looking first at it, then at me, and then back to the sign. Very calmly and deliberately she said, "Before I break every last bone in your body and suck the marrow out, I want you to tell me what this diner is doing here."

If I didn't think well, I did think fast, and I said that Mike's was probably some chain that was expanding into Texas, like us.

"A chain, huh?"

"Yeah, you know, like McDonald's," I said knowingly, while I nodded my head for emphasis.

"McDonald's. Uh-huh. Okay, let's go to America's newest chain," J. said icily, "and see how McDonald's stacks up."

"Oh, uh, that's a bad idea. You know that first place was just the worst . . ."

It was no use. J. had already pulled up in front, parking exactly where we had that morning. We walked inside, and there stood Mike his ownself, grinning from ear to ear. I thought he was going to hug us.

"Yep, just as I thought," I said before J. could say anything. "These places are all the same."

J. stared at me for a full minute while I tried to look sincerely confused. "Give me a coffee, black, no sugar, to go," she said to Mike, "and make it fast." She stomped back out to the car.

We looked at each other, and Mike winked at me, then turned to the coffee maker.

Chapter 26

We put in some hard driving for the rest of the night. For once, J. was the one who wouldn't talk. I tried to sleep but, what with the wind and the choppy ride (built for speed not comfort), hardly dozed off.

An interesting quirk about J. was that she would never speed, regardless of the circumstances. Maybe it had something to do with her law enforcement background, but I doubt it, since that didn't stop her from doing much of anything else. Just as the sun climbed the horizon, we stopped at a Valero for gas.

J. checked the oil in the Vette, and I bought a cup of coffee and some doughnuts. I walked back to the car as she pretended to flirt with the attendant, asking him if he was local, what it was like around there, and how far it was to Albuquerque. He was polite, but he kept looking at her as if something was off and he couldn't quite place it. It was hard to blame him. Although she still looked good, the past thirty-six hours hadn't been kind ones to J., and it was beginning to show.

J. may have taken more upkeep than me, but we both looked like a couple of refugees from Detroit. She paid cash for the gas, went in and got some coffee, and then we were back on the highway. I shared my doughnuts with her. We passed a billboard of Billy Stan Freeburgh, staring menacingly down at passersby, with his index finger raised in admonition. The day began afresh.

Chapter 27

Two or three hours outside of Albuquerque, J. suddenly began talking again.

"I need makeup."

"Huh?" I asked.

"I need to stop somewhere and get some makeup," J. said with exaggerated patience.

We were blasting along, still headed east toward a land whose boundaries I figured even the vultures skirted, and looking at J., I wondering what made her think I even remotely cared.

She continued, "It has to be someplace big, like a mall. I want to go to a Saks or—"

"I'm not going anywhere near a mall with you," I said and looked back out the window at the telephone poles that snapped past like so many missed opportunities. J. didn't say anything else, so I thought maybe she'd given up on the makeup thing, but as soon as we hit Albuquerque, she started scouting for a mall, and when she saw one, pulled into the parking lot.

"This'll have to do," she said.

"What?"

"Come on. We're there."

"There?"

"Here."

Seeing nothing to gain by sitting in the car, exposed to the afternoon sun and watchful eyes while J.—and more importantly, the key—went into the mall, I started to get out, but then J. asked, "You staying? Fine. I'll leave the key so you can listen to the radio."

My comatose hopes began to stir.

"Whatever." I tried to sound disinterested.

She gave me a smile of pity or something else.

"Not a chance. See ya in a couple of hours," J. said over her shoulder as she walked off.

I watched her stride across the parking lot, surprised at how much distance each giant step ate up and, as usual, I was strangely impressed. J. was a force to be reckoned with. A weird force, but a force nonetheless.

I couldn't figure out this penchant she had for dressing like she was going to a job interview or something. She could play the petite, demure sexpot—well, okay, not petite, but demure sexpot—to a tee in a crowd of strangers, but one-on-one, she took control. Totally.

I abandoned my thoughts on J.

When we got into Albuquerque, cell service had reappeared. During a momentary lapse of insanity, I decided to call someone from home and see what, if anything, was going on. I didn't want to call Mom or Gianfranco. For some reason, ever since I'd stolen the car and the money, I felt a little more kindly disposed towards Ralph and had begun to call him, at least to myself, by his nom de choix, Gianfranco.

I finally decided to call James, a friend of mine from college.

"Colin? Man, where've you been?"

"Dark side of the moon."

"Well, there's people looking all over for you. They're probably lookin' there for you now."

"Yeah, I'd guessed. Mom and Gianfranco?"

"Who?"

"Ralph. Mom and Ralph?"

"Who's John Frank?"

"Our gardener. From Italy. You two should get together."

"Uh, yeah, right. Your mom called, sure, but not just her, and no, it wasn't your dad or the gardener. It was two big burly guys. Dark car, dark suits, dark shades . . . said they wanted to talk to you about your new car. I didn't know you got a new car."

"Uh, yeah, sort of . . ." I trailed off, wondering how—

"You're always gettin' a new car . . ."

"Yeah."

". . . and I'm still drivin' mom's minivan . . ."

"Uh-huh," I groaned.

". . . that we used to take on vacation back in the nineties . . ."

"Well . . ."

"I wanna trade parents . . ."

"Okay."

". . . and then maybe I'll get a new car . . ."

I hung up. Maybe calling James wasn't such a good idea after all. Pretty much all he did was sit in his room, smoke dope, and watch CatDog and Samurai Champloo cartoons all day long. But he didn't hallucinate. And even if he did, I doubt it'd be two burly guys in dark suits looking por moi. It sounded like he'd seen Dale and Howard, two guys that were always hanging around my stepfather's office. They're the ones that got this whole Gianfranco thing started in the first place, and Gianfranco must have had them visit everyone I'd ever met. An idea had been tugging at the back of my mind during my exchange with James, and now, with time to kill and J. the conqueror out of my sphere for at least another hour, I decided to try it.

I walked back to the car, got into the driver's seat, and fumbled for the hood latch under the dash. I found it after about ten minutes and was rewarded with a heavy clunk as the hood released. Getting out of the car, I went and stared in consternation down into the engine bay. The motor was crouched between the fenders like an iron spider, replete with a web of belts, wires, and hoses that sprouted from every surface at different angles. Each and every part of that engine was a tangible reminder of my failure in high school Auto Shop class: Oh, the horror.

I felt confident and a little vindicated in the knowledge that no one from this planet could stand in the presence of anything of such fugitive design and not be cowed. I was wrong.

"Problems?"

Hunched over as I was, in an ignorance-induced apprehension, I sort of twisted around, looking over my left shoulder and squinting my eyes against the afternoon sun, a la Quasimodo. When I saw who, or I should say what, was addressing me, I froze. Officer Friendly had materialized by my side.

"No, no. No problems," I blurted out.

"Why's the hood up, then?" he asked, understandably.

I stood there for a minute with the realization that life as I knew it had ended, not with a bang, not with a whimper, but with a question. All in all, that seemed reasonable enough to me. Acceptance that I was about to be irrevocably smashed on the windshield of fate seemed to have a calming effect, and I felt much better. I stood up and, turning around, addressed the policeman.

"Well, actually, I am having a bit of trouble. This bright red chunk of Americana here belongs to my uncle, an uncle that not only is unaware of its accompanying me to go shopping but who will kill me if he finds out. I lost the key somewhere in the mall. So, I was wondering if you could help me start it?"

Against the backdrop of recent events, asking an officer of the law to help me steal a car seemed, well, not normal but not exactly abnormal either. If I was going to steal a car twice, it would certainly be this one.

I tried to give him a look that combined friendly boy-next-door honesty with good old down-home stupidity in one convenient package.

"I think I'd like to see your license right about now," he said.

My one shot having failed, I now realized, with more than a bit of trepidation, that when he called in my license number and realized that not only had I already stolen this car but I was also trying to include him in the festivities, things were about to get ugly. I was going to have to spend the rest of my days in the big house where large men were going to give me prison tattoos with ball pen ink and make fun of me for not knowing how to hotwire a car, let alone not just shooting the cop and going about my business.

"Right now, to be exact, sir," he said with that fake politeness cops use when they're about to jack you up. I realized that I had been standing motionless, staring at him with my mouth open and looking as guilty as I was.

I fished my wallet out and tried to hand him the whole thing, but he didn't take it.

"Hand me your license, sir."

When I opened my wallet to get my license, he let out a low whistle when he saw how thick the bills were in it.

"That's a lot of money for a guy your age to be carrying."

"About two thousand," I said.

"That's a lot of money for a guy any age to be carrying."

"Well, you know how it is: shop till you drop," I said lifelessly.

"You should talk to my wife. Okay, uh, Colin, step over to the car, please."

We got into his car, and I looked around. I was strangely calm. I was beginning to feel at home sitting in the passenger seats of various vehicles with men I didn't know.

He punched my identification numbers into his computer. While we waited for the information to load, he baited me. I guess he was trying to do the "Good Cop/Bad Cop" routine by himself.

"The address on your license says you're from Dallas. You from Dallas, sir?"

"Yes."

"You're a long way from Kansas. You a runaway?"

"Kansas? What are you talking about?"

"I was making a joke, sir. You know . . . Dorothy? Wizard of Oz?"

"Oh, a joke. No, I'm on vacation. Kansas wasn't on the itinerary," I said.

He looked at me. "Vacation? What person in his right mind would want to vacation here?"

"What's sanity got to do with it?"

"Just answer the question, please."

"Told you. I'm visiting my uncle."

"I don't know, but it just seems kind of odd that a college kid would choose to spend his vacation here, even with his uncle."

"I'm kind of an odd person," I murmured, looking out the window. About that time, the computer beeped, and my entire driving record, which took four screens to accommodate, appeared. He whistled through his teeth again.

"Now that's what I call a lot of tickets. Your daddy must have a good lawyer."

"My dad is dead," I answered, looking him straight in the eye.

This bothered him, which was more than I'd expected. He dropped the tough-guy act. "I'm sorry. I shouldn't of said that."

I shrugged my shoulders and looked back out the window. It didn't much matter, and I figured that any time now he was going to get to the last screen and be informed that not only was my driving record as long as a sermon on Christmas but that the latest addition held roughly the same standing in relation to the rest of my record that Christmas does to the rest of the year.

He cleared his throat, "Well, nothing much here. Let's go into the mall and see if your key has been turned into security."

He cleared the screen.

I was barely listening. Some mistake had been made, and contrary to usual, it was in my favor. His computer either didn't have access to the

Dallas Police Department files or, more unlikely, it just hadn't been updated yet. I didn't want to go into the mall, but I didn't want to arouse more suspicion either, so I followed.

After deciding that I was involved in no wrongdoing, the cop got very chatty and introduced himself as "Wentworth, Ken."

I had completely forgotten about J., and as we entered Saks, I was suddenly aware of a low, buzzing noise inside the store.

Wentworth Ken and I rounded a corner and saw a large crowd milling around the makeup counter, talking excitedly. And then I saw why. Every orifice in my body clamped shut.

J. was sitting on a tall stool, right in the middle of everyone, getting a complete makeover. Problem was, instead of being dressed like her demure little self, she was dressed like a lumberjack: boots, jeans, buffalo plaid shirt, the works.

I stopped dead in my tracks. I didn't think she could shock me anymore. That's one problem with thinking. Just as soon as you get an idea in your head, another one comes along and makes it obsolete. Others can do what they want, but as for me and my house, we will stop thinking.

Wentworth Ken just said, "A man wearing makeup . . . I just don't get it. More homosexuals land out here every day. Must like the weather or something."

"She's not gay," I said absently.

"What? She who?" he asked suspiciously.

I froze for a second and then said, "He, I mean, just a hunch." It sounded like a question.

Wentworth Ken snorted. "You had my job and saw the things I see day in and day out, you wouldn't be so sure of everything."

We walked closer, and I suddenly found myself praying J. wouldn't see me, so of course she did. I don't think reverse psychology would work on God, but sometimes . . . She also noticed Wentworth Ken by my side and tensed up. The girl that was applying the makeup observed this and said chattily, "This is no time to get nervous now, I'm just about to apply the Tenacious Base Coat that will make sure your wife always appears cool and refreshed, whether she is or isn't . . ." her voice trailed off in concentration.

For her part, J. looked like a coiled spring, ready to snap at any moment, and seemed to be controlling herself with some difficulty.

90

A short, balding man next to us shifted his weight and spoke to his wife: "Loretta, I don't care if your nose falls off, all your teeth come out, or anything else. If you ever ask me to go here or anywhere else and try on a bunch of makeup for you, your bags better be packed and the car runnin', 'cause I'm gonna kill you."

Loretta smiled and sighed a matronly sigh. "Harold, I wouldn't dream of that and you know it. You are far too much of a man," she said, rolling her eyes.

Overhearing this, another man nearby said, "I don't know, but he doesn't exactly look like the futile and frail type to me."

A woman standing next to him nodded. "He is kind of cute, though," she said, "even with makeup."

"Well, we're not accomplishing anything standing here watching the freak show. Let's go find your key," Wentworth Ken said and walked off. I left with him, looking over my shoulder at J., who followed me with her eyes in the mirror.

We went down to the security office, and after about fifteen minutes of fumbling around, the man in charge said that no one had turned in anything except a walking stick.

We looked all over the mall for the nonexistent key, which began to get rather strange because I started looking for it, too, and kind of expected to spot it. Eventually we gave up and, exiting another door, returned to the car.

"Well, sorry we couldn't find your key. I'm not going to do anything about you taking your uncle's car, and I'm not going to hotwire it for you. But," he said slyly and pointed down to the right side of the motor, "see that round thing bolted to the side of the engine?"

"Yeah?"

"That's the starter. See that big red wire and the small black one next to it?"

"Yeah?"

"Well, if you take a screwdriver and touch both of them at the same time, right where they connect to the starter, I think you'll be pleasantly surprised." He was smiling and nodding like a positive idiot now. He got in his car, waved, and drove about fifty yards. Then he stopped and backed up to me. "Make sure it's in neutral before you try that trick I showed you. See you around."

"Thanks," I said. "I'll be around." I felt like the earth had reversed its rotation, all screwed up and twisted. He drove off.

I started laughing. I had my chance. I looked around in the car for a screwdriver. All I found was a quarter, but it looked like it would bridge the gap perfectly.

I knocked the car out of gear, making sure that my feet were clear in case it started to roll. "Starter, restart us!" I exclaimed and jammed the quarter down onto the two terminals. The engine coughed once, and then the quarter turned red hot. I yelled an obscenity at the top of my lungs, and it lashed back at me from across the near-empty parking lot.

An elderly couple walked by with disapproval in their eyes. I looked at my thumb, where I was greeted by the sight of George Washington's head in profile branded into my flesh. Looking closer, I could just make out the word "YTREBIL" in perfect block letters.

I nodded to myself in sudden realization of the symmetry of it all.

Chapter 28

J. walked out of the mall, dressed to kill in a white linen caftan and tan sandals, came up to the car, and informed me that I was a worthless, no-count ass.

"What's the idea, huh? Where's the cop?" she asked, looking around the parking lot for surveillance vehicles or something.

"He's gone."

"Gone where? I hate cops."

"Uh, you're sort of a variation on that theme yourself," I reminded her. J. looked at me uncomprehendingly.

"What 'theme,' exactly, am I a 'variation of'?"

"Now that you mention it, several." Seeing that this didn't exactly smooth any ruffled feathers, I hurried on. "You are a game warden, remember?"

"Well, that's different. We don't go around handing out parking tickets or making people stop speeding."

"No, you go around making sure that people only slaughter one species of animals as opposed to another," I said. "And only at certain times of the year."

"There's a bit more to what I do than that—"

"I can imagine," I interrupted.

"But you still haven't told me what you and Dudley Do-Right were doing in the mall," she finished.

"He thought I looked suspicious so—"

"He took you shopping."

"No. He thought I looked suspicious, so he took me into the mall to ask security if I had done anything that they knew of. When they said no, he let me go."

This didn't entirely pacify her, but she accepted it.

"Out of curiosity, what exactly prompted you to dress like Paul Bunyan before getting the makeover?" I asked.

"You know, if you thought more, you'd ask a lot fewer questions."

"If I thought more, I wouldn't be in this situation," I said.

J. looked at me and nodded.

"Well, what do you think the general reaction would have been if I'd gone in dressed like this and asked for a makeover?" she asked.

"They'd have done it?"

"Precisely. And what do you think the general reaction would have been after the counter girl stripped all of my makeup off and saw me exactly as God made me?"

"Screaming hysterics?"

"Well . . . yeah, probably. So, I went to the men's department first and bought some clothes, changed, and went to the cosmetics counter to buy makeup for my wife. Smart, huh?"

I still had serious doubts about the intelligence of dressing like a woman, kidnapping a car thief, and heading for Graceland on the open road, but didn't mention them.

"Sure," I said. "Smart."

"I also wanted to make sure that I didn't get caught again like we did at the Alamo, needing men's clothes and not having any."

"The Alamo?"

"Yes, the Alamo."

"The Alamo-themed 'motel no tell,' you mean."

J. looked at me, but before she could respond, Wentworth Ken drove up again and, looking at J., asked me how things were going.

"Fine," I said.

"Made yourself a friend, have you?"

"Yeah, I guess you could put it that way. Made her myself!"

J. wasn't saying or doing anything. She was hardly breathing.

"Did it work?" he asked cheerily.

"Not yet."

J. looked at me. I could see the muscles on the sides of her jaws clenching and releasing as she gritted her teeth. Wentworth Ken seemed interested in J. and looked at her closely.

"Have we met before, ma'am?" he asked.

"I don't believe we have," she returned shakily.

"You look awful familiar," he said.

"Well, maybe you've seen her around," I said, and gasped as J. grabbed my thigh with her right hand. I would have sworn that I could hear my femur cracking.

Wentworth Ken noticed that she had her hand on my leg and asked me why he might have seen her around. I don't know what it is, but something about life without parole hardens a man's sensibilities.

"Because this is my aunt and, as you may have guessed, she lives here. I called her on my cell to bring the spare key."

He started laughing and said, "Boy, your uncle's sure gonna be glad when you're gone." He was still laughing as he drove off.

"Me too," I said, and a voice in my head said something that I have since forgotten.

J. waited until he was gone and then said, "So, that's what he thought was so suspicious. You were trying to start the car. If he'd known how ignorant you are of most everything, he'd never have worried about you trying to steal it."

"I stole it once, didn't I?"

"Well, don't try it again."

I said, looking at my seared thumb, "Count on it."

J. looked at my hand, my face, and back to my hand, then started the car, put it in gear, and off we drove, just me, my aunt, and my angst.

YTREBIL, my ass.

Chapter 29

We stopped at a store, and J. left me in the car while she looked around. One thing I had to say for her, if she'd been a lab rat, they would've been proud of her. She learned quickly by trial and error. Instead of just the key this time, she'd popped the hood then disconnected the coil wire, which accompanied her into the store. That way, she said, even if I did manage to hotwire the car without charring myself in the process, it still wouldn't start. She clearly didn't give me the same amount of credit for my abilities to learn from negative stimuli as I did her.

She'd been gone for about twenty minutes, and the sun was burning the nape of my neck. All the while, people walked past looking at the car, whose hood was still up, at me, at the car . . .

Eventually, she came out, and I was fairly relieved to see that the store manager wasn't chasing her. She had a plastic bag full of stuff that presumably she'd paid for. She dropped the sack behind the seat, replaced the coil wire, slammed the hood shut, and got in.

I thought that we were leaving town, but instead, J. drove a few blocks over to some Italian restaurant. After parking the car, she got out, yanked the coil wire off again, and walked inside.

I waited for a few seconds, and then the door of the restaurant opened and J. stuck her arm out, motioning me inside. I sighed heavily.

Once inside, I was shown to the table where J. was seated. I looked around, noting the well-appointed interior, and reached the conclusion that this was the type of dining establishment that needn't worry about its clientele writing on the bathroom walls.

The maitre d' sneered condescendingly from behind his perch, and after about ten minutes, the waiter arrived, fashionably late.

"My name is Gianni, and I will be your waiter this evening. Will you and the . . ." he smiled thinly, "ah, gentleman be dining?" he asked.

"Yes," I said. J. and the waiter both looked at me.

"Yes, thank you," J. said.

Gianni looked at us as if we were a pair of shoes that he found to be particularly disappointing.

"I'll give you a few minutes to look over the menu."

A little while later, a surly guy that was about my age casually strolled over and set down two glasses of water, sloshing them all over the tablecloth. We never saw him again.

After about ten more minutes, Gianni wandered back over to take our order.

"What will the lady be having today?"

"I think I'll have the veal marsala with a side of fettucine alfredo, scampi for an appetizer, and the house salad. Oh, and a split of Chianti."

"Uh, I think I'll just have a cheeseburger and water."

The waiter and J. looked at me like I was a leper. He stalled for another moment, to see if I was joking, and then informed me they didn't serve "American" food. I ordered ravioli, and he left to fill the order. I swear I heard laughter coming from the kitchen.

I looked across the table at J. and wondered why we were here. I'd come to notice that J. rarely did anything without reason. I didn't have long to wait.

"I've got a problem," she said.

I gave her a look I normally reserved for bodybuilders and other types of self-created absurdities and cleared my throat politely. That old Sword of Damocles was clearly hanging over my head.

She seemed to be waiting for me to comment, so I didn't speak, move, or think. After another pause, she continued: "A problem that, frankly, I think you can help solve."

A fly buzzed around, noncommittally, and I, too, avoided eye contact. I faked a yawn.

My glass was running low on water, and I looked around for the water boy, in vain, in vain. All in vain.

"Can you sing?"

"No," I lied. "Tone deaf from birth. Tragic."

"That was more of a rhetorical question. You sing quite well. I've heard you."

"Fine, I can sing. So what?"

"Well, I'm sure you've noticed how many Elvis impersonators are working right now. And as far as I'm concerned, that is a fantastic way to pay tribute to the King. You know what they say: 'imitation is the sincerest form of flattery.'"

"I didn't know they said that. Who exactly are 'they' anyway?"

J. rolled her eyes and continued. "Much as I'd love to, I can't sing, and so I really can't impersonate Elvis. It's just impossible," she said, looking perplexed.

"That's the single most intelligent statement I've heard you make. You look nothing like, uh, the King, and you're about as musically inclined as a car wreck. That's not to say you're not a wonderful—"

J. clamped her hand over my mouth to shut me up.

"That's not the main reason," she hissed. "The reason is that Elvis was—is—a man," she finished, fairly dripping disappointment. "More to the point, he never wore women's clothing."

"That," I said, "is a matter of opinion."

J. cuffed me on the side of head, making my ears ring.

"Say something like that again and I'll break one of your fingers," she promised. I decided to get J.'s mind off of digital incapacitation and back on the Elvis predicament.

"So okay, what's the problem?" I felt that asking that was akin to lying down on the highway, and I sat, waiting for her next little surprise.

"Well, it's two-fold. First, of course, Elvis is a man." She paused and I looked down at my hands. I decided that silence was the better part of valor. "And second, there's a million Elvis impersonators. They're all men too." She waited for me to grasp her point.

"Truuuue," I said. I felt like someone who is driving around, lost, in his own hometown.

"But," she said, pausing for effect, "there are absolutely no Priscilla Presley impersonators. Zero."

That statement, and the idea behind it, shrieked through my head like a thousand-channel broadcast.

I excused myself, went to the bathroom, and caught Gianni leaning against a stall, smoking a joint. He tried to hide it, but I walked up to him, snatched it out of his hand, and bogarted three long, enormous hits. "Put it on the tab," I said.

Chapter 30

I don't think I can give a very accurate portrayal of the rest of our repast, or the rest of the afternoon, for that matter, but I do recall it being extremely pleasant.

J. evidently felt that I'd had enough abuse for one day, and instead of putting in any hard driving, contented herself with adopting a leisurely pace and chattering along about any number of things that, as usual with her, had no basis in fact or reality. A little after dark, we pulled into Milagro, found a motel, and got two rooms. I lay in bed and tried to figure a way out of my little predicament. Leaving was, I suppose, an option if I wanted to leave the car with J., which I didn't, and if I could think of any place to go, which I couldn't. She evidently trusted me enough by now to let me get my own room—I suppose the run-in with Wentworth Ken took care of that, but then again, she'd also rendered the car unstartable and therefore undriveable. What she didn't know was that I'd been more afraid of him than her. Classic example of my life: layers and layers and somewhere, buried deep, a kernel of truth. Maybe. All I knew about the truth in this situation was that I was young, lost, and drunk most of the time. Not necessarily in that order. I tried to make myself pick up the phone and call my mom or an ex-girlfriend or anybody, but once again was surprised at how much effort it seemed to take. Too much.

I opened the chest of drawers in search of the ever-present Gideon's Bible. I figured all that was lacking in making this a completely miserable evening was a little traditional guilt. Read the Bible, maybe think about how life was when dad was still around. No Bible. Relieved, I shut the drawer.

I went out to the pool and sat down under a light, over by the NO LIFEGUARD ON DUTY sign. Thinking back over the past couple of days led my mind back even further to life before this, coddled, surrounded with money, cars, anything and everything, with zero motivation to do anything other than get knee-walking drunk every night and give my parents—particularly Ralph/Gianfranco—grief; a strange, new heaviness crept through me. I'd felt it a little at times, but nothing like this restless, fitful fever. It was harder and harder to breathe, and my head was light and dizzy. Sitting alone in this oasis and surrounded by concrete, trimmed shrubs, trees, and manicured grass, the cool, blue water of the pool was hypnotic. Too cool and too blue to be real, I decided. It scared me, but I don't know why.

I closed my eyes and different, older memories began to separate from one another, in no particular order, though maybe not all of them were mine. Anyway, I drifted in that space for some time, my eyes and body feeling heavier and heavier still as my field of vision narrowed down to a pinpoint.

When I opened my eyes, the pool looked a little different, and as I puzzled over that, an old man, dressed in torn and dirty dress slacks and a once-white, button-down shirt two sizes too large, shuffled up to me and asked for a cigarette. I told him I didn't have any, but he kept on insisting, so I tried to give him five dollars.

He said he didn't want five dollars; he wanted a cigarette. Finally, I got fed up with him and flagged down a cigarette girl dressed in a flapper costume, carrying a tray stocked with Camel, Old Gold, Torchlight, and Raleigh. I asked for a carton of Merits, but she just laughed a little and gave me a pack of Old Gold. I handed them to the old man, and he lit one up, inhaled deeply, and let the smoke drift out of his nostrils and mouth in sheer contentment. I noticed his worn-out loafers and no socks and how the little toe of his left foot pressed against a hole in the shoe.

"What're you thinkin' about?"

"Nothing," I said.

"Yet you're thinking, all the same."

I decided to level with him. "I was wondering why I feel like I do, down, useless, like I'm trying to roll a boulder up the road and it keeps trundling off to one side or the other and getting lodged against the curb." I looked at him as he took another drag.

"I know," he said. "I know that feeling."

"And?"

"And what?"

"What am I supposed to do about it? All of it?"

He looked down at his clothes, the frayed belt he wore and the tobacco flecking his tattered shirt, then across at me with a strange look on his face, as if he'd just read his own obituary or something. I don't know.

"Telling you will do you no good. Lessons are earned, not given."

"Oh? Why's that?"

He leaned toward me, and he smelled like cheap wine and old sweat.

"Because they're all upside down." He leaned back, the strange look on his face gone and replaced with smiles, a satisfied, almost childish look, as if he had left and was suddenly someone else. Then he continued. "You know why?"

"No." I was starting to wish he'd go away.

"Me neither." He started laughing at me. The sudden shift in topic and personality, just as it seemed like I was going to get something, infuriated me. Standing up, I slugged him in the side of the head as hard as I could, catching him unaware and dazing him. Then I pushed him into the pool. He couldn't swim, and I wouldn't help, but I would watch as he flailed and splashed for what seemed like days and then sank beneath the surface. It was over.

He was floating facedown, three feet or so under the water, with his arms outstretched, like he was flying down a hall trying to touch both walls at once. Feeling nauseous and heavy again, I sat down on the edge of the pool and dangled my feet in the water. I thought maybe if I swirled the water around with my legs, I could make him move a little. Then I wouldn't feel so bad. The cigarette girl came up and pulled her costume up over her head and off. She was younger than me and pretty, with blonde hair and blue eyes and little beads of sweat over her upper lip.

She sat down beside me, and we both looked down at him, shifting slowly underwater as if to some lullaby we couldn't quite hear.

"I don't know why I did that," I heard myself say. I noticed she was smiling at me and breathing kind of hard. She stroked my leg gently.

"Don't worry about it, baby," she said. "You did it because you could." She curled her lips back in a smile, revealing coal black teeth.

I woke up with a start. Everything was just like it had been in my dream, except there was no girl, and from where I was sitting, I couldn't see into the pool.

I got up very slowly, being careful not to look into the water, and went back to my room and turned the TV on, to some religious show.

There was Billy Stan Freeburgh, railing away and trying to tell me that if I sent him some money, he'd fix it with God so that nothing bad would ever happen to me again and I'd get everything I'd ever wanted. I watched that whore all night long.

Chapter 31

J. had evidently asked for wake-up calls because I most certainly got one. I had finally gone to sleep, though I don't know when, and woke up sore and cramped, still sitting in the chair in front of the TV.

I watched the static for a few minutes, trying to figure out why they call it "white noise," but gave up, then walked out to the pool and watched the steam rise off the water in the morning chill. Over by the chair where I'd sat the night before, someone had left several beer cans and a crushed, empty cigarette pack. A spasm tore up my spine, and I bunched my shoulders against it.

J. stepped out of her room, and we went to the restaurant for breakfast.

"Sleep good?"

"Yeah," I lied, looking at the water.

"Think about what I mentioned yesterday?"

"I don't want to talk about that right now."

We passed the rest of our time in the restaurant more or less in silence. I felt considerably better than the night before, but that's not saying much.

Chapter 32

After breakfast we loaded up and hit the road again. We drove for a while with nothing much to see and nothing to talk about. And then, right outside of San Ignacio, we saw the wreck.

A huge billboard of a girl in a bikini, smearing suntan oil all over her bronzed body, looked joyfully down on the mayhem. The caption, which I'm still trying to figure out, read, "IT'S NOT ABOUT JUST DESSERTS!!"

From the looks of it, the guy driving had gone to sleep and hit the guardrail, rolling the car and thoroughly messing up everyone in it. Or maybe he was gawking at the girl. We were the first ones on the scene, and steam and smoke were still roiling from under the car hood.

"Oh no," J. said. She seemed genuinely concerned.

"Keep going."

"Are you crazy? Those people need help."

J. pulled the car over and we got out. She was right. They did need help, and after forcing myself to look at them as people, as opposed to one more impediment, I guess I was ready to help also.

It was a man and his wife and their two sons. The woman was talking to us about not having time to stop, and if we could help her get everything loaded back up and the kids in the car, then maybe they'd make it on time.

J. tried to explain to her that they'd had a wreck, that the woman was in shock and needed to sit still, but it didn't seem to sink in. The back of the car was covered with stickers from places like Six Flags and the Grand Canyon and other national parks. I had forgotten that some families actually still took vacations together. About the best we ever did was take different Uber rides to the same airport.

The two boys were just kind of out of it, though one of them was yelling, "We had a wreck!" The other was looking at the girl on the billboard. They didn't seem to be hurt or anything. J. led each by the hand

104

to their mother, who was suddenly very angry. She busied herself dusting them off and asking if they were okay and was swearing to them, by everything animate and otherwise, that in about an hour and a half they'd catch a plane to Phoenix and leave What's-His-Name to explain the details. The boys didn't say much, although the younger one had started crying.

I chalked all of their reactions down to shock. I guess the father was the one in need of the most attention because J. was crouched over him, alternately pushing on his chest, two short powerful movements, and giving him mouth to mouth.

"What's that woman doing to him?" the woman demanded.

"She's helping him, I guess. You were in a wreck. Go take care of those boys," I ordered.

She did what I told her to, and then I was relieved to hear sirens off in the distance. I was watching J. work over the man and was struck by how efficient and caring she seemed. I guess anyone that big can't be all bad. Her wig was a little sideways on her head, and she had a runner in her stocking, but suddenly I felt very proud of her. Taking her to Graceland didn't seem like that big a sacrifice anymore, although I decided we'd have to hit quite a few more car wrecks to convince me that being an Elvis impersonator was an idea worth considering.

The emergency vehicles rolled up, and to my horror, I noticed that amongst the assorted vehicles was a news team, complete with cameras and a van with a microwave dish. We were about go live in front of I don't know how many people, and my assumption was that J. wouldn't have time for a quick powder and hair realignment.

I was right. I swear the news crew was filming as they poured out of the back of the van. They were like a bunch of film students on speed. There were only three of them, but like the loaves and fishes Jesus worked over—plenty and then some. The paramedics pushed J. aside and started checking out the father. After a couple of minutes, one of them yelled at J. and asked her why she was doing CPR on a perfectly healthy, albeit dazed, man.

The reporter tried to get him to say something, but he was too mad. The paramedics were able to get rid of the reporter, so he streaked over to the furious mother and started firing questions at her at the rate of like, three thousand a minute, but suddenly she was crying too hard to talk coherently. I was next on his hit list and made a statement in Spanish, for some odd reason, before I even realized it.

I was beginning to notice that when action was required of me, either under stress or due to, the results usually came from deep, deep left field.

My interview went something like, "Sir, are you related to the family?"

"*Chocolate caliente durante dos semanas.*"

"What?!?" the reporter yelped.

The cameraman translated. "Hot chocolate for two weeks." They all looked at me.

"Tell the paramedics we have another zombie," the reporter said, and then he spotted J. sitting on the back of the Vette, smoking a cigarette and looking off past the horizon.

"Ah, miss, could I have word with you?" Evidently, he had received so much negative reinforcement by this point that he was approaching J. very carefully, indeed. Of course, her size could have had some bearing on that also.

J. snapped back to the present and looked him over carefully. He and the other two members of the crew, looking over his shoulder, were sort of half-crouched in front of her, ready to run or report, whichever option seemed most prudent. Mass media's answer to the fight or flight instinct.

"What?"

"Would you mind if I asked you a question?" He licked his lips nervously.

"Another question, you mean?"

"Ma'am?"

J. looked at him and then cocked her head to the side as if telegraphing, *Here is a particularly useless specimen.*

"Oh, right," the reporter said. "I get it."

"What kind of 'questions?'" J. asked.

"Like what happened here?"

"I don't know. We were driving by, saw the wreck, and stopped."

"We? Who else was with you?" he asked.

J. motioned to me with her cigarette. All three of the news team looked at me and then back to J., a little dubiously.

"We, ah, we thought he was in the wreck also," he finally said.

"He can give that impression."

106

"Well, um, it certainly was good of you people to stop and help this family," he started up hopefully.

"We're just on our way East. We saw the wreck and we stopped. He," she said, motioning to me, "is an Elvis impersonator."

The news crew turned as one and inspected me once again.

"Oh," the reporter said.

"And, um, what do you do?" he asked J.

"Oh, I'm his, uh . . ."

"Yes?"

"I guess you would call me his . . ." J. was dragging it out, and everyone, including me, was leaning forward to hear what she was going to say.

"I guess in polite company you would call me his . . ."

"Yes?"

Heavy breathing and licking of lips.

". . . manager," she finally finished. Everyone kind of sagged in anti-climax, and then she told the cameraman to get away from her with the camera because we had to go.

We got in the car. As we were pulling away, the cameras were pointed at us and rolling, and the reporter yelled, "Where are you folks headed?"

"Graceland," J. said and then hit the accelerator and dumped the clutch, showering pebbles, bits of broken glass, and other roadside flotsam and jetsam onto the astonished onlookers. An acrid, white smoke settled over the crowd and obscured them from our view.

Chapter 33

"We made every major network," I said, looking up from the TV.

We were in Oklahoma City, Oklahoma, the "No Tolerance" state, in the Plains Chapeau Motel and, contrary to what their license plates say, it was not "OK!"

"What?" J. had just gotten out of the shower and was now standing in a puddle and a towel. She needed a shave.

"Every major network. I knew we shouldn't have stopped."

"We had to. But how—"

"That little family unit just happened to be State Representative Billy Stan Freeburgh cum televangelist-on-the-rise traveling incognito looking for smut," I cut her off, looking back at the TV as yet another replay of J. crouching over the representative was aired. It looked like a rape-in-progress.

"Looks like he found some," I finished grimly.

J. looked at the TV in disbelief.

"I knew there was something familiar about that guy. What'd you say he was doing?"

I ignored her question. "You probably thought he just looked like something you picked up in a bar one time or another."

"I told you I'm not gay. He does have nice sideburns, though. Add a couple of inches and they'd look like Elvis's."

"Why don't you call him up? After this he'll probably be looking for a job," I said. "I mean, after he's had your tongue shoved halfway down his throat, how could he refuse?"

"Very funny. I can't believe I saved Billy Stan Freeburgh's life. God does move in mysterious ways. By the way, you gonna tell the manager what their sign means?"

"No, I'm not, and yes, He does," I said, getting up to leave. "And another thing. You didn't 'save his life.' The paramedics said he was just disoriented." I walked to the door.

"Where are you going?"

"Back to my room," I said. Dragging the Moral Majority to the brink, though not difficult, is quite tedious. The TV station replayed my interview. Hot chocolate for two weeks. Oh man.

"What's all that about hot chocolate?" J. asked me before I got out the door.

"One of only two things I learned in three years of Spanish classes. Good thing that's what came out."

"What was the other thing?"

"*Mi lápiz es grande. ¿Te gustaría ver mi lápiz?* My pencil is big. Would you like to see my pencil?"

J. started laughing and plopped down on the bed. It was a couple of moments before she could talk, rather she just laughed and shook her head. "Yes, I think you're right. That statement definitely would have caused us some problems. They probably have a team of psychologists in Washington right now, poring over what you said and trying to figure out just what you meant: is it a homosexual plot to discredit Freeburgh? Was the car wreck planned by outside forces? And, and, dare I say it? Does the slut have AIDS?" J. finished, laughing uncontrollably. It was fun seeing her laugh like that, and I fought, had been fighting, to keep from admitting to myself what was obvious: J. really was one hell of a girl.

"I'm glad you find it so amusing. Now me, I figure we're in pretty deep as it is, being on TV and all."

I was thinking again of Gianfranco and Dale and Howard, or Gino and Guido, as he called them, and also thinking it was great that mom hadn't called in an Amber Alert. Doing that and giving a description of the Vette—assuming she knew about it—would've crashed this party in all of the wrong ways. I had been careful to turn off the "find my phone" option, not to use any of "my" usual credit cards—the Valero card was so new I figured it'd be a month before the first bill generated—or do anything else to reveal my whereabouts, and now this had to happen. Dale and Howard, the idiot twins, were hired, nurtured, and directed by Gianfranco, my loving stepfather. Their collective I.Q. was about seventeen and a half, but they were the kind of guys who didn't mind calling in to the home office for directions. Add to that the fact that they each were built like my grandmother's General Motors refrigerator and things began to make a negative spin for the worse. They'd already been to see James, my friend at school, so I knew they were on the case, so to speak.

Back in my room, the light on the telephone was flashing. The directions on the phone informed me that, when the light was flashing, I had a message at the front desk; the number of times it flashed between pauses told you how many messages. Four. I called the front desk and asked if I had any messages. The girl said that three were from my mother saying it was urgent that I call home. The fourth didn't leave a name or number. They just wanted to know if a guy and a woman in a red '65 Corvette were staying there, and if so, what was the address of the motel and our room number. She said she could give them the address but wasn't allowed to disclose room numbers without the guest's permission. Did I want her to give it to them if they called again?

"No!" I yelled and hung up. I ran next door to J.'s room, but she didn't answer when I pounded on the door. The most revolting, disgusting music imaginable reached my ears, and I turned slowly and looked across the parking lot. "Lounge" in blue neon met my eyes. Of course. It'd be about high time for J. to go to work. She was having to push hard to pay for our meals and rooms. I'd been paying for the gas—otherwise, we wouldn't have stopped at Valeros exclusively—but that was about it. How an Arizona game warden had become so proficient at dancing with drunk men while picking their pockets was a question beyond my powers of comprehension. Probably just as well.

I started walking across the parking lot then stopped. What if Dale and Howard were already here? As soon as they saw me—or J., for that matter—they'd move on us. I looked across the street and, of course, there was a Valero, a sort of combination restaurant/gift shop operation that sold everything. Having a sudden burst of desperation, I walked over and went inside, because when I'm down, spending money makes it all better.

I wasn't disappointed in the selection, and when I left, I was the proud new owner of one pair of imitation leather cowboy boots, one pair of boot-cut black 501s, and a black, western-cut shirt with pearly snaps, red shoulder panels, slash pockets on the chest (complete with cowboys on horses lassoing imaginary doggies), and embroidered on the back, the Yellow Rose of Texas. I bought a straw hat with a quail-feather hatband. To complete my dope psychobilly ensemble, I bought a belt with a buckle on it that looked like a hubcap. The manager threw in a string tie that consisted of a strap of black cord and a chunk of Lucite with a rattlesnake head suspended in it, jaws gaping wide to show off its fangs to their best advantage. He said he was having trouble moving them. Indeed.

Back at the room, I slipped into my new identity and surveyed the wreckage in the mirror, noting that I looked like Roy Rogers in a Dale Evans acid-enhanced nightmare. I took a deep breath, stepped outside, and walked with purpose towards the bar sign that flashed across the parking lot.

I was almost there when the old woman from the desert stepped from the shadow of a Winnebago, bringing me up short as if I'd hit the end of a rope.

While I waited for her to speak, I looked her over. All I could see of her clothes was a long gray tunic, bound at the waist with a rope. She still appeared to be a thousand years old, but in the light of the full moon, her skin was soft and translucent, and her hair gathered the pale moonlight and held it.

"Do you know me?"

The question was as unexpected as it was sudden.

"Yeah, you're the lady who helped me in Arizona and New Mexico. How was Texas? You sure move—"

"Then why did you help that man on the road?"

"You mean Billy Stan Freeburgh—"

"Yes."

Now her eyes glowed like those of a cat staring out from utter darkness, bright blue-green orbs of refracted light.

"We didn't know who it was."

"Would you have stopped if you had?"

I knew the answer she wanted, but I decided that, with her, the truth was best.

"Yeah, I guess so. They needed help."

She looked at me for a minute and then said, "Well, yes. When I was here, maybe I would have too. Times change."

I nodded my head.

"Now, my first question. Do you know me?"

I shut up and thought it over for a minute.

"No, ma'am. I guess I don't."

She smiled.

"The two men who want to find you will be here soon. Stay with Julie."

111

"Thanks," I said. Then she reached toward me and handed me a black, flat-brimmed hat like Stevie Ray Vaughn used to wear. Even had a Concho band.

"Wear it," she said and turned to go.

Before I thought about it, I blurted out, "Does Julie have a real, I mean, a man's name?"

The old woman stopped and looked me over once more. "Of course," she said. I didn't try to watch her go. I'd learned that much at least.

I tossed the straw hat like a frisbee into the bed of a parked truck and put the black one on. It fit perfect.

Chapter 34

As I walked into the bar, any hopes I'd had of making a discreet entrance vanished. The girl charging cover looked at me and jerked her head back so hard that she hit it on the wall behind her, then got on the intercom and called for security, the manager, and no idea why, a priest. Two of three came.

"What's goin' on here?" The manager, who looked like a cross between Lizzy Borden and a kangaroo, wanted some answers.

"Nothing," I said. "Came in for, uh, a cold one and to, uh, shoot some, you know, pool."

"Is there a full moon tonight? Huh? Is there? I swear, first that lumberjack-lookin' bozo comes in and plays ten dollars' worth a Elvis songs, and we only got three, and now you, you . . ." The security guard, who looked like something you'd find in a used pet store, had taken over briefly, but found that words failed him. I suspect the experience was not new to him, so he just stood there with his hand on the butt of his revolver.

The manager took the helm again in what was beginning to resemble tag team interrogation.

"Well, yes, it is a full moon tonight," I offered.

"Well, alright. You can come in, but don't talk to anyone you don't know and don't cause any trouble."

"Okay."

"Oh, and stay away from the juke box!"

I nodded in agreement.

"And no damn daincing!"

No damn prob, I thought.

Once inside, I leaned my back against the far wall. I looked out onto the dance floor, but didn't see J. I checked all the couples at the tables, but once again didn't see her. There were four or five guys standing at the bar, and, sure enough, the "Lumberjack-lookin' bozo" turned out to be J. her own self. I couldn't believe it. Out in public and wearing men's clothes too; that made twice now. I walked over and took a stool next to her.

"Feeling okay?" I asked. J. gave me a puzzled look, but when recognition made its entrance, she smiled at me.

"Maybe I should ask you the same thing," she said, looking me over. I decided to direct the conversation away from my fashion scream.

"What's with the outfit? I thought you had a moral objection to dressing like a man," I said.

"I wouldn't call it 'moral.' But I do object to wearing dirty clothes. That Billy Stan Freeburgh got dirt and saliva all over my dress, and the other one is filthy as well. I need some new ones."

"Yeah, okay, we'll see what we can do," I said.

"And now, if you don't mind, what's with this get-up? Nice tie. Does it bite?"

"Uh, I don't think so, or not anymore at least. Look, we have a serious problem."

"Oh?"

"Yeah. My stepfather has two guys that do—odd—jobs for him. They work outside of the office, if you know what I mean."

"I don't know what you mean," J. said.

"My stepfather makes a lot of money. A whole lot of money. Problem is, he's real weird about it. No one in the family seems to know why. I mean, it's supposed to be legit—and is, as far as I know—but he acts like it's gangland."

"Is this some kind of threat?" J. was acting cool, but I could tell she was getting a little mad.

"Yeah, sort of," I said. Then I realized what she meant. "No, not like you're thinking. These guys—twins, actually—are looking for me. Today they called the motel. They know where we are. They're on their way."

"And you're giving me a chance to run, because you like me so much," J. said with sarcasm. "Nice try."

"No, I'm not. They are looking for me because I sort of don't own the car we're in," I said.

"Come again?"

About that time, the girl at the front got on the intercom again and called for the manager and security. I could see the door in the reflection of the mirror behind the bar, so when Dale and Howard came in seconds later, I had my back to them. I was feeling very tense.

"There they are," I whispered. J. just sort of looked at me.

"So run to them. But if you tell the police I kidnapped you, I'll tell your stepfather that you offered to pay me to commit—and video—an indecent act with you, which I accepted."

"You still don't get it. For starters, as long as he wasn't involved—or you couldn't prove that he was—you could tell my stepfather anything you wanted and he wouldn't care. Second, if I wanted those guys to recognize me, I wouldn't be dressed like this," I motioned to my outfit. "And third, if those guys do spot me, we're both in trouble."

J. thought about this a little and then said, "Okay, back to the car. You say you don't own the car? As in, you stole the car?"

"Well, I didn't exactly steal it. I traded something for it," I said.

"And what, exactly, did you trade for it?"

"My stepfather's Mercedes." J. absorbed this for a little bit, and I watched the twins. They had taken a table and were carefully looking the crowd over, one person at a time. They hadn't seen us yet. J. cut in.

"You know, you are far less intelligent than I ever gave you credit for being. I mean, granted that shirt and the rest of that crap make you look pretty stupid, but all that can be taken off. No, your stupidity goes clean to the bone, doesn't it? Trading a Mercedes for a Corvette. They probably never even told your old man. I wonder how much money the salesman made off your dad?"

"Stepdad. That doesn't seem very relevant right now. You don't like my clothes? So what? If Dale and Howard spot us, they'll probably give us a couple of concrete overcoats and take us swimming."

"That doesn't make any sense at all. According to you, they're supposed to bring you home, not drown you."

"Yeah, well, you never know. They aren't real bright, and they watch a lot of movies."

"Well, that makes little sense, and anyway, we're in a desert. Not exactly primo drowning country."

I thought back to my dream by the pool. "It's not impossible. Anyway, I'd be hard-pressed to tell you one thing concerning us that does make much sense," I said.

"Fine, we'll get out of here. I'm not tired, and getting a little closer to Graceland is all good anyway."

It was my turn to stare in disbelief.

"Graceland? Are you kidding? Every man, woman, and child in America with internet knows that's where we're headed. The Republican party probably has hit squads mobilized in Tennessee right now, not to mention Gianfranco and his band of merry morons. It's over, got it? Graceland is out."

"John-who?"

"My stepfather."

J. looked thoughtful.

"This predicament needs a diversion," she said. "Then it'll be a party." The jukebox cued up "Suspicious Minds," courtesy of J., for about the twelfth time. I buried my face in my hands and hoped that when the end came, it would come swiftly and come surely.

Chapter 35

I looked up in consternation, scared of what J. was going to do, and I found myself gazing at a large, heretofore unnoticed, moose head. He looked down from the wall, his regality undiminished, though he was only twenty percent present. Not a bad showing. I wondered briefly how J. would look attached to a wall and I smiled. Given the opportunity, perhaps I'd spend the extra money and have just her skull mounted, the tasteful and understated "European Mount" that I so admired. Off to the left of the moose there was a racoon, sort of looking up and over its shoulder with a sad-faced look that said, "What did I ever do to you?" My reverie was interrupted by J. leaning across the bar and asking the bartender if she could borrow the phone. He said no, and for her to use her cell or the pay phone in the men's room and not to stay on it more than three minutes.

I began to hope that whatever mayhem J. was planning would somehow include the employees of this establishment. The weight of their oppression was taxing. I needn't have worried, though. J. motioned for me to follow her, and after she had made it to the restroom undetected, I followed.

"Hello, police? Yes, please transfer me to the Chief of Police. What? Fine, the Assistant Chief will do. Thank you." As the call was being transferred, she scratched her ribs just below the underwire of her bra. Add that to the 90000 trillion things I've never thought of, but it struck me how uncomfortable those things must be. I was still looking at her breast when she said, "Yes, this is James Simpson," snapping me out of it. "I don't expect you to know who I am. Anyway, a friend and I were just over at the Plains Chapeau Lounge enjoying a cocktail when two identical twins, dressed as if for a funeral, approached us and asked if we'd like to buy some nude photos of various and assorted elected officials. Naturally enough, we were shocked and reported them to the manager, but he merely laughed and said that if it weren't for the generous—I don't know who, they just said 'elected officials,' no mention was made of civil servants. As I was saying, evidently the management is in on it too—and you don't care. Hmmm. Well, he showed me a particularly provocative photo involving what he said was the Chief of Police's wife and a couple of domestic—" J. frowned as if in thought. "Well, I don't know if was or not. I've never seen the strumpet. We're from Boise, Idaho. You will? Fine. The two, er, salesmen are seated in the lounge. Yes, of course. My friend and I are dressed in identical Hawaiian plaid shirts and Bermuda shorts. We'll be at the bar. Thank you." She hung up. "Well, they're on the way."

"Great. What do we do now?"

"I'm going to wait by the door, and you're going back to the bar and hope the twins don't recognize you. When the fun starts, just walk outside, and I'll pick you up."

"You'd better," I said, having an unpleasant flashback to the night in New Mexico when I almost left her to the Bubba Pack.

I went back up to the bar and ordered a vodka tonic and waited. I'd been hanging on to a pill bottle full of muscle relaxers I'd found in the Benz before I traded it off and thought now was a terrible time to take one . . . so I took two. J. went up to the front and leaned against the wall, looking out into the street. After a few minutes, she perked up, then walked briskly outside to the accompaniment of screeching tires and bullhorns. Deputies flooded in through every door, including the fire exit, and began rounding up employees. Four rushed the table where Guido and Gino were sitting and tackled them, yelling "Freeze!" and other similar commands that are impossible to obey when one is in free fall. I hesitated, drained my glass, and headed out the front door. The last thing I saw as I left was one of the twins, his face to the floor, but staring at me and yelling in recognition. I tipped my hat and smiled, already feeling a bit woozy.

Chapter 36

J. picked me up as planned, and we eased onto the highway. More squad cars were converging on the bar from every possible angle, as were TV crews.

"We need to ditch this car," J. said.

Unlikely as it might have been after self-medicating, a spasm hit me between the shoulder blades, causing me to twist halfway around in my seat before I knew it.

"What? No. What? No way."

"Everybody is looking for it." I thought it over but had to agree with that, although it took an act of will, which I'm splendidly ill-equipped for. This trip was getting further and further out of hand with every passing mile, every passing moment. We were entering the philosophical hood of one my high school English teacher's favorite authors, HST—el gonzo himself—and we were definitely pushing the envelope of crazed road-trip technology.

All my real clothes, including yet-to-be-worn stuff from Bone and Wool, had been abandoned at the motel. All I had were the clothes on my back. That the trunk contained a duffle bag with a little less than $10,000 helped my state of mind, but didn't alter the fact that people were pulling up next to the car just to stare and point at me. For once, people were ignoring J. in favor of gawking at me.

I didn't know how long it would take for the authorities—or at least what passed for them in this town—to figure out that they'd been had, but it couldn't be long. We were piling up some serious bad karma, and the fact that I don't believe in karma didn't help because I was sure it believed in me. J. was talking, but it sounded as if from far away, and though I did not have a positive mental outlook, I felt strangely calm.

"We don't have a choice. We've got to make a plan and think it through . . . Oh, what's that?"

J. had been in the serious planning stage one minute and the next was peering at the Antioch Baptist Church where it looked like there was about to be a wedding. That or the Baptists had begun having Saturday night services for those sleepyheads who couldn't make it for Sunday morning.

"What are you doing?" I asked as J. began to pull into the crowded parking lot.

She pulled around back and parked the car.

"I just love weddings."

Chapter 37

She dragged me out of the car and pushed me toward the church; my legs felt like they were prosthetic.

"What the hell's wrong with you?" J. asked. I just shook my head, which made my scalp itch. We walked into the back, and J. signed the guest register, if signing it "Priscilla Presley" counts. It occurred to me that I seem to be a magnet for people who would prefer to be someone else. Then again, I was sort of getting caught up in the spirit of things, so I signed it "Hank Williams, deceased."

The ceremony hadn't started, and most everyone turned to look at us as we came in. No one so much as batted an eye. We chose the bride's side because there were fewer people on it, and they seemed, on the whole, to be cleaner than the groom's support team.

We sat down and J. immediately began to tell me what changes she would have made in the wedding decorations, but I wasn't listening. We didn't have long to wait before some pre-recorded music of a country song about a John Deere tractor, or at least the color of it, was started, and the groomsmen and bridesmaids began to file down the aisle, walking slowly and grimacing in concentration as they tried to match speeds and move in a stately manner to the front.

Next, a sour-faced girl of about seven came along with a basket of rose petals that she was supposed to sprinkle lightly and evenly for the bride to step on. Apparently, this didn't fit her program, because she didn't drop any until she got down to the front, where she up-ended the whole basket, leaving the petals in a mound in front of the preacher and the young, nervous-looking groom as she stomped back the way she came. I pegged her for the stepdaughter.

J. wasn't paying any attention to this, though, because she was too busy eyeing the bridesmaid's dresses. She elbowed me in the ribs.

"Those dresses aren't as bad as I would have guessed," she whispered.

"That's comforting. Maybe they'll let you try one on after the wedding." J. didn't say anything to that, but looked at me for a long moment. Then we sat there for a few more minutes discussing our options.

J. took the position that if the twins were really that big a threat, we should ditch the Vette and get something a little more inconspicuous, and specifically something with a top.

I, on the other hand, though in full agreement, didn't feel that I was ready to part company with God yet.

We were left at an impasse. J. mused about how much more comfortable, not to mention drier, our trip would have been if I'd just kept Gianfranco's car. She said the thought that she missed an opportunity to roll through the gates of Graceland in a Mercedes was disheartening. I didn't commiserate.

"What model was it?"

"The Mercedes? S Class AMG 63."

"Damn. You think we could trade the Corvette for a Mercedes?"

"If I wanted a Mercedes, I would've kept the one I had. Besides, anyone with a Mercedes isn't going to trade for a thirty-some-odd-year-old Chevy."

"You did."

"Yeah, but it wasn't my Mercedes. It's easy to make a bad trade with someone else's stuff."

J. thought about this for a moment. "The Mercedes would have had navigation, Bluetooth, the works. Right?"

"Yes, Julie, it did."

"Aaarggh! We could have punched in the coordinates and called ahead to let them know we're coming."

"They do know we're coming. Remember the wreck? The TV crews? The man you molested? Another thing, the Benz was Lo Jacked, so they'd have found me—us—easier than we'd have found Graceland."

J. shrugged. "Whatever. Drop it."

The wedding still hadn't started, and people were beginning to squirm around and make the muted sounds that every restless crowd makes. Everyone involved in the ceremony was present, except there were more groomsmen than bridesmaids, and J. concluded that one of them must be late.

She went to investigate.

I stayed put. After reviewing my situation, I decided that if I ever got back into any kind of sensible interaction with ordinary society again, I'd go for counseling. On a high-speed run across four or five states—back and forth, mind you—in a stolen Corvette with a transvestite/game warden/Priscilla Presley wannabe for a side kick . . . Well, it wasn't like it could hurt.

J. came back and said it was time to go. I'd long ago given up questioning her on such mundane matters, as to the whereofs and the wherefores. J.'s sense of timing and propriety just weren't in sync with the rest of humanity.

We walked out to the car while J. cast furtive glances back over her shoulder from time to time. I guess I knew something was up but couldn't concentrate long enough to ask what. When she was positive no one was following, she gave me a conspiratorial look and said, "Voila!" She held up a new dress for my inspection, a dress that just happened to look exactly like the ones the bridesmaids were wearing. She jerked it back down as a car roared into the parking lot and stopped.

A flustered girl jumped out of the car and asked us if the wedding had started. We said no, they were waiting on the missing bridesmaid.

"That's me! Do you know where the dressing room is?" she asked.

"Down the first hall on the left as you enter the building," J. said helpfully. "Second door on the right."

"Do y'all go to church here?" she asked.

"I did once," J. said.

"Thanks!" She galloped off.

"Your dresses are divine," J. called after her.

Chapter 38

After ruining the wedding, we went straight to a gas station so that J. could put on her ill-gotten gain. Unfortunately, it wasn't a Valero, and pretty much all they carried was automotive related, nothing relevant to buy. While I waited on J. to finish dressing, the attendant stared at me like I might be a shoplifter.

J. yelled from the bathroom that she needed a t-shirt. We didn't have anything in the car, but there was an auto parts store across the street, so I crossed over and went in. There wasn't much of a selection, but I bought the most tasteful one they had, which, unfortunately, wasn't very. It was bright purple and had a drawing of guy hanging his head out the window of an eighteen-wheeler. The caption read: "POTHOLES BUST MY NUTS!!" I never did figure out just what it was advertising.

I took it to the gas station and handed it to J. through the door. She came out looking slightly vexed. The dress that had looked moderate and stylish on the girls at the chapel looked horrendous on J.

There is nothing more unsettling than seeing two extremes portrayed by means of the same example. For starters, a hem length that was tasteful on girl-sized girls hit J. right above the kneecaps. Then, of course, there was the slight disparity in body shape and weight distribution between J. and most every female since the homo africanus model was phased out. J. was only able to get the zipper halfway closed before the huge muscles in her back and arms impeded further progress. I would have laughed, but the spectacle was just too freakish.

I stood there feeling I should help, while J. fooled around with the dress, trying to somehow overcome the laws of nature, specifically those that pertain to mass and volume. She finally just rolled the top down around her waist and pulled the t-shirt on, ending up with a very eclectic look that matched mine in weirdness, point for point. We were a pair, and in this, no comfort was to be found.

Chapter 39

Repositioning herself into the dichotic world of transvestitism made J.'s spirit soar. As for me, seeing her thus was just business as usual. I was past having any particularly negative reaction to seeing her dressed as a woman and, in fact, preferred that to her lumberjack outfit. I guess I'd found the point where seeing her in drag—with a five o'clock shadow and the odd chest hair poking through her top—seemed more normal than distressing, and the otherness in such huge doses had an anesthetic effect on me. J. seemed at ease regardless of what gender she dressed as, but she obviously preferred women's clothes. This struck me as odd, because although I always treated her as if she were gay, she never really did anything to prove that she was or wasn't—quite the opposite really; if anything, she seemed to be asexual. Probably better for everyone concerned.

We still hadn't come to a final decision as far as the Vette was concerned. For all I could see, the main problem wasn't the law, as I had previously thought, but was my stepfather. As I said, it's funny how identical things can be so different.

I tried to figure if I'd exchanged one set of problems for another or just taken the ones I already had and pumped them up, à la growth hormones. J., as usual, wasn't the least bit concerned about the car or Gianfranco or anything else that wasn't involved with her triumphant cruise through the gates of Graceland, dressed like Priscilla Presley and evidently with me in tow, singing lead. I wondered if this was really my life, and if so, how'd it get so twisted?

Chapter 40

Though my musings had been shadowy all along, darkness fell, and we put some distance between ourselves and the scene of our last transgression. About 10 p.m. we stopped in Clearview, Oklahoma, for gas and decided to call it a night. Or a day. Anyway, we got a motel and that was that.

I had been mulling over our options and decided that in the morning I'd take some of Gianfranco's advice. He always said that the best defense was a good offense. He's very original. Anyway, I figured that after all the offenses I'd committed, being defensive made sense, and since things were as they were, we could use a little information, so I might as well be offensive. Or . . . I don't know . . . whatever. With that decision behind me, I lay on the bed, and much more tired than I'd thought, fell immediately into dreamless oblivion.

I woke early and tried to figure what the best course of action would be. I could call another one of my friends, but the chances that any of them knew anything I didn't were slim. Same for everyone at his office. In spite of her calls, Mom was so far out of the question that she never even occurred to me. Then it hit me to go to the source. I'd call the man himself and see what gives. I used his 1-800 number.

"Transcontinental Conglomerate Incorporated. How may I direct your call?"

"Ralph Singleton, please," I said.

"I'm sorry, sir, there is no Ralph . . ."

"Betty, this is Colin."

"Colin! Where are you? They are looking all over for you," Betty said. Then in a conspiratorial voice, "Are you okay?"

"Yeah, fine. Patch me through to Ralph, okay?"

"Okay, but you know he prefers to be called—"

"Gianfranco, I know. You're still Betty though, right?"

"Oh, of course. Your father—"

"Stepfather."

"Oops. Sorry, Colin. Anyway, he said it was a good thing I don't have to give my name out on the phone. He said I have a 'blue collar' name," Betty said without malice.

"I think you have a lovely name," I said without conviction.

"Then why don't you ask me out?"

"You know why," I said. I hoped she did, because I sure didn't. She was about my age, maybe a little older, very attractive, owned her home, and had graduated from the university in three years. What's more, she had her own convertible, and she'd actually paid for it. Which may have been the problem. I liked Betty, but she fairly dripped responsibility. If I ever did ask her out, it'd probably be the end. She dashed my hopes for an easy resolution all the same.

"No, Colin, I don't."

"Well, how about if I told you that right now I'm sharing the comforts of the road with a six-foot-three game warden from Arizona who likes to dress like a woman?"

"I'd say you're lying."

"Even if I told you I've been kidnapped?"

"Especially if you told me that. You stole the car, Colin. Not some Arizona game warden in drag."

"I'm telling the truth," I said.

"I'll put your call through," she said icily. Just as she put me on hold, I heard her sigh in exasperation or disgust—maybe both—and I was alone on the line for a couple of minutes, during which I was subjected to a recorded bio of my stepfather, which, for the most part, was totally bogus, unless the "Old Country" refers to Ohio.

"Gianfranco, here. Tell me your problems and watch me solve them."

"Colin here. Stole a car, picked up the world's strangest hitchhiker, and am driving cross-country in search of the American Dream, sowing the seeds of discontent, and reaping the whirlwind damn near every time my foot touches pavement," I said.

"Colin, hang on a sec."

The line went dead and round two of Ralph/Gianfranco's dream biography came back. It was pretty interesting hearing all about how he had organized the resistance movement in Italy during Mussolini's 'reign of terror' and had to be smuggled out of the country in the hold of a cargo ship bound for Albania. He must have been all of four at the time. He was just beginning his epic traverse—which incidentally is still "sung about in all the small villages" of the Po River Valley—when he got back on the phone.

"We know where you are. Gino and Guido are closing the gap."

"Who?"

"Gino and Guido. You know them: they're the twins. You always asked me what exactly it was they did for me," he said in a flat, sotto voice.

"Did you get two new twins? The only ones I know anything about are named Dale and Howard . . ."

"Same twins. Only now they're named Gino and Guido."

"Ralph . . ."

"Gianfranco." He rolled his r's now. I sighed.

"Look, this nom de office thing has gotten totally out of hand. Why don't you just get some secret invisible playmate or something? Go to Italy, get it out of your system. What's Mom's name this week?"

"Same as always. She's worried sick about you, you ungrateful little wretch. Is that any way to pay me back for all the things I've given you and your mama? It hurts me here, in my heart. By the way, who's the bimbo who called the police on my boys?"

"Uh, good question. I'm still trying to figure that one out . . ."

"You took my money, you traded my bambino in on a fifty-five-year-old Chevy, and now you call home for forgiveness. How have we come to this . . . ?"

"I didn't call home for forgiveness. I called home to see what you told the braindead buckaroos to do and to tell you to make them go away," I said.

"Oh. Fine," he said, snapping back to business. "Their orders, specifically, are to find you, drug you if necessary, and bring you and that car that I had to pay for back to Dallas. That was really stupid getting on TV like that. Led us right to you. That false clue about hot chocolate didn't fool me for a minute. All we had to do was call a few motels and ask about that car. Two hours with AT&T and *bingo*! We knew right where to find you."

"How'd it go with the police?"

"They couldn't find any evidence. We're suing for false arrest. I'm gonna own that town."

"Yeah, great. You need a town like that. You can change the name to 'Salerno.' Salerno, Oklahoma. Has a nice ring to it. You can have a statue of your travails in the Caucasus cast for the courthouse lawn, or something. Oh, and thanks for the car."

"The car is registered in my name. If you don't meet Gino and Guido in Dallas within the next twenty-four hours, I'm going to call the state troopers and report it stolen."

Ralph/Gianfranco hung up.

I put the phone receiver back into the cradle and stepped next door to J.'s room, where J. was idly filing her nails.

"What's the news?"

"Well, good and bad. The good news is that we are no longer driving a stolen car," I said. "My stepfather paid for it."

"Big of him. And the bad?"

"That in twenty-four hours, he's going to report it stolen."

"So, in twenty-four hours, we're going to be driving a stolen a car again, huh?"

"Yeah, unless I take it back to Dallas and turn it over."

"Well, what it's going to be?"

"You giving me a choice?"

"Maybe. What happens if you don't take the car back?"

"We keep going till we get to Graceland," I said. "Or till we get caught."

J. smiled at me.

"What happens when you get back home?"

"If I go now, probably not much. Handed all kinds of punishments that won't be enforced. Back to college maybe."

"And if you don't go now?"

"I honestly don't know. My mom and my stepfather had a son a couple of years ago. He's always gotten the lion's share of the attention, but he's getting more and more recently. Gianfranco's been telling Mom that if I don't come around, he'll cut me out of the will."

"So? Wills can be contested. I'd think it's rare for a stepson to be entirely cut off."

"Rare as a game warden who knows as much as a North Dallas lawyer? Anyway, as I see it, getting cut out of the will is a distinct probability. I think I went too far this time."

J. looked at me to see what I was going to say next. When I didn't say anything, she said, "Yeah, you get to choose. If you need to go, then go."

"Give me a minute," I said and stepped outside. I walked out into the parking lot and looked at the car. Making sure I kept my share of the will was a lot of incentive to just go back. If I played my cards right, acted real sorry, and apologized for all the trouble I'd caused, I could stay in the will and probably keep the Vette too. That's what made the most sense. That was the only option that made any sense, and anyway, this had to end, I told myself. It was the responsible thing to do. My mind was pretty well made up, but I was still thinking about it when I remembered the old woman, and then I saw her, standing out on the edge of the parking lot.

But now, unlike the other times I'd seen her, she looked frail and gray, a shadow of her former presence.

I walked over to her. She was hugging herself with both arms and staring at me. The light was gone from her eyes.

"Are you okay?" I asked. "What's wrong?"

"Cold," she said. "It's so cold."

"It's got to be a hundred degrees out here," I said. "You must have a fever." I moved to put my arm around her.

She pulled back from me. "Make the choice," she said.

I stared at her for a moment longer, but my decision was made before I consciously thought it and had been gaining traction on me for some time now. As I watched, she began to visibly improve. She stood straighter, tossed her head, and the tangles fell from her hair. The familiar light shone in her eyes and she smiled. "Yes," she said. "Very well."

I walked back into J.'s room, and she turned to face me. "Get in the car, chick."

"What?" J. asked.

"We goin' to Graceland."

J. squealed and kicked her feet up and down like a toddler doing the happy dance.

Chapter 41

We got in the car and pulled onto the highway, headed east. J. drove along, just over the speed limit.

"I think that gas we bought was watered down."

"I knew we should have held out for a Valero. What's wrong?"

"This car's missing worse than Jimmy Hoffa."

"Who?" I asked. J. looked at me. "Just kidding. I think he's pushing up the daisies in my stepfather's garden." We both laughed.

The car was running pretty bad. We were right on the outskirts of Checotah and decided to look for a mechanic. We didn't have a whole lot of luck driving around, so we went to the first place we found, the Lake Eufaula Inn on the south side of town, got a couple of rooms, and went down to the restaurant to eat.

After an uneventful lunch that consisted of nothing I'd ever seen in any of the four food groups, we went back to J.'s room and started calling garages.

It was after 2:00 p.m. by this time, and after repeated failures, we finally found one that agreed to fix it that day.

It was supposed to be right off Main Street and it was, but when we got there, it had a "Gone Fishing" sign on the door.

J. looked at her watch. "They're not going to catch anything this time of day." Not seeing anything else in the ghost town, we wound up back at the room and started all over again, had zero luck, and then decided to try the food at Lin Cuisine IV. J. asked the hostess where the other three were, but she just looked at us. The food was the usual hinterlands Chinese . . . you know, heaps of MSG and everything looked the same. Afterwards, we drove straight back to the motel. It was just getting on to twilight. J. called down to the front desk, and the night clerk gave her a new number, which she dialed.

"You're not going to call, are you?"

"Yes, I am. Why wouldn't I?"

"Well, for starters, it's after nine o'clock at night."

"So?"

"So, they'll be closed," I said.

"So?" J. said, dialing the number.

"What?" the guy on the other end of the line yelled so loud I could hear him across the room.

"Um, is this Phoenix Motor Works?" J. asked, making a face at me. She switched over to speakerphone so I could hear.

"Yeah, Mr. or Mrs . . ." the mechanic trailed off.

"Ms.," J. affirmed.

"Okay. What d'ya need?"

"Are you open?"

"Course I'm open. Would I be answering the phone if I wasn't open?"

"I don't know. What are your hours of operation?"

"Eight to six, six days a week," he said.

"And you're still open? It's after nine."

"Eight p.m. to six a.m.," he said gruffly, overemphasizing his p.m.'s. and his a.m.'s

J. looked at me again, and I just shrugged.

"Isn't that kind of strange?" she continued. J. was having a hard time.

"Just ask him about the car," I said.

"Lady, do you have something in mind, or are you just gonna ask me stupid questions all night?"

"We have a '65 Corvette that needs a little attention. It's not firing on all eight cylinders. Maybe it needs a tune-up."

"Maybe it needs a tune-up, maybe it needs a new engine. Maybe it needs a new owner. I don't s'pose I'll know till I see it, huh?"

"Well, no, I guess you won't. Where are you located?"

J. got the directions, scribbling them on the back of a sanitary napkin she had in her purse "for the sake of authenticity," and we were off, me of the questionable intelligence and she of the dubious sanity.

We arrived at Phoenix Motor Works about forty-five minutes later than we should have, due in part to J.'s lack of familiarity with the town and my reluctance to handle the directions physically. Trying to navigate from the smartphone was a bust, too, because evidently, Google didn't accept the existence of said auto shop. Anyway, I attempted, with mixed results, to read what she'd scrawled on the, um, feminine hygiene aid from the dash where I had immediately thrown it upon receipt from J., and this caused some awkwardness.

Eventually, we found the street and the garage thereupon, then knocked on the black metal door, three times with a long pause between each strike of fist to metal and three in rapid succession, as per his instructions.

A sliding peephole that was about six inches wide and two inches tall slid open, and the same surly voice that we had had to put up with on the phone asked our business.

"What?"

"We just talked to you on the phone. We're in the Corvette," J. said.

"What Corvette?"

"The one that may need a tune-up, new engine, or new owner," J. said. It was a telling indication of our dependence on this clown that J. didn't kick the door in and conduct the conversation tête-à-tête, so to speak. She was certainly capable.

"How do I know you're who you say you are?"

"What does it matter?" J. fairly screamed.

"Let me handle this," I said to J., then turning to the door, I asked, "Would it be better if we came back after whatever drugs you're obviously taking have worn off?"

There was a long pause then we heard the sound of an assortment of locks being opened and the door swung slowly inward. The mechanic turned out to be a smallish man in his mid-thirties with sideburns that straggled down the sides of his face to the middle of his jaw, where they gave up the fight and lay, diminished and in defeat. He was wearing a work shirt that had "Michel" embroidered on it. I was a little disappointed that he didn't look like Lon Chaney, and said so.

I was rewarded with strange looks all around. The mechanic spoke first.

"Did someone mention drugs?"

I looked around and wondered how I had ever allowed myself to get to such a strange pass; I suppose only my weakness had kept me going.

"No, not really," J. said.

"Oh," the mechanic seemed disappointed. "Really are here about fixing a car, huh?"

"Yes, we really are," J. said irritably.

"Whew. Well, bring it in." He stepped out of the door and waved us in, looking us over carefully. He whistled to himself as he eyed J.'s t-shirt and chiffon skirt approvingly.

We pulled in and got out of the Vette. J. tried to explain what the car was doing, using a series of grunts, screeches, and other primal noises that she seemed to think would put things into perspective. I looked around the garage, taking in the fact that there were no machines, no tools, no anything that most mechanics keep in their shops. It was pretty much just an empty warehouse. But over in the far left corner of the shop, there was something huge, bulbous, and mostly hidden under an olive drab canvas tarp.

"Yeah, well, I hear what you're saying, but I'm not, um, accepting any work right this minute. As you can see, I'm pretty full up." He motioned to the empty room with an expansive sweep of his right arm while J. and I tried to figure out what he was supposed to be working on.

I spoke up. "You working on whatever is under that, uh, that—"

"Tarp?"

"Yeah, tarp," I said.

"Are you, maybe, interested in what is under that tarp?" He sounded like the Big Bad Wolf in Little Red Riding Hood. "Did you come to find out about what's under the tarp?"

I was starting to feel like LRRH and was getting positively freaked by the whole scene. I turned to the door, but J. caught me by the arm.

"Yeah, Michel," she said, "we came to talk about what you have under there."

He looked at J. for a second.

"Michel? Were you looking for Michel?"

"I thought you were him," J. said. When he didn't say anything, she added, "Your shirt says 'Michel' on it."

"Oh, that's because it belongs to Michel. My name is Mervyn. All my shirts are dirty. You still want to look under the tarp?"

"Sure," J. said.

He smiled.

"Good. Come on," he said. "I'll show you." He led us over to where the tarp seemed to skulk in the shadows, and then he grabbed a corner of the heavy fabric. A strong, musty odor pervaded the room, and I was thinking to myself, "Any moment now, something's going to jump out from under there and rip your face off." He jerked the tarp back, and our astonished eyes were met with what seemed to be acres of chrome shining dully under a thick layer of dust.

A 1959 Cadillac convertible had materialized like the Ghost of Conspicuous Consumption Past and, frankly, it moved me. It felt like a homecoming, of sorts. J. seemed to feel its hypnotic draw too as she walked slowly around it, running one long, perfectly manicured nail down the side, leaving a narrow swath of pink revealed like a freshly-skinned grapefruit. J. hummed a few bars from "Burning Love."

"So how do you like it?" Mervyn asked.

"How much?" J. returned, as if in a trance.

"10,000 samoleans," he said. J. looked at me.

"What do you think?" she asked.

"We don't have that kind of money on us," I said with a twinge of guilt. It's telling of my all-out enchantment for the Cadillac that I even thought about it all.

Mervyn walked over to a low coffee table and turned on a jam box to some classic rock station. "Lowrider" was playing. He looked past me at the Vette.

"How about an even trade? I trade you one classic car that I personally guarantee to be completely free of defects of any kind—with no interested parties trying to relocate it—for a classic Corvette that may, for all I know, be on its last legs. Huh? Whatd'ya think?"

"We don't have a title or any paperwork on the Vette," I said.

"That's okay, neither does the Caddy! But hey, I've got a buddy that you can get in touch with tonight. It's a simple deal. You cough up 200 bucks and *bam!* you get a title to the Cadillac."

"So, this friend of yours owns the car?" J. asked.

Mervyn paused for a moment and appraised us once more. "You guys didn't come from Max, did you?" Mervyn asked.

"No, I came from Dallas, and that," I said, pointing to J., "came from Rosie's Roadside Grill, a.k.a. The Portals of Hell. Who's Max?"

Mervyn looked us over again. It was clear he was sorting out his options. He'd already admitted he wasn't entirely legit, but he hadn't said anything downright incriminating either. That was about to change. "Well, I may be making a seriously bad career move here, but I'm a damn good character judge, and you two sure don't look like any cops I ever saw. Max is my business associate. We're in the business of providing quality automobiles at a reasonable price for deserving and select clientele of good folks with good tastes that outweigh their wallets, if you know what I mean, and I think you do. Max's end of the partnership is in the area of acquisitions. I do the selling. What's wrong with her, anyhow?" Mervyn motioned to J. "If y'all are cops, can she be the one who slaps the cuffs on?" He winked at J.

I took the lead again. "So, what you're telling me is that this car is probably something that rhymes with 'swollen.' Fine, that bothers me not one little bit. You also mentioned that for $200 your associate could provide a title. Great. As for her, I don't know what's wrong with her. Female trouble maybe. Maybe not. Personally, I think she just needs to find herself."

Mervyn looked at J. as if she were a side of beef and licked his lips. "Maybe I have a better idea. Why don't you take the car and leave her? I can sell the Corvette and wire you the money after you've settled down somewhere. As for finding herself, she can do that right here. This is a real nice town. Not really big enough to lose much of anything."

The thought of trading a road-weary transvestite for a '59 Cadillac in mint condition appealed to my emerging philosophy of Transitory Entropy, the main (in fact, only) tenet of which is that, at any given time, physical existence has the ability/probability to make a hard left turn headed for points unknown and deposit you in a situation with which your previous experiences have no connection or affiliation. Also, any decisions you make while in the realm of Transitory Entropy stand, and what's more, no one will be the wiser. They'll think you screwed up all by yourself.

"Um, boys? Boys!" J. had something to say. "I don't mean to get in the way of all this fantasizing, but where he goes, I go." She pointed at me.

"Now, honey, let's not—"

"My name is not 'Honey' and don't you—"

"Well, what is your name?" Mervyn interrupted.

"You may call me Ruth. Now where is the man with the title?"

Mervyn evidently saw the writing on the wall and began to give me directions to Basil's, a club where we would meet his "business associate," whose name Mervyn wouldn't divulge.

What he didn't see was J. taking his jam box and stowing it in the back seat under some clothes she'd gotten out of the Vette. I tossed the duffle bag with the money in it into the Cadillac's trunk. We traded keys and knowing looks, and then J. and I left. That was the last time I ever saw the Vette.

Chapter 42

The Cadillac ran pretty good, but you could tell that it had been a while since it had been driven. We stopped at the first Valero we came to and made the attendant check the oil and tires and all that junk.

While he did that, I walked in and looked around inside. They didn't have the best selection I'd seen, but compared to an ordinary gas station, they were still way ahead of most.

The attendant filled the car up with High Test unleaded, saying that it would burn cleaner. As it was, the car still smoked for a little while, and we could smell old metal and oil heating up and dust billowed off the car behind like a cloud of evidence while we drove around looking for the bar. We followed Mervyn's directions to a tee and still got lost. Despite her appearance and all the effort she'd made to look and behave like a female, J. was like every man in the world in one respect. She'd have rather bled to death in a strange town looking for the hospital than stop and ask for directions.

Chapter 43

After what seemed like years, we found Basil's. It was quite possibly the seediest looking place I've ever seen, despite the swanky name. If a big budget movie was being made about a bar where the law was outlawed, it would have been set in a place that looked like that place. It was made from cinder blocks with rusted rebar poking out here and there. Burglar bars were installed over every opening, for reasons which entirely escape me. Maybe to make the clientele feel more at ease. Perhaps this was just a stopover for those weary souls bumping around between prison terms, a place meant to instill a homey, familiar setting for those who figure a life without bars is no life at all, only an interlude.

In any event, J. and I were as out of place as Santa Claus at a bris. We went ahead and walked in, but had to stand just inside the doorway for a half a minute to let our eyes adjust to the oppressive darkness. The odor of stale beer and vomit swirled around us like mist rising off a cesspool. "Born to be Wild" was playing on the jukebox, which J. immediately went and inspected.

"We are truly in Hell," J. said. "There isn't a single Elvis song on the jukebox." So this place has that going for it, I thought to myself.

The bar was packed end to end with the burliest, hairiest people I'd ever seen. Mixed bag. There was enough leather being worn to cover the floor of Texas Stadium, with plenty left over for the soda fountains. A neon sign over the bar said, "Check Your Attitude at the Door," but was ignored by one and all.

I recognized immediately that large quantities of alcohol were in order, and when our waitress stomped up to the table, I was ready.

"Yeah?"

"Give me four shots of Jack Daniel's in a glass and a beer."

She didn't even blink. "A beer. This is a bar. We have lots of different beers. You get to choose."

"Okay, whatever is the coldest beer you've got."

"Fine. What do you want, Cinderella?" She seemed to have developed an immediate hatred for J.

"Bring me a glass of milk," J. said sweetly. The waitress just snorted and left. She brought the drinks—including a tall glass of milk—back to the table and slammed them down, sloshing the contents over the sides of the glasses.

"That'll be eighteen dollars." J. gave her a twenty and she left. She didn't bother to return our change.

J. and I looked around, trying to figure out if the guy with the papers was in the bar yet, and if so, who he was. It was for this reason that I was surprised to turn around and find a tall, bird-like woman standing right next to our table, staring at us intently. She was dressed in a black leather motorcycle jacket, black jeans, and knee-high snakeskin cowboy boots. Maybe the fact that she and I were sort of dressed alike attracted her; I have no idea. No one spoke, and then she just sat down and started talking.

"I don't know what it was drawed me to him, well, then again maybe I do—I guess it was his tattoos that really got me inersted at first, but there mighta been more to it than that . . ."

We were at the bar to pick up a title, but instead, we'd found a companion. I guess seeing us sitting there waiting for Mervyn's friend from the underworld to come and sell us the papers had triggered some buried matronly instinct.

As usual, everything we were doing had the appearance of being one thing, and the reality, well, the reality was our own private label.

She said her name was Lucille. The miles lay on that woman like layers of asphalt on a county highway where the mayor and the contractor are brothers-in-law. Her age was hard to guess, but I put her at a hard forty. In dog years. She ordered a double Black Jack and Coke. The maternal figures on my roster were piling up thicker than slime at a political rally.

"I've always been one of those hard-to-keep-down types, if you ask me. 'No regrets' is my motto. Why, I've ripped the rearview mirror off a ever car I ever owned and some I didn't," she said, leaning back into her chair and studying us. "Anyway, back to them tattoos. He had all kinds of 'em. I met him at the diner I was workin' at—served him coffee and read them tattoos. Musta' cleaned that part of the counter he was sittin' at a hunnert times. Hank, he said his name was, and next week he was back, and I'll be damn if he didn't have my name in block letters on his arm. Musta gotten it off my name tag. So, we took up together. I guess you could say I was a bit hasty, but somethin' about seein' my name on that man's arm made me wanna wiggle. Of course, like all men, he started goin' weird on me, but quick. He always had been a little funny. First time I saw him with his shirt off, I saw he had a big bullseye tattooed right between his shoulders. That didn't really bother me none—I kinda liked th' colors and stuff. So, things went on more or less like they always do—go to work all day so's you can go home and drink a twelve pack. But then he came home one day with a new tattoo—'D.N.R.' it said. I figgered it was some ol' gal's initials an' I lit into him good, more outta habit'n anythin' else. 'Naw, honey,' he hollered from the bathroom where he was hidin', 'Ain't no gal's initials, it's a medical term . . . ol' Doc Sparks was talkin' about it t'other night at th' bar, said it stands for "DO NOT RESUSCITATE."' Well, that one threw me for a while, after I figger'd out what 'resuscitate' meant, but I guess it wasn't the worse thing I ever saw.

"He could tell I was gettin' jumpy, so he didn't do anythin' too strange for a while. Hung around the house, got a couple of skulls an' daggers and stuff like that put on various parts of hisself.

"Then, it happened. You ever notice that when a feller goes completely rabid, it sorta happens slow for a while, and then just really happens?"

J. and I nodded synchronously in agreement. I didn't have a clue, of course, but figured that eventually she'd get around to explaining it.

And she did. While she talked, she began to remind me of this story I read in a high school English class about this guy who kills a bird and then feels this need to go around telling people about all the bad things that had happened and how his life was, you know, completely screwed up and stuff. I never had quite figured out the point of his story, but it seemed to be something like, "You never know what's going to happen until it does, and maybe not even then, but remember that sometimes a bird isn't just a bird," but maybe that wasn't it either. I never could see why he didn't just go buy another one or something.

Lucille's chainsaw voice clobbered its way into my head and put me back into my misery.

"So, there I am one night at th' diner, sorta cleanin' the counter real good." She laughed and winked at J. "And in come Hank with this funny grin on his face, like he'd just drunk a pint of rot-gut or found a mess of baby possums. Then he sits down right next to th' guy I'm cleanin' around and puts his right leg on the counter, still grinnin' like God's own personal idiot. Well, I asks him what he wants, and he pulls off his shoe and sock. By now, I figger he's on a six-hour vacation with Jim Beam and friends. Then I look down and seen his newest tattoo. It started right in th' middle a the top a his foot and said 'TAG GOES HERE' and had this bright red arrow pointin' down to his big toe. 'Hank,' I said, 'that does it. I'm leavin'.'

"'But, Lucille,' he said, 'you used to like them tattoos. Why shoot, when I got that one with your name put on my arm, was when you 'cided to move in with me.'

"'That's right,' I said. 'And it's a good thing you got my name on your arm, cuz now you go back and have "GONE FOREVER" put right under it.' And leave I did, right then and there, just walked outta that café and down to the bus station . . . after gettin' a little travelin' change outta th' register, of course."

Lucille finished and took a long drag from her cigarette. "Just cuz I don't write on bathroom walls don't mean I got nothin' to say."

We just stared at her. J.'s smoke had gone out due to neglect. I felt a sudden urge to take massive amounts of controlled substances. Anybody who says that drugs are abused by people who want to escape their lives is one hundred percent correct. I think some of us have earned that right.

I realized in one of those rare flashes of lucidity that, like the man who killed the bird, Lucille had singled us out for reasons only she could fathom and that she would stay with us until her plans had been realized.

"So, what's y'all's story, anyhow?" Lucille was addressing us at random, looking from J. to me and back to J.

"Well, we're waiting here for a man that we bought a car from to meet us here with the title," J. said.

"Bought a stolen car, huh?"

"We most certainly did not buy anything stolen—" J. started, but Lucille cut her off.

"Oh, of course not, honey. Why lotsa lawyers and banker-folk like to come down here to this here execative lounge. Hell, happens all the time, I 'magine."

I was beginning to see that Sarcasm and Brutality, her truculent sister, were Lucille's constant guides and companions. J. was taken aback, and I could tell she was at a loss as to what to do.

141

If Lucille had been a man, J. probably would have just popped her in the mouth and that would have been that. As it was, J. could tell that Lucille was far too much the type of woman who, when challenged, would not only respond in kind, but would win, though cities be leveled and multitudes slain. Lucille'd probably do the leveling and slaying, whether it was necessary or not. I had to give Lucille credit for one thing, and that was the fact that when she figured out J. wasn't going to do anything, she let it drop. She wasn't looking for trouble, but she wouldn't run from it either. As for confrontation, she couldn't have avoided it if she'd lived alone in a concrete bunker a thousand feet underground. Some people are born to it, can't and won't live any other way.

"Well, perhaps there is some question as to the whereabouts of the car's owner," J. allowed.

"That's more like it," Lucille said. "What this table needs is a little more honesty."

I was looking around the room for our "contact," as Mervyn at Phoenix Motor Works had chosen to call him. I had seen just enough spy movies to make me suspect that he'd arrived at least thirty minutes early so he could watch us and stuff, make sure we weren't with anyone else or talking into hidden microphones.

"Awright, your turn now. Fess up and remember, I was cornerin' cowboys in the hog lot 'fore Woodstock, so tell th' truth."

"I'm sorry?" I asked.

"I can see that! You're skinny to boot. What I want to know is what in th' world someone that looks like he just fell off the hood of a Lincoln town car deeeeluxe with a silver spoon shoved up his ass is doin' out on the town with Miss Purebred Lust here."

J. decided to intervene. "Not that it's any of your business, but we are en route to visit the home of the Eternal King of Rock and Roll, the Man Himself, Elvis D. Presley. If you have a problem with that, or wish to make any statement that casts aspersions on The King, I'll be forced to ignore my longstanding rule against using violence against women and thrash you within an inch of your sordid life. Maybe less." J. finished her impassioned speech and sat back in her chair, breathing heavily.

Lucille didn't say anything for a long minute or two, and when she did, she sounded thoughtful.

"I never been talked to like that ever, not by man nor woman. I didn't never figger I'd ever let anyone, either. I still have half a mind to drag your ass outta here by that hank a hair on your head, and there's only one thing stoppin' me: what you did was in the Defense of The King." Lucille pulled another cigarette out of her case. Less sincerity and thought have gone into the drafting of peace treaties than went into her last comment.

"But what does the 'D' stand for? Elvis' middle name sure didn't start with no D," Lucille said. "It was Aaron. Elvis Aaron Presley. God bless him an' the momma what bore him!"

"D stands for Delightful," J. shot back. This pleased Lucille.

"I guess I'll just have to come along and pay my respects too."

J. and I looked at each other, and then I looked off out into the crowd. I knew there was nothing I could do to affect the outcome.

"Wait a minute," J. said. "You can't come to Graceland with us."

"Oh, sure I can, honey. I don't have no place to be for at least another fifty-five years, maybe more if God ain't payin' any more attention'n He seems to be. Besides, I just wouldn't feel right 'bout lettin' you two run off in a stolen car without someone of my . . . experience . . . comin' long to help guide you through the trouble spots. And believe me, darlin', if I weren't there, there'd be lots of trouble spots."

Lucille's thinly-veiled threats were like a Victoria's Secret catalog: a lot was left to the imagination, but not so much that you missed the point. J. certainly didn't miss it. She just shrugged her shoulders and said fine, come to Graceland with us, but I knew that she had put ditching Lucille into the top priority section of her brain.

"Now I s'pose y'all are waitin' on Mervyn's 'business associate' to appear outta nowhere and provide y'all with the magical papers that are gonna say you own a certain car?"

J. and I looked at Lucille. I started with "How—"

"So you know Mervyn," J. finished.

"Course I do, hon. Everyone here knows Mervyn."

"How'd you know we're here to get a title from Mervyn's partner?" I asked.

"I bet you been to college. Am I right?"

"Well, yeah," I said. "I haven't finished or anything."

"Well, good for you. Don't you even think 'bout finishin'. Them college teachers'll scramble your brains, and don't you think for one sec they won't, hon. It's their job. It don't make 'em bad people, jes' makes 'em dangerous."

"What does this have to do with my car?"

"That car belong to you? Well, ain't you th' lucky one? I always wished I had a titty-pink '59 Caddy to call my own," Lucille said wistfully. There was a second or two of silence during which certain things that had been floating around in my head suddenly slammed together.

"I don't suppose you're in 'acquisitions' are you?" I asked.

"Why, yes, you could call it that. I really like to call it stealin', though, m'self." Lucille seemed pleased that I'd finally figured out something all by myself. "My real name is Maxine, but you can call me Max," she finished.

"An alias. I see. So, what's the news on the papers?" I asked.

"Couldn't get none. It'll take three, mebbe four days."

I didn't really have anything to say to that, so I just sat there.

"Let's get out of here," J. said to me. Then turning to Max, "We'll meet you back here in three days." We got up, and as we walked out, I turned to see Max, sitting alone at our table, staring up at the ceiling into darkness.

Chapter 44

Back at the motel, we went to our respective rooms. I tried to sleep but couldn't, and after pacing the floor awhile, went outside. Across the street, a Valero beckoned like an old friend. I walked on over and bought a twelve-pack of Heineken beer, and noting that the sign on the door said it was "a Class C Misdemeanor to drink on the premises," cracked one open and washed a couple of Hydrocodone down with it, wondering if it was still a misdemeanor. I opened another bottle and started walking up the street.

Around four beers later, I came to a cinderblock VFW hall sporting a huge, old combat jet mounted on an iron post in a corner of the parking lot. It was about ten feet from the bottom of the jet to the ground. I walked around and under it. On the bottom side of the left wing, someone had elegantly spray painted, "GOD IS JUSTICE AND LOVE"; underneath, in another hand, was scrawled, "DEATH FROM ABOVE."

I was trashed by now, so I threw the twelve-pack on top of the wing, for motivation, and then started looking for some way to climb up. I had just about given up when I saw a metal garbage can full of trash at the far end of the parking lot. I walked over, up-ended it, and carried it to the plane.

Standing on top of the can, I was just able to reach the top of the wing and pulled myself up. I fished a beer out of the carton and stood there looking up at the stars that shone like cold, incandescent spikes thrust through the endless night. I started feeling dizzy and sat down with my back against the cockpit and my legs stretched straight out, parallel to the wing.

After a couple more beers, it occurred to me that, to get it right, really get it right, I should be inside the cockpit. I tried to slide it back. It had been sealed with silicone or something, but after a few minutes struggling with it, the canopy jerked open with a rust-laden screech and I climbed inside. Most of the instruments were gone, and the rest were smashed and broken. One of the ones left showed the profile of an airplane, wings superimposed over a straight, horizontal line. Looking at the wings in relation to the straight line was supposed to show the position of the plane relative to the horizon. The left wing on the gauge tilted down at a crazy angle of about forty-five degrees. The compass had no needle.

I downed another beer and wondered what carries an airplane in one piece through who knew how many combat missions and, later, student pilots and other chance encounters, only to wind up nailed down to a parking lot out in the middle of nowhere like some trophy.

I was feeling that old, familiar weight, and my thoughts became less focused and finally I dozed off. I dreamt I was walking through one of those French gardens where everything is arranged just so, every tree, flower, and bush trimmed and forced into a symmetry of maddening exactitude that nature never intended. The farther I walked, everything became more, then more menacing. There was no breeze, nothing rustled in the bushes, no noise of anything living, not even insect.

I came to a bush of black roses that partially hid a small stone doorway in the wall of the garden. Stepping through the door, I walked down flight after flight of stairs, burdened with the knowledge that, as I descended, on the outside, ages rolled on, cities were built, flourished, then crumbled into dust. I turned once and looked back, thinking maybe it could be reversed, then turned around. Far down the stairs, a light was growing larger and brighter, and the air became increasingly humid and salty. I continued down until I finally came to light pulsing through another portal. I stepped through.

Out of the quiet of the tunnel, I found myself on a deserted beach. The sand was scorching hot, and a deafening wind howled like the souls of the damned off the gray-black sea. Turning to escape the way I'd come, the wind forced me to my knees then completely down, and with my face in the sand, I realized, finally, that nothing was there to shelter me. Still the wind raged, and I, with my arms stretched out in front of me, watched as the sand stripped the skin and muscle off my body, down to the pink-white bone. Around me the wind howled and howled like a conquering beast.

As I lay there, the sand began to pile up around me and fill my rib cage until only about half of my skeleton remained above the sand. I knew my bones would bleach in the sun for ages before anyone came to gather them up and take them back into the garden.

I forced myself awake and shook my head to clear it. Though I hadn't been asleep long, my legs and back were cramped, and the hangover was already starting to come on.

My watch said three-fifteen. I looked around the cockpit and up through the canopy, running my fingers through the tangle of my hair. The stars spiked down colder than before.

Chapter 45

The night ended rather badly, and I couldn't get to sleep after my nightmare. Getting down from the jet had been a little difficult, but then again, there's always gravity. Afterwards, I took what was left of the beer and sat by the pool, thinking about how things were going and why, things I rarely thought about, although sometimes, looking out of the car while J. drove, I thought about the other times I'd driven down other stretches of highway, past little crosses and bouquets of flowers left by the survivors of those lost to the road, and I'd think about how nothing ever really seemed to change. And at those times, I felt like maybe I wasn't really in a car at all, that maybe I was sitting somewhere, quietly remembering another time or another trip, maybe another life.

Then one look at what was driving the car would blast me back into reality.

When she and I drove on, through the vacant country, past the parking lots of dying towns, the vestiges of a rich and vibrant life were everywhere to see, like the time we were super lucky to see an abandoned drive-in theater, its screen straining drunkenly against the guy wires at an angle to the highway, as if leaning an attentive, albeit battered ear to the murmurings of the road, the murmurings of times long past.

I wished I had some reason for this trip that would, if not make it seem right, at least make it understandable, but I didn't. The best I could come up with for stealing a couple of cars and driving all over creation with a transvestite was, why not? It really just didn't matter that much.

I'm sure Gianfranco felt differently, of course, but for him there was money and his rather twisted sense of family honor involved.

J.'s entire world seemed to revolve around Graceland and sorting out whatever it was that compelled her to dress and act as she did. As for Max, maybe she felt that it was time for a change of scenery. I really never asked her. So out there by the pool, my reasons all seemed tidy, if not typical.

Morning light came, and I got up and went to my room, showered, and put on my psycho-ranger costume. My rattlesnake head looked a little testy in its Lucite coffin, and I wondered aloud whose idea it had been to try to sell those things. But whoever it was, they'd sure had my number.

Chapter 46

The motel offered a "Free All-U-Can-Eat Breakfast Buffet" to guests, and when I went to the dining room, I ran into J.

Getting a cup of coffee, I went to her table where she was reading a paper. She looked refreshed, and I wondered if she ever had bad dreams.

"Hey," I said. She put down her paper and looked across the table at me. She was wearing half-glasses and looked sort of like a stern, motherly type. The hair on the back of my neck resisted the urge to stand on end. She smiled and took a sip of orange juice.

"Good morning. Did we sleep tight?"

"No. I had . . . dreams."

"About Max?"

"I don't think so," I said.

"Now, what are we going to do about Max?"

"Take her with us, I guess. What else can we do?"

"Ditch her somewhere."

"Ditching people who don't want to be ditched is harder to do than you might think," I said. "Besides, why bother?"

J. didn't say anything, just put her coffee cup down and gazed at the pool outside.

The Max topic didn't come up again after that, and I went back to my room. I had stored the duffle bag containing my stash of money under the bed. I removed $500 from the bag because I needed some new clothes, badly. I wanted to take the Cadillac, but naturally my guardian transvestite had the key. I guess she figured that, if she let me keep the key, I'd leave her. I guess maybe she was right.

I was about to call an Uber when I heard knocking at my door. I went and opened it, and there was J., showered, refreshed, and ready to go.

"Let's go shopping," she said.

"You're reading my mind again."

150

Chapter 47

J. was leery of driving the Cadillac until we got the fake papers, but she wanted to drive it so bad that we went ahead and took it to the Checotah Mall anyway.

Because of our rather eclectic ensembles, we got quite a few looks apiece as we entered, but as soon as we got inside, we split up. J. went off in search of a big department store. I was looking for the most expensive place I could find.

I finally found a small store called Monte's, which carried, according to the sales clerk, "Only the best of the best of the best."

The quality of their clothing was okay, but the price was just what I just looking for: sky-high.

I was scared to use my stepfather's credit cards because I figured he'd have at least canceled them, but since he bought the Vette, I doubted he'd have reported the cards stolen. Anyway, I decided on cash and carry.

I picked out about three hundred dollars' worth of slacks and shirts—or to put it another way, I got three pair of slacks and four shirts. The salesman asked me what I wanted to do with the clothes I'd worn in. It was clear that he thought they should be burned. It was also clear that he though I'd just spent a lot of money on clothes that he found much more suitable; the jury was still out concerning my judgment. I wanted to throw them away, but I also felt a strange attachment to them.

"I don't know. Throw them away . . . wait. Don't throw them away. Put them in with my other clothes." As he was about to comply, though, I said, "No, don't put them with the others. Put them, oh, I don't know, put 'em in a separate bag."

He waited briefly to see if I would change my mind again, and when I didn't, he complied.

They didn't sell any shoes that I was interested in, so, barefoot and wearing a pair of khaki pants and a new button-down, I left. It was clear that, in his eyes at least, I was unrepentant.

The Allen Edmonds shoe store was downstairs, and though I soon discovered that an escalator is unbelievably hard on bare feet, I persevered. I had to wander around a bit, then found it and went inside.

A smallish salesman in his late forties bustled up, shaking his head from side to side.

"May I help you, sir?"

"I, uh, need some socks," I said, a little uncertainly.

"Yes, sir." I'm not sure if this was agreement or compliance, but he didn't seem fazed. I gave him the benefit of the doubt.

"And a pair of shoes."

"Yes, sir."

I bought a pair of brown loafers with tassels, and as I was leaving, a thought struck me.

"Do a lot of people come in here barefoot?"

He looked at me for a moment. "No, sir. Will there be anything else, sir?"

Chapter 48

I walked around the mall some more and then decided to wait in the car. I watched all the families bustling in and out of the mall entrance, chatting with each other or arguing or not really speaking much at all, and it all seemed so unfamiliar. I began to wish J. would hurry up.

After about fifteen more minutes of family watching, I spotted J. walking out of the mall, furtively glancing back over her shoulders. She labored towards me with a sort of jerky gait that made her look stiff or something. A couple of guys with walkie-talkies left the mall from different doors and were pacing briskly around, talking into their radios and looking all over the parking lot.

One of them spotted J., said something into his radio, and started running after her. She had a pretty good head start, though, and made it to the car, lurching and staggering like Quasimodo in drag.

She finally reached the car and fell over the back door into the seat, tossing me the key in descent. I fired the car up and we sped away. In the rearview, I saw more security guards converging on the parking lot. One sprinted diagonally across the lot, trying to cut us off at the exit, so I let him get in front of us, and then I wheeled the car in behind him and made a bee-line for the next exit down. I think maybe my sojourn in the VFW hall parking lot had bestowed some dog-fighting skills on me.

I looked into the backseat where J. was struggling into an upright position and could see that she had on about six different layers of clothes, one outfit per layer. I shook my head and drove us back to the motel.

Chapter 49

There was a message for us at the front desk, from Max.

We called, and she said that she was still waiting for the papers to be finished, and that if we wanted to, we could go to the country club for dinner. J. asked Max how she had ever managed to become a member of a country club, and Max told her: she'd had an entire life story forged, from birth certificate to college diploma. The name she chose for this sham was Annabella Something-or-Other, and after Max told me and J. her "life story," I had to admit I'd have wanted her in my country club too. She might be a car thief to us, Max said, but to the good folk at the Bayard Country Club, she was an Italian heiress with seriously heavy connections in the Vatican.

We didn't really want to spend any time with Max, but I was kind of down, and J. said that going to a country club might cheer me up, make me feel at home. I figured I'd at least see some people like I used to be around. I actually don't like snarky, rich, pretentious people any more than they like themselves, but I can relate to them. We decided to take Max up on her offer.

Max said she'd steal a nice car and pick us up around eight.

At five after eight, J. and I were sitting in her room, watching Pay-Per-View and having an argument about whether or not we had to pay each time we switched titles.

The honking of a car horn interrupted us. When I looked out the window, my heart about tore loose from my ribs. Gianfranco's black Mercedes was crouched like a beast of prey outside the motel door. I ran to the bathroom and tried to wriggle out of a window that would have been too small for a mouse with latex bones. It was over and I knew it. About that time, I recognized J. and Max's voices in the room.

"Well, where's the all-American boy off at now?"

"When you honked, he jumped up, took one look outside, and ran into the bathroom," I heard J. say.

154

There was silence for a moment while this information was assimilated, and then Max said thoughtfully, "He's sorta skittish, ain't he? Reckon it's account of me or you?"

"A little of both. He's led a sheltered life," J. said. I got out of the tub, brushed myself off, and walked into the room.

"Have both of you brushed your teeth?" I asked. They looked at me with one of those we-know-what-you're-up-to looks and then smiled smugly at each other. J. suggested that we quit wasting time and go to the country club. A sense of utter futility, combined with a feeling of mild anticipation, stole over me.

We walked out to the car, and with a shudder, I realized that my intuition had been right: this was Gianfranco's Mercedes. I didn't know how he'd managed it, but he obviously had somehow worked things so that J. and I fell right into his hands, via Max and the Phoenix Motor Works.

Gianfranco had been right all along when he used to tell me that, with a little money and a lot of people working for you, you could accomplish anything.

I couldn't see through the tinted windows, but didn't need to. I knew what was in there. I thought about running, but suddenly realized the hopelessness of it all and gave up.

Max smirked at me and, stepping in front of me, opened the back door, motioning me to get in. I stepped around the door and looked inside. Nothing. No one.

"Where is he?"

"Who?" Max asked me.

"You know exactly who," I said, feeling hurt and betrayed. "Gianfranco." Max looked at me and then at J.

"John-what?"

"Franco," J. answered. "Colin's got this fixation that we are being chased by his father–"

"Stepfather," I corrected.

"Stepfather and a bunch of thugs," J. said lightly. "There were these two guys in a bar, but I'm not even sure they were after us, or anybody, for that matter."

"Then why'd you run when I said they worked for Gianfranco?" I asked.

"Didn't want to risk it. But I haven't seen them in a while. What they're supposed to do to us when they catch us, I haven't the foggiest."

"First thing they'll do is drag your ass down to the secondhand store and put you in a nice, pre-owned leisure suit, if I have my way," I said through clinched teeth. J. tut-tutted me, and Max looked at us both as if for the first time.

"Look, if you wanna have yoreselfs a little lover's spat, don't go off an' skip it on account a me. But I'm hungry as a broke-out chain gang wanderin' 'round in the desert, and I'm goin' to th' country club an' eat. Now, y'all comin' or goin'?"

J. was, I guess, about as hungry as I was, because she grabbed me by the arm and shoved me into the back seat of the death-car. Then she got in the front seat and looked at Max.

"We're coming."

Chapter 50

The ride to the country club was pretty uneventful. J. and Max sat up front and tried to stump each other with Elvis trivia, and I sat in the back, looking around at the car, which was definitely Gianfranco's. I found one of his business cards stuffed down in the back seat, between the cushions. That day at North Dallas Classic Cars, I thought I'd seen the last of this barge forever, and now here I was, riding to the High Plains CC in it.

I'd always thought life was an incredibly bad idea.

We got to the gates of the country club, and when I saw the cattle guard, I knew we were in real trouble.

It was a little after dark now, and the entire grounds were lit up with those huge lights like they have out on the highway, the ones that cast that ghostly, blue-gray tint over everything. I don't know if that particular shade has a name already, but I think it ought to be named "Hades Blue," or something like that. The gravel of the drive crunched like broken teeth under the tires of Gianfranco's car as we pulled into the valet parking.

A gardener was stomping around in what was supposed to be a flower bed, making desultory jabs with some pruning shears at this or that plant. When he saw us, he walked over and opened the doors of the car and then took the key from Max and, without wiping his feet, got in. He pulled off to park it.

I looked at Max. "When Gianfranco sees what you just let that guy do to his car, he's going to make a sizable deduction from your paycheck."

J. rolled her eyes. Max looked at me curiously, and then she spoke very slowly. "Honey, if I hear just one more little ol' peep outta you about this John feller, I'm gonna take a chainsaw and trim you down a bit."

J. laughed a little, and I shrugged my shoulders.

"Whatever," I said. "We can do it your way."

We walked into the clubhouse, which was actually a converted Quonset hut, and looked around. I read in a bathroom somewhere that no one ever went broke underestimating the taste of the American public; I figured he'd been here.

J. turned up her nose, and my hopes rose as I realized she was about to refuse to stay. Then she spotted a velvet painting of Elvis, dressed in a white jumpsuit like my grandfather used to mow in, and decided it wasn't all that bad. I gave up hope.

The mâitre d' came up and seated us, calling Max "Annabella" and, in general, making a subservient fool out of himself. He mentioned how often he'd been going to mass. By his count, about six hundred times in one month alone.

"Well, I'm sure that's not nearly enough," Max said to him and winked at us when he slunk off. We watched him go.

We were seated, according to the layout of the dining room, at a very good table. It was a lot bigger than the number in our party required. Several people looked at Max and pointed. Knowing glances were liberally applied.

J., ever the talkative sort, jumped right in. "So, Max, what's good here?"

"Well, honey, I'll tell you. The chicken fried steak is good, the hamburger's better, and the fried catfish is to die for," Max said dreamily.

I grabbed the menu. That didn't sound like the food offerings of any country club I'd ever been to. The waiter came over, and Max ordered the fried catfish. As did J.

I ordered a martini. I didn't have a clue how it would fall out, but I wanted to be well-fortified when Gianfranco and the double dunces joined us. J. and Max talked awhile about this and that and eventually started quizzing each other over Elvis trivia again.

My martini came in a tea glass. Instead of an olive, it had a lime in it, and it was straight-up cheapass gin.

The food came, and one glance told me that it, at least, had been prepared by a master. I sat and ordered "martini" after "martini" and watched the doors, waiting for the end of the trip. But nothing happened, other than J. and Max earning a new respect for each other. I earned a liquid lobotomy.

I looked over through a double-vison haze to where J. and Max were tearing into the food like a couple of unhinged vultures. I ordered another martini. I could feel the gin-loonies trying to pry the lid off the top of my head. It was touch and go.

"How come so quiet, hon? You still waitin' on them bad guys? I sure hope one of 'em has some interesting tattoos," Max said.

J. started laughing and said, "I guess it'll take 'em a while, since we *are* in their car and all."

I didn't say anything. I thought that maybe, if I ever came into my trust fund—which at this point was highly unlikely—I might spring for a little brain augmentation surgery for both my girls. Or maybe a little head ventilation via small arms fire. I saw great possibilities in both.

"What are you thinkin' about, darlin'?" Max was verbally assaulting me again.

I looked at her, or both hers, actually, as my dinner was starting to catch up with me, and answered, "Uh, whew. Um, I was thinking, about, I was thinking about what I'd like to do for you guys. You've really been great."

J. and Max looked at me and smiled. "Yer drunk, hon," Max said.

"Completely gone, dear. It's time you laid off that stuff," J. finished for her. "Besides, we have now come to the planning stage of the evening. It really is time we talked about getting the papers on the Cadillac." She took my drink from me.

"Say no more, doll, say no more. I rushed to the printer, an' I got 'em right here in my purse. Y'all got th' two hunnert dollars?"

I didn't say anything as I pulled out my wallet and counted out twelve or fifteen twenties and threw them across the table. Conversation was momentarily suspended in the dining room as the money floated in a see-saw motion gently down into Max's lap, around the table, and onto catfish bones.

"Paid in full," J. said to Max. Then she turned to me. "Where'd you get that money?"

"I've had it," I said. Damn that *in vino veritas* bullshit.

"All along?"

"All along." I pulled out a wad of twenties and hundreds and held it up in front of J. and Max. "I've got enough unbacked federal reserve firepower here to kill me, put Max in a coma, and make Julie wear men's clothes."

"And you've let me, on my less than adequate income, pick up the tab for the last several days?"

"Well, I am the kidnappee, and you are the kidnapper. I doubt that when Patty Hearst was nabbed she had to chip in for gas."

"No," J. said. "But eventually she began to pull her own weight."

Max's eyebrows rose.

"Well, it's not like *I'm* not at risk," J. said. "When I acquired you, you were driving a stolen car. If we'd gotten pulled over, I could've gone to jail for that."

"Jail is nothing," I said. "I've been to jail, and after the last few days, jail seems like a rest cure." I nodded my head.

"Let me get this straight," Max said. "You're a kidnapper and he's a kidnappee?"

"Forget it," J. growled. Max looked at me.

"Colin?"

"Well, I'm operating on free will now, so I guess I'm not being kidnapped anymore."

J. gave me a kick under the table, but the alcohol protected me and I didn't feel it until the next day.

The waiter came over and asked if there was anything else we wanted. Max said no, and asked for the check. He said he could just put it on her tab and she said no, just put it on the table. He shrugged and walked off.

"Now, what about the car title?" J. asked.

"I'll bring them by y'all's motel in th' mornin', hon, and then it's Graceland Ho!"

I knew J. wanted the title tonight so we could ditch Max, but it was obvious Max knew, too, and she wasn't going to let that happen.

The waiter brought out the check and put on the table. J. and Max glared at me. I sighed and pulled out my wallet. I looked at the bill and handed the waiter a hundred dollars. Ben looked at me reproachfully as he disappeared into the waiter's pocket.

"Thank you, sir," he gushed.

Why so polite all of a sudden, I thought.

Max stared at me quizzically and then spoke. "Uh, Colin, hon, it's your money and all, but would ya mind tellin' me one teensy eensy little thing?"

"What?"

"Why'd you just tip that boy a hunnert dollars?"

"I didn't . . ."

"Colin here comes from the land of pretension, where they pay for their meals at the table," J. cut in.

160

"Oh. Well, that land of whatever ain't gonna float with Mary Lou up there at th' register," Max said. For me, I'd never seen a country club that had a cash register, either, except in the Pro Shop. You puts on the tab, you walks out the door.

We got up and walked to a counter by the exit, where I paid Mary Lou.

"Thank y'all so much," she said to no one in particular. Then she turned to me. "Next time you come in here, you tip me off so's I can wait your table" she said and winked. I said the next time I came in there she wouldn't have time to wait on any tables because the Rapture would be kicking into high gear and she wouldn't want to miss that. She turned to Max.

"We don't believe in no Rapture, do we, Annabella?"

Max, a.k.a. Annabella, said no, we don't believe in no Rapture. She and the pope had talked about it once or twice over a couple of cold frosties. Mary Lou turned to me with a smile.

"What pope was that?" I asked Max. She jerked her head towards me.

"What?"

"His name? Which pope did you have the 'cold frosties' with?"

The color started to rise in Max's cheeks, and J. walked out the door, laughing. I was left alone with Mary Lou and Max. Suddenly, I hoped that Max really did know his name. Mary Lou looked at Max with the firm, steady gaze of a penitent.

"Well," Max said, "the POPE!"

Mary Lou turned on me in triumph and said, "The POPE!"

"Oh, *that* one," I said and walked out the door.

Max came out a few seconds behind me and, in the persona of Annabella, told the gardener to go get the car, which he did.

As the Mercedes came around the corner, all the bad premonitions I'd had earlier came flooding back, and I suspiciously eyed J. and Max. The logistics of Gianfranco's being able to engineer Max's employment and subsequent entrapment of me were truly mind-boggling, and even in my drunken condition, I started to realize the impossibility of it.

The gardener opened the doors for us, and as I was about to get in, another car pulled into the drive. I glanced over my shoulder and saw a taxi with a couple of guys in the back seat.

Muffled shouts and bangings-around emanated from the back of the cab. The occupants seemed to be having some trouble getting the doors open and were yelling at the driver to unlock them. Near as I could tell, he was yelling back to them something about money.

The whole scene was captivating on some primal level, I guess, because I couldn't take my eyes off it. Max yelled at me to quit messing around and get in the car. At that second, the cabbie unlocked the doors, Max got out of the Mercedes to yell at me again, and the occupants of the taxi spilled out onto the ground. My worst nightmares were confirmed. Dale and Howard, or in the parlance of the enemy camp, Guido and Gino, were flailing around on the ground like a couple of coked-up game show hosts, screaming orders at me and at each other, with a steady stream of imprecations at the taxi driver, who was trying to back out and hurling abuse at any and all.

I looked at Max, but before I could speak, she said, "Honey, best ya' got in now. Them's the boys I stole this car from."

My grandfather used to say that one problem with being young is that no one can ever tell you something you don't already know. It seemed deep at the time. The twin terrors had managed to scramble to their collective feet just as J. reached out of the Mercedes and pulled me in. Max nailed it and headed for the cattle guard.

I looked back for Dale and Howard, but through the tinted glass of Gianfranco's car, there was little to see, just small articulate smudges.

We drove in silence for a few minutes, and then Max spoke.

"Well, I sure did want to take this fine piece of German steel through them gates of Graceland, but now we been made, best we ditch her."

I didn't say anything to that. J. cleared her throat.

"What do you mean by 'ditch' the car," she asked.

"Git rid of it. You know."

"Can't we just abandon it somewhere, like a mall or—"

"Where you got it?" I finished for her. They both looked at me.

"Nope. Can't just leave it somewhere. They'll find it," Max said. "Cops got all that DNA technology, and with the 'DNA and Me' finding people and kids they never knew existed everywhere, you never know who'll pop out of the internet and bite yer ass. Gonna definitely burn it."

"Oh yeah," I said, "good thinking. We better burn it, out here in the middle of nowhere, at night, so nobody'll ever find it."

Max didn't say anything.

"We can't do that, this car belongs to his father—"

"Stepfather," I interjected.

"Stepfather. Stealing it and letting them find it is one thing, but stealing it and melting it down is another."

"But I always destroy the evidence," Max said petulantly. "It's kind of my trademark."

"Not tonight," J. said. "Tonight it isn't."

Chapter 51

We finally won Max over, and she agreed to abandon the car at the first big truck stop we came to. We saw a cluster of lights, shining like an island in a stream of darkness. It was a few miles down the highway, and sure enough, when we got there, I recognized the logo of Valero. Home. No, more than home: sanctuary.

It was a big one and looked more like a small village than a gas station. I daydreamed that barefoot peasants ran to and fro, washing windows and pumping gas as merchants hawked their wares—anything could be had and in quantities more than one needed and, at times, wanted. Looking around the parking lot, I noticed a couple of women whose merchandise seemed to be available on more of a rental basis. Inside, truck drivers, the self-styled "knights of the road," swaggered around swilling coffee from big, plastic tankards that were refilled endlessly by simpering wenches bedecked in polyester. And somewhere, hidden behind mirrored glass and steel security doors, sat the Nobleman, ever watchful of his domain.

Max parked the car around back while I went in and bought a case of beer, a bottle of Tylenol PM, and some nonessentials—socks, a hand mirror, a box of cookies, some deodorant, a pair of flip-flops. As I walked up to the counter, I saw that they had one of those stainless steel food counters, about fifteen feet long, complete with the infrared lights and everything, to keep the food warm. Or maybe to cook it. Anyway, in all that space, all they had out was one turkey leg. It was dried and shriveled to the consistency of King Tut's thigh.

I put my selections down on the counter and pulled out the Valero credit card. A hard-edged waitress sauntered up to the register.

"Anything else?"

"Yeah. I'd like a turkey leg, but could I get a fresh one?"

"Well, the thing is, we gotta sell that one before I can make any more," she said.

"Don't be silly. That thing looks like it's been there two days," I said.

"Been there almost two weeks, not counting yesterday. But it's store policy. I can't make another one till that leg right there sells," she said.

I pretended like the counter was full of assorted foodstuffs and couldn't tell which one she meant. "You mean that one right there, behind all that other stuff? That one's going to be mine?"

She looked at me for a moment and then said, "Well . . . if you buy it, yeah."

"Okay, I'll tell you what. You charge me for that chunk of leather-wrapped bone, twice. Then, I want you to throw it away and make me a fresh one, okay?"

"No, I can't do that neither. We're not allowed to throw food away," she said.

"You won't be throwing food away, not really, because I'm going to pay for it. I'll pay twice. I just want a fresh one."

There was a small line starting to form behind me, from which the assorted sounds of impatience were beginning to emanate.

"What would I tell Stan, I mean, Patty?"

"Who?" I asked.

"My boss."

"Tell him—or her—that a guy came in here, bought the antique turkey leg, and asked you to wrap it up for him in a trash can," I said. "Tell him you were threatened. Tell him the entire Health Department came down here, did a Rockwell hardness test on it, and said that it passed if it was for tank armor, but not for human consumption. Tell him whatever you have to tell him to get me a fresh turkey leg!" By the time I finished, I was shouting.

She calmly let me finish and then continued with: "Well, I guess I can do that, but you have to walk out of here with it so I can prove with the video that I didn't just throw it away, or else he'll—she'll—fire me."

I began to feel a slow rage building deep in the pit of my stomach and realized that if I didn't get control, it was entirely possible that a turkey leg was going to drive me to kill a counter girl I'd only just met, all because her boss, name of Stan or Patty, might be watching on CCTV and fire her because she wasn't following some idiotic policy. I reconnoitered, taking the path of least resistance—you know, my usual modus operandi.

"Fine. I'll take that one, right there."

She sighed and got it out, but before she could wrap it up, I said, "Don't. Just hand it over."

She reached over the counter with the turkey leg, which I took with my right hand and gave her the credit card with my left. I made sure that the transactions were completed simultaneously.

While she ran my card through the machine, I slapped the turkey leg on the counter and hummed "Lost Highway," in 4/4 time.

Feet were shuffled behind me. The clock behind the counter ticked like a baseball bat struck against an old oak tree, an analog metronome. Finally, the machine printed up my receipt, and I signed it.

When I got outside, J. and Max were waiting for me. Standing there, with a case of beer tucked under one arm and munching on the desiccated leg, I think they realized the vastness of the gulf that was fixed between us.

Max had put the car on the side of the parking lot that faced the highway, and they'd called a taxi. When it arrived, we were all pleased to see that it wasn't the same driver from the country club.

Back at the motel, we gathered in J.'s room because it was late and all the bars were closed. It looked like Max would be accompanying us to Graceland after all and that J. was powerless to stop her. Seemed fair. They made our plans for the final push into Graceland, and we sat around and talked and drank. As the beer ran out, Max began to get madder and madder.

When we were down to the last can, her anger came to a head and she started ranting and raving about politicians and laws and policemen.

I asked her how she felt about game wardens, hoping to start a fight between her and J., but she just looked at me funny.

"They're fine, stupid," she said.

I said it just seemed like they were different sides of the same coin.

"No, they ain't. They get out there by theirselves and they work, protecting natural resources. It's those lawmakers who just sit around and don't never do nothin' but think up rules they hold over our heads but don't never follow theirselves that makes me mad. It's just like right now, tonight. I got to sit in this room, or in some other, when I want—need—to be out drinkin' with folks who'er like me. It's hard to follow a law that says you can't drink past two in the mornin', 'cause if you don't know yet, maybe someday you will, them's the hardest hours . . ." Max trailed off and

166

looked out the window. Then she said, "You're young. And you're stupid. And you ain't reached that point of your life where you can see th' light at the end of th' tunnel. But I have, and I don't want ta sleep any more'n I have to 'fore all that's taken away, out of my hands."

Max shoved herself up and out of the chair she'd been sitting in and stood in front of me and J., swaying slightly. She suddenly looked old and defeated. "In the mornin' I'll bring 'round the papers for that Caddy and we'll hit Graceland." Then she walked out the door.

J. watched her leave and then looked over at me; she laughed a little, but without sincerity. "Philosophical little tart, isn't she?"

Chapter 52

We sat around for a while longer, and then I went to my room to try to get some sleep before the next day's drive.

I turned the light out and got into bed, thinking about all the latest developments and wondering how long it'd take the twins to find the Mercedes. I thought I'd call Betty in the morning and tell her where we'd left it, then decided against it. Gianfranco had paid for the Lo Jack service; let them earn their money. I'd also tell her that we were heading back and to stop worrying about whether or not I was eating right and brushing my teeth.

My thoughts faded to black, and then a dream began to form. I was walking through an ancient town perched on a rocky coast ravaged by the green-black storm surge of the sea. The town was deserted, but only minutes before my arrival. Walking past cafés and restaurants, fresh food on the tables steamed in the cold air, and cars with engines running sat abandoned at signal lights while stores and houses stood open.

One house in particular caught my eye. I went inside and walked down a flight of stairs and through a low hallway that opened into a subterranean cavern.

In the middle of the cave there was a pool of clear, cold water, and next to that, a time-wracked bristlecone pine had sunk its roots deep in the rock. An owl sat in the top branches, and looking higher, I could just see the night sky. A full moon bathed the cavern in cold, blue light.

Stepping to the edge of the water, I stared into it, and though it was easy to see the bottom, I could barely make out dark shapes darting and swimming around and seemingly always at the corner of my sight. When I tried to focus on one, it would disappear, only to be replaced by another at the edge of my peripheral vision.

I dove in and sank. Nearing the bottom, I began to make out a shadow figure—a deeper shade against the darkness—floating a foot or so above the bottom and sitting cross-legged, back to me. Swimming around to face it, I found myself looking into the face of the old woman from the desert, wrapped in tattered clothes like iridescent coal. Her hands clutched her knees and her fingernails were long and razor sharp.

I looked around for whatever creatures I'd seen from the surface, but they were gone. Then the old woman began to talk to me through the water, and though tiny bubbles clung in her hair, none came from her mouth or nose. Even though it was of obvious utmost importance, I couldn't make out what she was saying. The harder I tried, the less I could hear, until all I heard was blood pounding in my temples.

She became more and more frustrated, then hurled herself upright and stalked across the bottom of the tarn as a cloud of gray silt rose around her, higher and higher until she looked like a cloud moving across the face of a smaller earth, or something else . . . I don't know. Coming to a door I hadn't noticed before, she passed through, looking back at me with a look that warned me not to follow. Then she was gone. All that was left to mark her passing was the fine silt that drifted sluggishly in the water and then settled.

I swam back to the surface and got out, my heart hammering through my ribcage. Looking back into the water, I couldn't see the door or where we'd sat, though the water was still and clear. A faint shrieking came from somewhere in the distance, getting louder and closer, making my head hurt, until suddenly I woke to my own screaming.

I sat up in bed and shook my head to kill the wailing, but it wouldn't die, then I realized there were sirens out on the highway.

I got up, washed a Norco down with a plastic cup half-full of room temperature Jack Daniel's, then turned the TV to a dead channel, volume up as loud as it'd go. Sitting there until graylight began pushing through the slats in the blinds, I listened to the frenetic hissing and crackling, desperate to find shapes in the chaos.

Chapter 53

Max called us at eight and said she'd pick us up at ten or ten-thirty. I called Betty to see which way the wind was blowing.

"Colin! Where are you?"

"I don't know, close to Hell or Tennessee," I said.

"Is there a difference?" she laughed. She didn't seem to be mad anymore.

"Don't know it."

"Well, Gianfranco is furious with you." Then she giggled. "How'd you manage to steal his Mercedes again?"

"Huh?"

"You know, from Guido and Gino?"

"You mean Dale and Howard?"

"Well, yeah, um . . ." Betty trailed off nervously. "Um, you do know that all calls are quote, recorded for training purposes, end quote, right?"

"Oh. Sorry. Just dumb, blind luck." I didn't want to explain about Max and get Betty all worked up and worrying. "What'd they have to say about that?"

"Oh, you know them. Gianfranco had to explain to them why he was mad. I swear, I don't see how much stupidity got dumped into one family. Makes me think their mom must have done something terrible in a former life. I bet she was a—" She stopped. "I'm sorry. You know how carried away I get."

"It's okay. Anyway, I got something a little more important than the vagaries of reincarnation going on here. Capiche?"

"Oh no. Not you too?" Betty asked.

"Sorry. Where are they now?"

"Don't know. Gianfranco told them to call soon as they found the car, and we haven't heard from them yet. Guess they're still looking," Betty finished, thoughtfully.

"Well, if they call in, you tell them that I left the car at a big gas station out by the highway. I'm not going to say which. Let's see if they remember the Lo Jack a little."

"A little?"

"Huh?"

"That last thing you said doesn't really make sense," she said.

I just shook my head, even though I guess she might have been right. "Whatever. Long night."

"Gotcha. Now, are you okay?"

"Yeah," I said. "I'm fine."

"Sorry about the other day. I shouldn't have gotten so mad."

"Forget it," I said.

"What are you going to do?"

"When I left, I was headed for Oregon."

Betty was silent while she digested this. Then she asked, "Why?"

"Well, you know, I thought I'd go to my grandparents'—"

"Your grandparents?" Betty asked in a kind of small voice. She had met them once.

I thought about it and decided not to waste my time trying to explain.

"I'm going to the airport and catch a flight back to Dallas," I lied.

"That's wonderful! You're doing the right thing. Now, um, is this traveling companion of yours I've been hearing Guido and Gino jabbering about coming with you?" Betty asked in that sly way people have when they're pumping you for info.

"No," I said. "She probably ought to go home too."

"No chance of me getting to meet the woman who captured your—"

"No, I don't think this one's going to work out," I said.

"Oh well. Maybe another time." She sounded a little relieved.

"Yeah, another time. Look, gotta go. See you soon," I said. Then I added, "I'd like that" and hung up the phone.

Chapter 54

Max arrived at ten-fifteen, and by ten-thirty we were leaving the motel. J. suggested I pay for the rooms, so I did and then climbed into the backseat.

We got on Route 66, and I saw that the Valero where we'd left the car was coming up. Wondering if Guido and Gino had found it yet, I said, "Hey, Max, pull over. I need to get some stuff."

"Let's drive a while. We can't be stoppin' and startin' if we expect to make any kind of time," she replied.

"Oh, come on. It'll take just a sec."

We were really close now. J., suddenly taking my side, said that we should stop and fill up, get some coffee, maybe a donut.

Max didn't say anything as she sped up. Then as she drove past the exit, I saw why she didn't want to stop.

Gianfranco's car was still there, but what had been a shiny, pretentious chunk of my stepfather's self-confidence the night before was now a still-smoldering, burned-out shell. The car looked like it'd been air-lifted out of Beirut or maybe been in a zombie apocalypse. Steam and little gusts of black smoke wafted up from various places. The windows were heat-cracked and blackened, and the windshield was smashed out. All the paint was crinkled and curled off the metal, and the tires were completely burned off. The wheels were melted flat where they rested on pavement.

Just beyond that visual joy-nugget stood eight members of the Checotah Volunteer Fire Department, one of them advancing warily on the car with what I'm pretty sure was a pair of Jaws of Life extended before him. The tool was bright, shiny, and looked like it'd never seen use. Behind him another guy had a fire hose trained on the car like a machine gun. Why they were going to cut the roof off I'll never know, but I'm guessing they just wanted to.

J. and I just stared at it as we drove by, and then I noticed Guido and Gino sitting on the ground. One of them was holding his head in his hands, and the other was looking at the car and then at the cell phone in his hand and then back at the car.

J. looked at Max. "You want to explain this?"

"Explain what?" Max asked innocently.

Obtuse might be an uncommon word, but it's hardly uncommon, I thought to myself.

"Explain why his father's car, which we left in perfect condition last night, looks like Satan just made a beer run in it?"

I could tell that J. wanted to break Max's back, and frankly, I sorta wanted her to. This little lark of mine had suddenly taken on a whole new dimension. I had just stumbled upon the Law of Hyper-Accelerated Devaluation. I'd never realized that the jump between $190,000 worth of car to a-buck-twenty-five-cents-a-pound junk steel could be so swift. Max looked at J.

"I thought it was his stepfather's," she said.

"Regardless, it's still a melted piece of junk!" J. yelled.

"Guess some a them vandals got to holt of it. I don't know," Max said and looked out the window. "Don't look at me—"

"Looks like you 'got to holt of it,'" J. mimicked Max angrily. "We agreed not to destroy the car."

"I didn't do nothin' to that car 'cept to leave it," Max protested.

I tuned them out and tried to figure out how Gianfranco was going to take this. Not very well, I decided. Yeah, it's true; I'm smart like that.

Chapter 55

We drove for twenty or thirty minutes and then my phone vibrated in my pocket like an angry hamster. I pulled it out and saw a number I didn't recognize, but it was a Dallas area code. Oh boy. Gianfranco. For some reason I answered.

"Yes?"

After a moment of silence, an automated voice came on: "This is the third and final notice that your vehicle warranty is about to expire."

Damn, that was fast.

J. was still mad, and I could tell that it upset Max, though I didn't know why she cared. My head was pounding from all the drinking I'd done the night before, and with the top off the car and the sun beating down, I felt a little dizzy. Max turned around and said once more that she hadn't had anything to do with burning the car, and though I didn't believe her, it really didn't matter.

I didn't answer her, but I'd been thinking about it since I saw the aftermath. On the one hand, the car was gone and there was nothing I could do about it; on the other, I figured if she did torch it, she'd never have another opportunity to do that to me again, so why mess with it? Besides, regardless of what she did or didn't do, I was starting to realize all of this was my fault. Everything.

"Forget about it," I said.

"What?" J. and Max asked simultaneously.

"Gianfranco's car. Forget about it. We're alive, it's dead, I'm yours. It was probably insured for twice its worth anyway."

J. turned the radio on, but there was no consistent signal, although a song fragment briefly surfaced just as she was about to switch it off. I glanced at it and was surprised to see the Bluetooth logo on the old radio. Figuring I could risk taking my phone off "Airplane" mode for a few minutes, I googled "Vintage car radio Bluetooth" and found that exact radio—which wasn't vintage at all—being advertised all over, from Zazzle to Amazon. Or maybe it was from Amazon to Zazzle. Anyway, this was an interesting wrinkle. I paired my phone, and soon J. was convinced that we were getting excellent reception. I cued up "All Shook Up" from my downloads and hit "Play." After the song finished, I played "Viva Las Vegas."

J. looked at Max and said, "This is nice!" a statement that Max emphatically agreed with.

"Must be a all Elvis station!" she gushed.

"Radio Free Elvis!" J. giggled.

I decided to let them believe what they wanted, then J. said, "I hope they play 'Can't Help Falling in Love,'" and Max gazed at her for a moment, an odd, almost tender look that I would have cause to remember later.

Anyway, I played "Can't Help Falling in Love," and before it even finished, Max said, "I wish they'd play 'Polk Salad Annie'!" So, I did, and then it became a game of "Wish a Song" as every time they mentioned a title, such as "Heartbreak Hotel" or "Blue Suede Shoes," I'd cue it up.

At first, J. and Max both thought we'd hit radio pay dirt, but then they began to see something mystical at work. As for me, obviously I was pulling these strings, but I was also having my own mystic journey vis-à-vis the old woman who kept popping up and disappearing at opportune moments.

Max floated the idea that maybe we were in the grip of something more powerful than we realized—which I could certainly relate to—and J. said, "Maybe."

Max said, "Maybe nothin'. I know it."

J. didn't respond directly, but then looked at the radio and said playfully, "All right. Let's test your theory. Magic Eight Ball, I wish we could hear 'Baby, Let's Play House.'"

Max looked at her in awe. "I've never met anyone who even knew about that one."

I was frantically searching for it, but autocorrect kept changing "house" to "mouse" for some damn reason, and just as they were losing faith, "Oh, baby, baby, baby, baby baby. Baby, baby baby, b-b-b-b-b-b baby baby, baby—" began to well up from the speakers.

Max and J. just stared at the radio enraptured, until a low growl from the centerline rumble strip made J. jerk the wheel to the right, but she was still focused on the song.

Elvis crooned:

> Now listen and I'll tell you, baby
> What I'm talking about.
> Come on back to me, little girl,
> So we can play some house.

Max looked at J. that way again, and Elvis whined:

> Well, you may go to college,
> You may go to school.
> You may have a pink Cadillac,
> But don't you be nobody's fool . . .

Even I began to think something magic was happening. Then suddenly, something about all of it just annoyed the hell out of me, and naturally, due to my inner jackass, I couldn't leave well enough alone, so as the two of them sang along dreaming about playing house, while the fine road seemed to glide beneath the wheels of the Cadillac, I suddenly switched it to Metallica's "Enter Sandman" and cranked up the volume. J.'s head snapped down as she looked at the radio, and Max just looked frozen. Then they looked at each other the way Amish parents might if little Amos or Isaiah showed up at the farm in a neon green unitard and a tin foil space helmet.

Before J. could touch the radio, I switched it back to the big E., and so for the next couple of hours, I had big fun manipulating the tech and convincing them that either the radio, the disc jockey, or both were schizophrenic. Getting bored of that, I shut down the tunes and neither seemed to notice or care; the spell was broken. J. hadn't said anything for a while and neither had Max, but after a bit she seemed to relax and cheer up. She looked over at J. furtively, with the same wistful look, and seemed about to say something but didn't. Instead, she glanced back over her shoulder at me.

"Hey, Colin, how come you was drinkin' so hard last night?"

I shrugged my shoulders.

"I mean, it's yer business and all, but it sure is a awful hard way for someone your age to live."

For some odd reason, that seemed to annoy J. "You ought to know," J. said and looked at her. Max didn't answer, but looked at her for a moment.

"Yeah, I guess I ought," she said in a quiet voice, "but I didn't never drink like that when I was his age," she finished a little angrily.

J. had stung her, that much was evident.

"Nothing else to do right now. If I go back to school, I might slow down," I said. "Maybe."

"In college?" J. asked sarcastically.

I glanced at her and decided, why bother?

"Well, ya know, drinkin' kills them brain cells," Max said as if she were confiding something. "Don't you never worry that you might kill so many of them cells you won't be able to learn no more?"

"No, I don't," I said, looking out at the country flashing past, just over the speed limit.

"Well, why not, hon? You gotta think about them things."

"Because of my theory of Cerebral Darwinism."

"Uh, cerberus which?" I'd thrown her with that one.

"Cerebral Darwinism. You're familiar with Evolution Theory, aren't you?" I asked. Max nodded her head yes, and J. turned around in her seat for a moment, but continued to look at me in the rearview mirror.

"Well, my theory of Cerebral Darwinism is similar. Keep your eyes on the road." Max nodded and I continued.

"So basically, I accept the fact that flooding your brain with alcohol kills brain cells. But what I think happens then is a form of survival of the fittest. The weak brain cells die, the strong survive. Therefore, by drinking like I do, I'm becoming more intelligent with every binge and actually improving my chances of succeeding in college." I smiled. "And life."

Max looked at me for a moment and then turned her attention back to the highway. J. had turned to look at me again.

"You've got problems, you know that?"

"Yeah."

"Big time," she said. Max looked over her shoulder at me. I was struck by how much younger she looked than from the night before. It was like getting out on the road was doing her some good. She looked, well, not exactly pretty, but not too bad. I dropped her age to thirty-eight. It occurred to me that Max was the kind of woman who was probably ignored in favor of the prettier girls in high school. Now, if she were to run into one of them, they'd both realize how Max had weathered the years better than they. She wore well.

Max looked at J. and commented on her makeup.

"What's wrong with it?" J. asked harshly.

"Well, nothin'. I was just wonderin' if maybe when we stop for lunch, you could give me some pointers?"

J. looked at her and smiled a little.

"Yeah, sure. Why not?"

I shook my head as the implications of that hemmed me in.

Chapter 56

We crossed into Arkansas at about one in the afternoon, and we immediately stopped at a little barbecue joint right off the highway. There was nothing else around it, and when we went in, it was empty except for the guy at the counter.

"Help you, folks?" He looked at J. as if he was wondering how many briskets he could carve out of her. "I got to warn you, though, we're fresh out of barbecue," he said. We stared at him, and he burst out laughing. "It's a joke! Get it? A barbecue joint that is OUT of barbecue!" He kept laughing until we all pretended to see the humor. "No, really, what do you all want?"

We ordered a couple of sliced beef sandwiches apiece, potato salad, and sweet tea, then sat down. J. also got apple cobbler and vanilla ice cream.

"Okay, Max, what'd you have in mind?" J. asked. Max swallowed a big chunk of her sandwich and squinted at J.

"Mind about what?"

"Pointers? You wanted some pointers on how to do your makeup."

"Oh yeah. Well, you know, just how to put it on an' stuff like that, so it ain't so obvious," Max said.

"How to put it on?"

"Well, like you. I can put th' stuff on, but then I look like a Indian or somethin,' you know, on th' warpath. But you wear a lot a makeup, and it looks good." She looked at J. closely, sort of squinting as if in deep concentration. "You wear a whole lot," Max finished.

J. cleared her throat.

"I see. Well, yeah, I can probably help you out, give you some, uh, advice," J. said, and Max nodded her head.

J. went out to the car to get her makeup bag. When she returned, they went to the ladies' room.

While they were gone, a bunch of highway workers came in. One of them walked up to me. "You own that car out there?"

I nodded my head yes.

"Where'd you get it?"

"Bought it," I said. "Three years ago."

"How'd you ever get money enough to buy a car like that?" he asked suspiciously.

"Well, it *is* several decades old," I said.

"That means it's a classic." His friends nodded to each other in agreement. It was clear they suspected me. Of what, I wasn't sure.

"I washed dishes."

"You what?"

"Washed dishes."

"You made enough money washin' dishes to buy a Cadillac?"

"I was real good. What's the point of this, by the way?"

"My uncle used to have a car just like that one out there—"

"Was he a dishwasher?" I interrupted. The man looked at me in confusion for a second.

"No, he wasn't no damn dishwasher! He's a sheep farmer."

"Lot of money in that?"

"In what?"

"Planting sheep."

"Hell, he don't plant no sheep!"

It occurred to me that maybe "planting" meant something different in Arkansas than it does back in Texas, but who knows? He sure did seem touchy on the subject though. "So how'd he afford the Cadillac?" I asked.

"I don't know. Anyway, he had one just like that one."

"And?"

"And it got stolen a few months back. Six or seven, I forget which," he said. "You sure you didn't just sort of borrow that car, 'stead a washin' dishes?"

My scalp started to tingle, and I could feel the blood drain from my face as the realization began to come to me—that killings happen over far less than this all the time. Billiards, for instance. People die in pool halls all the time, even when there's no money involved. As for me, I'm no good at pool, but I lie like a politician, and the possibility of lying one minute about washing the dishes and the next lying down at the City Morgue, being scrubbed down myself, seemed likely.

180

"Quite sure," I squeaked.

We stared at each other, and my throat tightened up so much I couldn't swallow. Then salvation came in one of its stranger guises: my favorite transvestite and Max, the made-over car thief, who, by the way, looked stunning. I dropped her age to thirty-two.

Several of the men whistled, and all of us stared as J. and Max walked up.

"What's going on here?" J. asked.

The highwayman who'd been interrogating me looked up at her and asked, "You with him?"

"Yes. Is there something wrong?"

They all looked at her like they suspected she'd asked a trick question. He looked from me to J. and Max and back again. "Lord, there must be something real wrong," he said.

"He's laboring under the misconception that my car belongs to his uncle," I informed her.

Max wasn't saying anything, but looked pensive. The roadworker looked at Max and J., and finally stopped at me.

"I think we oughta call my uncle and have him come up here, take a look for hisself," he said. "I expect he's got the title with the V–I–N number." That's just how he said it, too, with a big pause between each letter.

His friends looked at each other and nodded their heads in agreement.

"Go ahead," J. said. Max punched her in the shoulder.

"I hate to break up your plans for a family reunion, but we are on a trip to visit the Eternal King of Rock and Roll," Max said to no one in particular.

"Well, if you're in such a all important hurry, why'd you order all that food," one of the men asked, pointing to the food on our table. He did have a rather salient point, as all of us had ordered with a fair amount of exuberance. Max was silent.

"It was supposed to be to go," I said quickly.

"Yeah," Max said. "It was s'posed to go."

"I think you ought to go call your uncle," J. said. "Be sure to tell him to run right up here because you've got a problem with two women and a boy and you don't know how to handle it."

The roadworker in question, whose name I never caught, but whom I sometimes call Jack, looked at J. "Lady, I—"

"Shut up. I can't believe that two defenseless women can't travel through Arkansas without being accosted by the likes of you. Evidently, that movie—*Deliverance*—wasn't too far off track."

"Ma'am . . ." Several of Jack's friends were starting to look at him as if he'd tried to lift up a nun's habit. J. continued laying it on thicker and heavier.

"Call your uncle," J. said.

He whipped out a flip phone, dialed, and we waited. Nothing. He left a message to call right back.

J. smiled at him. "Maybe he's out in the woods with his banjo," she opined.

"He don't play no banjo."

"And he don't plant no sheep, neither," I mimicked. I don't know why. I just couldn't help myself. J. and Jack both looked at me, each with an expression as if they'd just smelled something awful. J. seized the moment.

"I never married, and until this day have never regretted it. But now, here in this barbecue joint where ladies clearly receive no quarter, and certainly no respect . . . What are you going to do next?" J. asked. "Make him squeal like a pig?" She motioned expansively towards me. "Say he's got a pretty mouth?"

Jack's compadres had had enough and walked en masse out the door, muttering to themselves and leaving him to face J.'s tirade alone. I once heard something to the effect that there's nothing like the wrath of a woman scorned, and though J. was never closer to being a woman than a televangelist is to being sincere, I think the analogy can be stretched to fit.

Jack's resolve to fetch his uncle quickly withered in the face of J.'s indignation, like cut grass in August. Maybe quicker. "Ma'am, I'm real sorry I ever said anything about it. Now that I think about it, the color's a shade different. I guess I'll be going now," he said. He hesitated a second to see what J. would say, but she just looked at him. "You all have a nice day." Jack left in full retreat.

"Well, that went off rather nicely, I think," J. whipped around and said brightly when she heard the door slam.

"Yeah," I said. "It did."

Chapter 57

We hurried through lunch, got back into the car, and I was allowed to drive, for some odd reason.

We'd been heading east on 66, and somehow I missed a sign. The next thing I knew, we were going down highway 71 headed for I don't know where.

J. was sitting up front. Evidently, she had told Max she was a game warden, because Max was grilling her about what it was like, was it exciting, dangerous and so on, which is probably why neither of them noticed that the traffic was getting scarcer and the road narrower.

As for myself, I was wrestling with the problem of how to get back on 66 without asking J. or Max.

My phone was off, and I didn't know if there was a map in the glove box or how to get to it if there was, and anyhow, there was no way to get it out without attracting any attention from the girls.

Speaking of which, things were getting weirder by the minute on that front also, as the more J. got into telling Max about her job as a protector of the wild, Max seemed to be getting more into J. Max was leaning over the seat as close to J. as possible, staring at her and, in short, looking like a schoolgirl in love.

I made eye contact with Max once, but she looked off, glanced down, and pulled away from J., who just kept chatting away.

J. of the unknown last name, first female game warden of the state of Arizona. Man, was she laying it on thick.

As is common with me, I slowly began to get the picture. J. was truly enjoying Max's attention. I think J. had been as surprised as me when she redid Max's makeup and found a very attractive, albeit somewhat rough, woman under there. With a decent cut from Bandit Salon—some place down in Austin where Mom always insists on going—and a nudge here and there in Nieman Marcus, Max would be smoking hot. Or more smoking hotter than she had become, though in an earthy, frontier woman sort of way. Yeah, I thought Melissa, Mom's favorite stylist, would bitch-slap some panache on Max's tired coif in ways that might raise the dead. I looked at Max again, and feeling a bit, um, firm, had to make myself stop thinking about her—and things that would never happen—and revised my guess about her age, downward to thirty. Then I tuned back into their conversation.

"Funniest thing that I ever saw in the field?"

"Yeah," Max said. "I used to sit around the café and listen to them old boys talk about huntin' and fishin' and how it was a life or death dangerous deal, or as one guy said, 'The difference 'tween us and them,' like Bambi's gonna come chargin' outta some thicket and maul a full-grown man with a gun."

"Yes," J allowed, "some of those guys take it a little more serious than's needed. I guess one of the funnier things I saw was a couple of years ago. It was about the middle of deer season, and I was at this café back home, called Rosie's."

Max interrupted with, "You been there, Colin?"

J. smiled generously at Max, turned to me, and winked. "Yeah, it's his favorite place to stop. At least when his wanderings take him to Wide Ruin," J. said.

I hadn't said anything, but pretended to get real interested in the road. Of course, Max wasn't ready to let any detail of J.'s illustrious past lie unmolested.

"You like it too, huh? What's it like? What're the folks that go there like?" she asked with genuine enthusiasm and interest, like a schoolgirl quizzing the star quarterback. That was a first for me, and her interest in J. pissed me off again.

"Freaks, one and all," I said. "Going to Rosie's is like having coffee with all the people that tried to get on *America's Most Wanted* and were rejected. Breakfast at Rosie's is like going out with the girl of your dreams and finding out that the faraway look in her eyes is the result of heavy Thorazine, shock therapy, and a dead puppy she loved."

Max winced and turned away.

"Rosie's is the place, ohh the place where all the nightmares come to play-ay-ay, and no one makes them go away-ay-ay—"

"Colin! Stop singing!" J. snapped.

"It was more of a chant, really," I said.

"Doesn't matter. You're scaring Max."

184

I caught Max's eyes in the mirror and did this thing with my eyebrows that makes them sort of go up and down, twice, really quick. She looked away.

"Relax, Max. I've left my axes somewhere towards the backsssess, or maybe somewhere towards my past-o, which, incidentally, tends to run together-o . . ."

"Shut up. Now," J. said. "I mean it." J. was looking over her shoulder at me while she patted Max on her shoulder. I shrugged.

"Okay. You were going to tell us a story," I said innocently. "The funniest thing your years as the Femme Pre-Eminent Game Warden in the service of the Arizona State Department of Wildlife lavished upon you."

"Forget it."

Max was ready for anything about J., and with the added bonus of anything that'd shut me up, she eagerly pressed J. to continue.

"You said you were at . . . uh, that place, couple years ago and . . ." Max trailed off, and I looked into the mirror again. She was looking at me with a strange look, fear or concern, maybe a little of both, and probably trying to second-guess the nature of my next tirade, but I felt all better, so I smiled a real smile for once and focused my attention on the road. J. took it from there.

"And these two guys came in, lugging all kinds of gear—guns, waxed-cotton duffle bags, mosquito netting, *two* tents, a portable shower—just everything. They looked like guys in a Cabela's catalog, except, ummm . . . what's the delicate way to put this?" she asked. "Except they were . . ." she paused for effect, "flat-ass ugly!" Max just grinned. "Well, everyone in Rosie's just stared at them.

"I was wearing my uniform, and one of them walked over and said hello, said he 'backed the blue,' looked me over again and said, 'and the green!' then asked could he buy my breakfast? I said no, but he paid for it anyway, and when he walked off, I saw he'd left a hundred-dollar bill next to my plate."

Max gasped.

"What kind of food they serve in there? They hirin'?" Before J. could say anything, Max laughed. "Okay, okay, I know he was tryin' to bribe ya'. What'd they say when ya' walked up and threw that money back in their faces?"

"I didn't," J. said.

Max shrugged and said, "That's my girl!"

J. smiled. "No, not that. I figured I'd need it for evidence in case anything happened."

"Yeah, right," I said.

"Oh," Max said. "Evidence."

"Anyway, as he was walking to their table, they all laughed, and I caught him say that he knew there'd be no trouble with the game warden. I decided right then that I'd camp out that night and find 'em first thing in the morning. And that God willing, there'd be trouble with the game warden."

"And?"

"And I did camp out that night, though I'm not crazy about it . . . you know, sleeping outdoors."

Max said, "Yeah, camping is sure hard on us girls . . ."

J. cast a sideways glance at me, but for once I kept my thoughts to myself and my mouth shut.

J. continued. "So they pitched both tents in a motte of mesquite trees, set up a portable blind right out in the middle of a clearing about sixty yards from their camp, built a fire, and then started partying. Watching them, I figured they'd probably shoot at anything that moved, so I moved off a bit, set up a digital video camera with a motion sensor to record whatever they did, rolled my sleeping bag out in the bed of the truck—snakes!—and called it a day."

Max and I nodded, more or less in unison.

"About an hour before sunrise, they woke up and banged around for a while, and then I could see the beams of their flashlights bouncing towards their blind, where they settled in."

"I started video recording and dozed off."

"What happened next?" Max asked breathlessly.

"Well, instead of coffee, I woke up to the smell of fresh marijuana."

"You rolled into the fire?" I asked in mock concern.

"Colin!" Max yelled at me.

"Well, how else did it get lit if J. was sleeping?"

J. quietly said that I knew it wasn't her marijuana.

"Yeah," Max said, "weren't none a hers!"

"So, then you lumbered over to their blind and hogged all their dope, didn't you?" I said. "Junkie . . ."

J. ignored me.

"I left the camera on because there was no way to prove they were smoking drugs as opposed to cigarettes—"

"Wimp," I said.

"Then what?" Max asked.

"I guess they went to sleep. It was still dark when a big herd of deer drifted into the clearing, milled around the two hunters for about an hour, grazing, jerking their heads up at every breeze, noise, everything prey animals notice. There must have been three or four big bucks—one of which could have made Boone and Crockett—and twelve or fourteen does."

"Weenie," I returned.

"Just before the sun broke the horizon, the breeze picked up a bit and the herd disappeared back into the trees, bucks first, like always."

"What'd ya' do to them two hunters?" Max asked.

"I walked over to their blind, sat down, and waited for them to come around. After a while they began to stir, and the guy who'd dropped Benjamin near my plate at the diner crawled out, sat down, and began twisting up a joint in serious concentration. Just as he finished, he saw me, flashed an uncertain grin, and then just handed it over."

"And?" Max and I said in unison.

"There was that and a little marijuana in a baggie, but not that much. I busted them for misdemeanor possession."

"Oh."

"Funniest part? Down at the station, I showed them the tape of them snoozing away while a herd of deer grazed around them."

"I bet they appreciated that."

"Honestly . . . that bothered them more than the possession rap."

Chapter 58

J. noticed it was taking an awful long time to get to Memphis and promptly deduced that we were lost. Phone service had been spotty, so I stopped at a handy Valero and went in to buy a map. In contrast to our previous experiences, this was a small establishment specializing in gas and oil with, oddly, a smattering of office supplies.

Behind the counter, a large, Brunhild-looking blonde shot me a friendly look, and to this side of her, an older man with both his legs in casts, two black eyes, and a half-healed gash across his forehead was sitting on a folding chair—which seemed like a bad idea to me—next to the coffee machine. She looked like something out of a Wagner opera. For that matter, so did he, maybe one the Valkyries were looking for.

"I'd like to buy a map, please."

She looked at me, and I thought I needed to explain. "I'm getting crappily consistent cell service out here, and I'm tired of being lost."

"Where you guys headed?" the girl asked.

"Well, Tennessee, among other places. Do you have one of those big road atlases, the kind that have about half the states in alphabetical order and the other half at random?"

"No, we didn't get none of those," she said.

"Well, give me a map of Tennessee then."

"Oh, that's just silly!"

I decided I hadn't heard what I'd just heard and shook my head.

"I'll tell ya how to git there. Now, you get back on this lil ol' highway and you take the third exit you come to," she paused, "or maybe it's the fourth. You're gonna know it cus about three miles down it sorta dog-legs back to the left. If she don't dog-leg, go on to the next one—"

"Miss—"

"Now, you stay on that till you come to Farm Road 1164—"

I had to stop her. "Look, I'll never remember all that. I'll just buy this map right here and—"

She snatched the map from my hand and smiled at me like you do to an infant you're teasing, and then she swatted me with it.

"Silly!"

I looked out to the car, and J. and Max were looking in at me like, *What's the problem?*

Brunhild forged on. "I'll just draw you a map."

She looked all over the counter and the store, then finally went into the back where I could hear her banging around. She came back after a minute or so with a piece of cardboard about a foot long and eight inches wide and went through the whole thing, explaining where to turn, what to look for, points of interest, drawing the whole time.

"There, she said. "Silly."

"Thanks, I'm sure—"

"Whatcha do is . . ." Now the old guy was involved.

His casts clanked together as he tried to sit up straighter in his chair, which creaked a bit and looked close to total collapse. "Get back onto the road out there . . ."

I really did want to be polite. "Yes sir?"

"Take either the third or the fourth turn . . ."

But he was talking very slowly and deliberately.

"Then you go to Farm Road 1164 . . ." He proceeded to run through the whole thing. It seemed like hours passed. "When you get back to the super . . ."

"Yes?"

"You just keep on trucking."

"Thank you, sir. I'll do that, sir."

Brunhild smiled and swatted at me. "Silly."

"Just keep on trucking," he repeated.

I stepped outside and looked at the "map." It had so many arrows, intersecting lines, X's, stars, et cetera, that it made me dizzy to look at it. Evidently, the only thing Brunhild hadn't put on it was anything to orient north. I went back to the car and explained to J. and Max that I'd been refused service, so we drove down the road a little farther to another gas station. I ran in and, refusing to speak, snatched a map off the rack and dropped a five on the counter and left. And thus, we got back on the right road.

Chapter 59

We drove all that day and stopped on the outskirts of Memphis, found a cheap motel, and got three separate rooms. I was paying for everything now. J. just scowled at me whenever I hesitated, and I was hitting my cash supply pretty hard.

After my shower, I flipped on the TV, looking for something, anything of interest, but most of the offerings were either soft-core porn or "reality" shows featuring canned drama between "friends" or some guy who was acting as if he was in mortal danger in the wilderness, all the while being recorded by a film crew doing exactly everything that he was, while simultaneously lugging who knows how much equipment. After a couple of minutes of channel surfing, there was a soft knock. Opening the door revealed Max, fresh from her own bath or shower, wearing a thin cotton dress.

"Can, uh, I come in for a sec?"

I opened the door a little wider, turned, and walked back into the room. Max followed me in and shut the door, then she sat down on the edge of the bed. I took the chair by the table, just as I noticed I'd stopped scrolling right on one of the porn movies I intended to skip when she had knocked. Great.

Max noticed, of course. "Oh. I can come back later, if . . . you know, you're busy . . . I mean, um . . ." she stammered. Understandably.

"I'm not busy," I said, figuring there was no point in explaining that I really wasn't looking at dirty movies.

"I gotta talk to somebody, and you're the only person I know here."

"What about Julie?"

"Well, it sorta involves her, if you know what I mean."

"You want to talk about her?"

"Not exactly. I just, well, yeah, I guess I do."

"Well, you're already getting better at it."

"What?"

"Talking. You're not talking like such a, well, like such a hick anymore."

"I been listenin' to y'all some, and I been to school too, you know. Or you don't. Anyway, I just, I don't know . . ."

"What's the problem?"

"I don't have anybody I can talk to, not really, and figured you bein' from Dallas and all that you might—"

"—have noticed you drooling all over yourself every time Julie's around?"

Max looked embarrassed, and I almost felt sorry for her. Almost, but not quite. She looked away.

"Yeah," she said hoarsely. Her face was red.

"Well, now that you mention it, yes, I have."

"Uh, okay. Well then, what'd ya think it means?"

"That you are one sick individual."

"I was hopin' that bein' from a big city and all you might be a little less—"

"Quick to point out a pervert when I see one? Maybe if you'd been discreet about it, instead of dropping by my room to announce it . . . Nah, wouldn't have mattered. Would you mind leaving so I can scrub myself down with lye soap and Draino?"

Max had started to cry a little and got up to leave. The realization that I'd gone too far and she truly didn't know that I was trying to be funny hit me hard.

"Sit down, Max. I was just kidding with you. I don't think you're sick. I shouldn't have said that. Really . . . I was kidding. I meant to be funny."

She turned at the door. "Really?"

"Yes," I said. "Really. I thought you'd know I was jacking with you."

She looked at me for a few seconds, trying—I guess—to decide if I meant it or not, and then she sat on the end of the bed, sort of like my girlfriend used to when she needed to talk.

"I don't know what I'm gonna do. I mean, I said I'd give up on men, but I didn't mean—" She stopped suddenly. "You and Julie ain't . . . that's not why you said those things, is it?"

"No. I was joking."

"What about you and Julie?"

"Nothing."

191

"Never?"

"Never."

Max didn't say anything, but this was truly far and away too good to let pass.

"She may dress nice and apply her makeup with the hand of a virtuoso makeup artiste, but I can honestly say that Julie and I are just friends, and not very good ones at that," I said.

"Then why are y'all on this trip together?"

"That's a long story."

"Tell me."

"A very long story."

"I've got time."

"Not for this story you don't."

"But—"

"Suffice it to say that, all appearances aside, as a woman I've never found Julie attractive. Let me rephrase. I've never found Julie attractive as a woman. For that matter, I've never found her attractive as a man, either."

"What're you talkin' about?"

"Julie. What are you talking about?"

"Julie. What am I gonna do?"

"Well, what do you want to do?" I asked. "No specifics, please," I quickly added. I was still stressing over her thinking I was checking out porn.

Max was bright red and looked like she was about to have a stroke. Maybe two.

"Lots of things. Sometimes I see her and I just want to run up and kiss her. Sometimes I think about goin' to dinner, you know, just me an' her. Other times, I jus' wish I could drive around with her forever. Mostly though, I just want to sit there and look into her eyes and her know I mean it."

"Well, maybe you can," I said. "You never know about Julie."

"It's funny you said that. Sometimes I think she sorta feels th' same way I do, but then she'll say somethin' mean. You know her better though. Is she . . . you know . . ."

"Is she what?"

Max looked exasperated and rolled her eyes. "You know what I'm saying."

"Not any more than you are."

"Not any more than I *was*. Or want to be. Or whatever. This is something I never even thought I'd ever have to think about," Max said. A single tear glided down her cheek. I dropped her age to twenty-eight and a half.

"Maybe you won't have to," I said.

"That'd be worse."

"No, not like that. Let's say you, um, girls, stay together and hang out after this trip. Let's say you go back to Arizona with her."

"Fat chance," Max said.

"For the purpose of argument."

"For the fun of it!" Max returned.

"Well, I'm all for fun. Anyway, J. lives alone. Didn't she tell you she had a cabin somewhere?"

"Yeah, it's a nice little two-story log cabin that she built herself. There's a tin roof, and when it rains it sounds—"

"Well, you'd be alone out there, no prying neighbors, or much else. Go into town a couple of times a month, a little more, a little less . . . You could probably sort things out pretty well."

Max thought it over.

"Yeah, I guess you might be right. Can I ask you somethin' personal?"

"I might not answer."

"Have you seen her, you know . . ."

"No, I don't know."

"Naked?"

I had to laugh.

"Oh. No, not really. Though I did see her in her underwear once."

"And?"

"Well, it'll probably disappoint you . . ."

"What is it?"

"She didn't have a single tattoo," I said.

"Oh," Max said. Then she perked up. "Blank canvas!"

Chapter 60

The next day we got up bright and early and crossed the Mississippi River into Graceland. Well, that's not entirely true. Memphis, Tennessee, really, but I'd never been able to separate Graceland from Memphis, like when someone says they want to go to China, as if there are no places or cities there, you just go to China. To me, Graceland, Memphis, Tennessee, was just one whole, a complete package. In my mind's eye, after listening day and night to J., and then Max, sing the praises of Elvis, I'd pictured it as some special place where all the people lived full and always eventful lives, creating bright memory after bright memory, each upon each.

Rolling through the outskirts, it was soon evident that Memphis was like any of a hundred cities, cleaner than some, dirtier than most. There were commercial signs, of course, all intending to cash in on the location, location, location, but there was nothing, I don't know how to put it, nothing real to signify that the man J. and Max and millions of others worshiped had ever visited, let alone called this place home.

We drove under a bridge where, on the impact-scarred concrete abutment, a smudge of red car paint marked the point where someone had died. Above that was spray painted:

Steven Franklin

9-25-15

R.I.P.

May flights of angels . . .

Underneath this were other names, his friends, I guess, a single ochre handprint and primitive animal figures like something discovered in a cave. There were various mottos and slogans as well, ranging from the sublime to the obscene, spray-painted in a bedlam of colors and styles, from the bottom to so far up that the topmost were lost in darkness, transforming the pillar into a post-modern stele. We drove by it in silence, and Max craned her neck around to watch as we passed.

Chapter 61

I assumed we'd just go straight to Graceland and get it over with, let J. do whatever it was she said she had to do—dressed like Priscilla, of course—and that would be that.

However, when we got to Memphis, neither of them seemed ready to finish it. Max wanted to stay at The Peabody hotel because J. had told her it had ducks in the lobby, so we went downtown, found The Peabody, confirmed the presence of the ducks, and after I checked us in, we stood in the massive lobby and stared at the marble fountain that really wasn't as large as I'd have thought, but then again, I don't know how large a duck fountain ought to be. A red carpet led up to it, and though there was the odd stain, all in all, it was close to immaculate.

At check-in the guy told us to have a look at the rooftop where a band was to play later that night, so we got in the elevator and, after a bit of confusion, realized that "S" was the button to push, although it'd have made more sense if they'd just kept to numbers.

The ducks were cool, but the rooftop was awesome and offered a panoramic view of Memphis, a stage for the band, and a huge neon sign that read, understandably, "The Peabody" in blood red letters.

J. took in the scene, breathed deeply, and said, "This place is infused with Elvessence." Max nodded in rapture.

"Elvessence?" I asked.

"Mmhmm," J. said. "Elvessence."

"That's not a word."

"Of course it is. I just said it."

"Okay, fine. It's a made-up word, then."

J. was still looking at the sign, but shot me a sidelong glance. "Name one word," she said, "that isn't a 'made-up' word."

I started to respond and then realized I'd been outwitted. Again.

After we put our stuff in our rooms, we left the hotel and drove around, trying to figure out just what exactly the Army Corps of Engineers had envisioned when they'd laid out the town. If the street system was intended to follow the general contours of the small intestine, then I guess they succeeded. In my opinion, though, it's the most God-awful mess of intersecting roads, loops, and dead-ends I'd ever seen.

We were more or less lost in Memphis for the better part of that day, but as we weren't actually trying to get anywhere just yet, "lost" is probably an overstatement. Anyway, we finally got back to the hotel in the early afternoon to take showers and naps and, in J.'s words, "Be fully prepared, both physically and mentally, for the fulfillment of our dream."

This "fulfillment of our dream" still didn't happen just then, though, because J. and Max took a vote and decided that going the next morning would be best.

Chapter 62

That night J. and Max wanted to go out. We went down to Beale Street and saw I don't know how many bars, most of which had someone at the door trying to entice us inside with offers of "no cover" or the "Best Blues on Beale," and though J. and Max didn't care where we went, none of them felt right to me. Every time they wanted to go in one, something held me back, and though they were frustrated a bit, they went along. It was obvious they were enjoying each other's company anyway. Then we found ourselves at the far end of the street, standing in front of a dark, no-name bar. J. and Max wanted to go back up the street, but I felt in my bones that this was the one. They looked at each other and decided to indulge me.

It proved to be much larger on the inside than it looked streetside, and it seemed as if we'd been transported fifty years backwards in time. The bar was filled with smoke and lit by a few low-wattage light bulbs hanging from the ceiling, and slightly by a sign over the bar that at one time had said "LIQUOR" in red neon. Now all it said was "QUO." A black light cast ambiguous silhouettes of the people in the crowd—their murky forms framed against the visible dark where they huddled together in isolated groups—throughout the cavernous room. The concrete floor and walls were cracked and beaded with condensation like some distillation of the hundreds of thousands of hard and desperate hours that had passed there.

J. and Max looked skeptical, but I was set on it, so we took a table in the corner and waited. A waitress walked over, took our drink order, and never came back. This was repeated by two others. Finally, J. got mad and stomped up to the bar to get them herself.

An old black man was stooped over a table next to ours, and when J. walked past, he raised his head and said, "Merciful."

I stifled a yawn, and the old man looked over at me and smiled. "Ya' sleepy, huh?"

"Bored," I answered.

"Not used to such slow movin' times, eh?"

I tried to think of something to say to him that wouldn't be entirely rude, but gave up. "Guess I'm just not ready for the grave."

"That so?"

"Yeah."

"Then you in the wrong place."

I didn't answer.

About that time, four skinny black guys and two very big women strolled in, looked around, and then walked over to the man sitting next to us. They talked quietly for a few minutes and then walked into the back. When they came back, they were lugging guitars, clarinets, saxophones, and all kinds of other stuff.

They got up on stage while a flurry of waitresses swarmed around them, stashing plastic cups half full of liquor on any flat spot they could find that wasn't occupied by a musician or an instrument.

I ordered two drinks from a waitress as she whipped past me.

The band got busy setting up, and after about fifteen minutes, the lead singer stepped up to the microphone.

"'Scuse me, folks."

And then, with no sound check, no do-overs, and no apologies at all, they ripped into a two-hour set that made me reevaluate life as I knew it.

I've racked up a lot of time in a lot of clubs, usually drunk, but sometimes not, and I've always paid attention to the band. If they suck, I leave. This bunch, whose name I never caught, was unlike any I'd ever heard. For starters, the lead singer had a voice that sounded at times like the smolder of aching flesh, cheap bourbon in a plastic cup, speculative rage, like a bastard file coated in molasses. Sometimes cold and hard, other times heated to incandescence, but always possessed and seemingly driven by all the pain in the world, ancient, enduring, and insatiable. How a man that skinny could carry the weight of that voice was beyond me. The women sometimes sang, sometimes wailed back-up, and always swayed to the smoky rhythm in their full, unblunted power that aroused every man in the house including, and perhaps especially, me.

In my ignorance, I thought my experience with the blues, all of which was confined to what the cover bands played in the Deep Ellum bar area of Dallas and the same seven songs they play on iHeart Radio, was vast. But the slicked-up pretty boys of Dallas and Fort Worth, for all their posturing, wouldn't have stood a chance down here, and as for the commercial fodder served up on corporate radio, you could set your watch by which song was playing.

The crowd was a gyrating mass of need and want, fueled by hunger and a shared spirit, locked into the band in a psychic feeding frenzy. Every note they threw out was snatched up, sucked dry, and absorbed. Instead of satiation, the crowd thirsted for more. Poseurs from north of the Mississippi trying to put their shoulders to that wheel would have been broken on that stage, and that, at least, would have been fair.

During the break, the old man leaned over towards me.

"Hey, boy! Still tryin' ta stay awake?"

"I'm up."

He looked at me, and then at my beer.

"Not hardly."

I went to the bar and yelled to the girl that I'd have what the band was drinking. She looked doubtful, but reached under the counter then poured me a drink out of a brown bottle that had no label. I remembered those old westerns where everybody always had a bottle of whiskey on their table, and I told her to give me the bottle.

"I can't do that!"

"Why not?"

"This shit a buck-fifty a shot," she said.

I pulled out a hundred-dollar bill and put it on the counter.

She looked at it for a moment and told me to wait and then walked over to where the old man was. She leaned down close to him and said something, motioning back to me a couple of times. The old man glanced over at me, but it was too dark to see whether or not he said anything. She came back, pushed the money back to me, and handed over the bottle.

"Goodbye," she said.

I turned with the bottle, remembered, then fished another hundred out of my jeans, put one in her tip jar and walked up to the stage and dropped the other into a guitar case that was lying open. No one on stage even glanced down at me.

J. and Max lifted a couple of eyebrows apiece when I came back to the table, but they didn't say anything.

The old man next to us looked me over as if for the first time, and then motioned me to join him. I gathered up my bottle and two cups and went and sat at his table.

He poured a couple of drinks out of the bottle.

"If you gonna try ta keep up, you best off right here," he said. He also said his name was J. C.

I thanked him.

J. C. looked at me for a moment then said, "You ever wander around, 'lone and lost?"

"Yeah, it's happened."

"Ever have a woman to help you through?"

"I guess," I shrugged. "In what way?"

"Don't matter what way. Any way."

"Old woman?" I asked, not knowing for the life of me why.

J. C. smiled and leaned back, laughing and tapping his fingers on the table. "Boy, she ain't always old."

Then one of the singers cried out, and I and the rest of the crowd howled back, and as it all started again, I thought of the old woman from the wilderness and finally it came to me that I'd been witness to power, a real power, walking unveiled.

Chapter 63

That's the last thing, in the strictest sense of the word, that I remember. In the freeform, impressionistic sense of the word, there is much, much more.

Darkness and smoke, of course, and later, the wet, clammy floor. But first was the feeling that something had cut the connection between my mind and body. J. C. poured and we both drank while the music throbbed through me, bridging the gap caused by the whiskey, or whatever it was, between thinking and doing. My mind was filled with images of rivers and mud, God and pain, of slogging through stands of cypress trees while water splashed around my thighs and moss hung down to blind me, or to point the way. Dogs howled and children screamed, and I thought about the pain, not just mine, or just anyone's, but all of it, a nightmare four hundred years in the making. And I figured that, until the end, I could just never apprehend, let alone understand, it.

And I danced. Not well—because I've never liked dancing nor felt comfortable at it—but with abandon and with women I'd never seen enter the bar, who'd come with men who just laughed and clapped and poured more drinks, and J. and Max were there to the end, though for me, just in flashes and always watching.

Every now and then, when I whirled past the table, I'd see J. C. laughing and pouring more whiskey and always yelling at me to keep up.

The walls closed in as the music faded away, and I lay on the floor with my ear pressed to the concrete, listening to the throb of all the sins and blessings borne by the soul of the city intermingled with my heart's blood-song coursing through my veins. And I sank down and down, deeper than ever before, into a place so vast and still that even the darkest of dreams dared not enter.

Chapter 64

There's nothing quite like a moonshine whiskey hangover. Some liquors—like rum—cause more pain, but none has the tenacity of homemade whiskey.

J. and Max first came down to my room around seven or so and started banging on the door. I answered around nine or ten.

"Well, if it isn't John Barleycorn," J. snorted.

"Arraagh," I said.

"How do you feel?" Max asked.

"How do I look?"

"I was hopin' you felt better'n that," Max said kindly.

"I guess Graceland is off for this morning," J. said, looking at me not unkindly. "And anyway, I'm going to go look for something to accentuate my outfit so it'll be perfect."

Max looked at J. lovingly.

"You brought a special outfit just for the tour?"

"Of course," J. said.

Max looked down at her faded jeans and wrinkled shirt.

"Oh."

She bit her lip. I was too hungover to withstand any more pain, and though as with most, I usually have an endless capacity to bear the sufferings of others, I wasn't up for it that day. I rolled over in bed and grabbed my jeans off the floor. I took four hundred dollars out of my wallet and gave it to Max.

"Go get something nice and tasteful. No boots or spurs or anything else that might make someone think you're a person of the cows. Let Julie pick it out."

"Well, Colin, I . . ." Max started.

"Don't," I said. "Noise must not happen in this room today."

J. smiled and, placing her hand in the small of Max's back, guided her to the door.

A thought struck me, and I reached back into my wallet and got out my Valero card.

"Better take this too. And be careful. There's humans out there."

Chapter 65

I went into the bathroom and turned on the shower, then went and lay down on the bed to wait for the hot water to come up. Dozing off, I slept all afternoon and, at some point, a dream stole quietly upon me.

I was in a small mountain village, surrounded by evergreens and boulders. It was high and just below the tree line, and though it was late summer, the cold air stung my face and burned in my lungs. As I walked, the aromatic smell of smoke from someone's cookfire clung low to the ground.

A stream flowed down one side of the path and collected in a pool at the edge of the village, where a bridge made of rough-hewn stone crossed it, and suddenly, a wounded elk burst out of the trees and onto the path in front of me. It was bleeding from the shoulder and struggled to stay on its feet.

Some children from the town came to me. The oldest boy was carrying an old bolt-action rifle and marching towards me; he stopped and stiffly presented it to me. The other children watched in expectation.

The elk was standing lock-legged in the road, but as I began to walk towards it, the elk leapt into the stream and was swept down to the pool by the bridge.

I ran down to the water's edge, watched the flow and eddy, and waited for the elk to surface.

Minutes passed, then finally the elk made it to the other side of the pool, dragged itself ashore and lay down, gasping raggedly for breath. At first, the injury didn't seem all that bad, but as the elk moved, its wound tore open and thick, clotted blood coursed down its side and transformed the dry ground into a rich red mud as the animal slowly returned to dust.

I walked across the bridge and tried to make the children wait for me, but instead they followed. There were no sounds except the water and the labored breathing of the stag, and the children joined hands and made a half-moon shape behind me, with me in the center.

Stepping closer to the animal as it lay on the ground, I raised the rifle and aimed carefully to shoot through its head, but the gun exploded in my hands, and as white fire surged through my skull, I realized I'd been forever blinded.

The children were giggling when they left me, and I crawled in circles trying, with no luck, to get back to the sanctuary of the village. Realizing the futility, I made my way back to the dying elk. I could feel its shallow breathing and almost taste the odor of our comingling blood as I lay close, hoping to steal its body heat for whatever remained because, though I'd never see again, I could smell the coming nightfall.

Chapter 66

I woke up and was afraid to open my eyes for several minutes, but finally did and had to squint against the late afternoon sun that glowed against the wall, the color of molten steel. The room was hot and stale-smelling, and I'd sweated clean through my clothes. Even the sheets were wet. I decided it was time to get up and about.

Opening the bathroom door, clouds billowed out, and as they cleared I saw that I had managed to steam the paper completely off the walls. It lay in a great, rubbery mass on the floor and hung in foot-wide strips from the ceiling. Pretty sure it looked like a brain tumor, or maybe a dinosaur tapeworm, though I've never seen either.

I shut the water off then called room service and told them there was a problem with my room and I would need a new one immediately. Hanging up, I realized more was needed, so I called back and asked them to bring up a large bottle of Pedialyte, some Advil, and two double meat cheeseburgers. I told them to put it on my Valero card. They said they didn't take Valero and I'd have to wait a couple of hours at least before changing rooms. Typical, of course. You can always gauge the luxury level of a hotel by the number of services they either don't offer or do offer but charge for; the higher the room rate, the fewer services are available gratis.

After eating half a bottle of Advil and half a burger, I went on into the bathroom where I rolled the wallpaper into a huge ball and shoved it into the corner, showered and shaved, got dressed, and waited for J. and Max. It didn't take long.

They came up and banged on the door for me to let them in so they could show off Max's new things. J. must have added some to the money I gave Max, because she had about three new outfits, and per usual with J., they were sharp. How a game warden from Arizona ever got that kind of taste in clothes, particularly women's, was beyond me.

After I'd seen everything, J. suggested to Max that she go get ready for the tour. J. stayed in my room.

"Here's your card back. We filled the car up and bought a camera, but paid cash. Thanks anyway."

"Why didn't you use the card?"

"No reason," J. said.

"Whatever," I said. "Well, I saw what she got, so what'd you get?"

"Just a hair comb. Found it at an antique store."

"That all?"

"Well, the lady said it had belonged to Priscilla," J. said.

"Surely you don't believe that?"

"Oh, I don't know. I'd have bought it anyway. Hang on." J. walked into the bathroom and flipped on the light. "Holy shit!" She stuck her head out the door. "Colin?"

"Max looks pretty good," I said. "Jealous?"

"What happened?"

"I left the shower on too long."

"You were in the shower long enough to steam the paper off the walls?"

"Of course not. I turned the shower on and fell asleep. Now, are you jealous?"

"Of . . ." J. looked back into the bathroom, and then turned back to me. "Oh. Max? Maybe."

"I wonder who she might be dressing up for?"

"Stop right there. I know she was in here with you the other night," J. said and looked off. Things seemed to be headed that way again.

"Boy *was* she. She was definitely here the other night. *All* here." I laughed and added one more "Whew!"

"You know she isn't just another college girl for you to treat like a slut, Colin," J. said with anger rising in her voice. "Case you hadn't noticed."

"Well, I've noticed a lot of things about Max, but that's not one of them," I said lightly. I whistled a few bars of "Love Me Tender."

J. started grinding her teeth together and flexing the muscles in her jaws, while this huge vein swelled up through the makeup on her forehead, so large that I could see it pumping with blood.

"Yeah, like what, you little son of a bitch?"

"That she wants one us of badly," I said and waited for a few long seconds. "And it ain't me."

J. took this in. "Come again?"

"Ain't me."

She waited for me to say something snarky, and when I didn't, the tension slipped from her body.

"Oh. Well, umm, well, what was she doin' in here for three hours the other night then?"

"Crying her eyes out over you, mostly. Is that a song title?"

"I think so."

"Well, if it isn't, it ought to be."

"I haven't done anything to make her cry," J. said.

"No?"

"No. Nothing." She looked at me again. "Have I?"

"Oh, only make her think she's on the verge of becoming a raging lesbian—present company excepted, of course. Can't see why the forced reevaluation of something as unimportant as one's sexual orientation, or reorientation, should bother her."

"I'm not gay," J. said absent mindedly.

"I know," I said. "Force of habit. And as for her, she isn't either. She just thinks she is. What are you gonna do, anyway? Are you gonna tell her?"

"No."

"Why?"

"Because she'd think it pretty odd for me to confess that I'm really a man and then dress up like you-know-who and go to Graceland."

I cleared my throat politely. "Well dammit, Janet, we can't have that," I said.

J. didn't bother to reply; she just looked off towards, but not out, the window, not at anything really. Maybe the fact that something as seemingly inconsequential as dress might wreak havoc on the lives of people we'd never know was unfolding in her mind.

"What are you thinking about?" I asked.

"I think it's my fault."

"No," I said. "I stole the car and did . . . other things."

"Yeah, but I forced your hand—so to speak—and now we're here and Max is involved too."

"Well . . ." I started, as J. looked over at me, "you're right. It *is* all your fault." I was grinning like a sixteen-year-old who'd gotten to third base on his first car date. "I'm glad that's settled."

You can always count on me to not take the blame.

Chapter 67

About that time, a quick knock on the door and Max glided into the room wearing a matching navy blue tailored jacket and skirt, linen blouse, ruby red clutch, and her face . . . well, her face . . . I about fell out of my chair. Twenty-five years old or I'm Cotton Mather. She told us later that she'd managed to slip into the hotel salon and asked the lady to make her look gorgeous. And that's just what the blessed woman did.

The stylist must have had the hands and the will of an artiste, as she'd cut off about four inches of Max's hair and worked it to full effect, leaving Max with one of those bouncy cuts that seem to be impervious to wind, water, fire, brimstone, or other acts of God and man.

While her hair was drying, they'd thrown in a free mani-pedi, given her a facial, and then applied—I think that's the word—her makeup. J. was good, but the she-devil downstairs was plugged into an elemental and clearly chthonic source.

J. and I just stared at her until she started to get nervous.

"What?" she asked, frowning down at her outfit. She tugged at her skirt a little, then lightly ran the flat of her hand down her ribs and stomach. "I look fat? What's got all over you two?"

I slowly shook my head, grinning like . . . well, like none of your business, and said, "Nothing, nothing at all. You look fantastic," feeling more than a twinge of jealousy directed at J. and I meant it. Max was smoking, smoldering, screaming hot.

I think J. was struggling with some kind of personal crisis, along the lines of wishing she looked that good and trying not to drag Max down to her bedroom. Not that Max would've put up much of a fight, I think.

So I intervened. "Julie, you best get dressed. You can find Max and me at the bar, sipping expensive champagne and looking très chic."

J. left with nary a whimper, but was looking over her shoulder and bumped into the doorframe on her way out. Max had watched her the whole time and then turned to me.

"I'll go to the bar with you. We're friends, but I done already told you that, if I can, I'm gonna be with Julie. I'm through with men."

I offered my arm, but when she just looked at it like, *"Yeah?"* I took her left hand and, placing it in the crook of my elbow, said, "Of course you are." Max looked at me narrowly. "No one's ever accused me of being a man," I finished.

Chapter 68

In the bar, I was having a hard time staying focused on the usual chitchat because, like everyone else in there, I couldn't keep my eyes, and mind, off Max. It wasn't that I particularly wanted her or anything, so much as I just couldn't get over how good she looked.

The waitress walked up and just smiled at her like "Hello, beautiful!" as Max warily noted the attention of several others—men *and* women.

Looking over the menu, I was suddenly hungry and figured that eating might take my mind off Max, so I ordered the calamari and a Heineken; Max ordered something called a "Hello Kitty." In no time flat, the waitress was back with the appetizer, and Max just stared at it.

"What," she asked, "is *that*?"

"Calamari," I said. "You know, squid."

She continued to stare.

"From the ocean . . . seafood that's good for you?" I added.

"Looks like deep-fried chicken assholes."

Looking at it from that perspective, I lost my appetite. She was right, though I don't know why that comparison would occur to anyone. But the beer was good and cold.

Max was fidgety and tense and barely touched her drink. I don't know if it was the calamari disaster or what, but our conversation was awkward and strange. This was all about to change.

My back was to the door, but I knew the moment that J. walked in. Max straightened in her chair, and all eyes turned to behold J., turned out like an incarnated Priscilla Beaulieu Presley, circa 1965. Specifically: a sporty, knit, baby-doll-style mini-dress in buttercup yellow, with opaque tights and white patent platform pumps. Accentuating this madness: a white vinyl clutch with a yellow daisy—or maybe a sunflower—clasp, white kid gloves, and cat-eye glasses. And yeah, she'd redone her makeup: high eyebrows, false black lashes, wide eyes with kohl eyeliner, pancake and powder to provide contrast (technical data courtesy of J. herself), beige lipstick, and a jet black, Ann Margaret bombshell 'do with all kinds of falls and hairpieces. Her new comb held everything in place.

She beamed at us like a lighthouse sent to save the damned. Problem was, Max and I were the only ones who knew who she looked like.

Chapter 69

On the way across town, a familiar question detached itself from the rest.

"Since we're so close now, tell me what it is you've got to do when you get to Graceland. You said that when the time came, you'd tell me. I've driven you across six different states, through rainstorms and droughts, ruined weddings, started and run from fights in bars, hotels, and the spaces in between. Max—hot as she may be—set my stepfather's car on fire. I've had recurring nightmares that will follow me to my grave and used my Valero card so much the numbers are almost worn off. In short," I said, "it's time."

J. gave me a long, evaluative look then said, "No, it isn't."

Chapter 70

We finally got to Graceland, and regardless of anything else I may have to say about it, I have to cede one point: for a private residence that has five people buried prominently in the back yard, it's about as tasteful as can be.

I paid for all our tickets, then we boarded a bus that took our tour group all the way across the street. I guess, given where we were, it was a fairly normal crowd, which I broke into two categories: normal folk, like myself, J., and Max; and the weirdos, à la the Domino's Pizza delivery man who said he "moonlighted as an Elvis impersonator and was waiting for that break from the Man."

Also included in our group was a reporter from the *National Enquirer*. She came in talking about free speech and freedom of the press and how she was the Chief Subordinate in Charge of the Elvis Files at the *Enquirer*. All of this was intended to place her as the Elvis Expert in our group, but looking around, I could tell there were few believers. Some of the more gullible took to her, though, and began asking her about recent Elvis sightings at laundromats and supermarket openings.

J. was mad at her because neither she nor anyone else had started screaming "Priscilla!" and begging for her autograph when we boarded the bus.

I toyed with the idea of a subgroup comprised of people who resisted immediate categorization, but scrapped it. There weren't that many of them anyway.

On the outside, Graceland wasn't what I expected. I thought it would be a flashy, modern house surrounded by miles and miles of manicured lawn, high-end cars favored by the eurotrash, palm trees . . . Instead, it was a fairly modest, old two-story colonial house that Elvis had bought then remodeled. It was fancy for its time and well-built, but wouldn't have made a guest house in my neighborhood back home. Placed in the middle of a landscaped, fourteen-acre lot, Graceland provided a soothing oasis in contrast to the rest of an area besieged with liquor stores, check cashing/title loan businesses, used car lots, vacant houses, a couple of burned-out restaurants . . . inner-city squalor that had metastasized into everywhere else.

Not so the inside. The interior decorator of Graceland must have been from the same school as the decorator who'd done the Alamo-style whorehouse back in Arizona. The interior got stranger the deeper into the heart of the house we went. J. and Max were enraptured and kept nodding approvingly to each other at various and sundry things that just made me wince.

Like the staircase. Both walls and the ceiling had mirrors covering every square inch of them. Narcissism run amok. I had to hold onto the railing just to keep my balance, and I still nearly stepped on some woman's head that I took for a reflection.

The pizza man, along with J. and the rest of the pilgrims, liked it, though. He looked at me and smiled. "When ahhm deliverin' mah pizzas tonight, ahhm gonna be thinkin' a that staircase, man. In homage." He really said that.

"Your cabin is two-story, ain't it, Julie?" Max asked.

J. nodded slowly, the head gears turning.

Our tour guide let us leave the dining room and took us into a hall that led to the back of the house. She said it was unfortunate, but that as the house was still a private residence, no one was allowed upstairs. She said we'd descend the stairs and go visit the TV room, where Elvis had ripped off Lyndon Baines Johnson's idea of having three television sets side by side so that he could triple his audio/visual intake by watching every network. All three of them.

About that time, the lady from the *Enquirer* mentioned, in sort of an offhand way, that the real reason no one was allowed upstairs was because Elvis was still alive, but that he was a hopeless drug addict and they kept him locked up in what used to be his old bedroom. She went on to say that he had ballooned to 427 and 3/4 pounds, and that all anyone ever saw of him was one grubby, paw-like hand that snatched his opiate-laced pizzas and deep-fried Twinkies through the feed slot in his door.

The tour guide bore this patiently and started to lead the group on, but J. said, "Wait a minute."

Then she walked over to the reporter and, grabbing her by the lapels of her suit, picked her up so that just the tips of her shoes scraped against the floor.

"I've been ignoring the stories your filthy-trash magazine's been printing about the King for twelve years. And when I finally get to Graceland, of the one million people who have come through it, I have to get stuck on the tour that has you on it. I'm only gonna say this once: Elvis died in 1977 in this house and they buried him. End of story. Got that?"

The reporter, eyes wide as saucers, nodded yes, she got that. J. set her back down to a smattering of applause from the rest of the group.

One of the other women, evidently afraid that she might be next, cleared her throat.

"Ma'am?"

J. turned and looked at her.

"I don't, um, you know, really think Elvis is still alive either. But, but the way they say he died . . . I just don't think the King would've gone like that. I mean . . ." she trailed off.

"I don't know," J. said. "But my grandfather said that the bravest, fiercest Indian fighter he ever met died in a rocking chair, so I guess the way you live your life doesn't guarantee the end will justify itself."

Several people in the group nodded in agreement. The tour guide reverently said it was time to move out.

Chapter 71

I was the last person in our group, and as I waited to go down the stairs, I heard a faint rasping noise. My eyes followed the curve of the banister, and I looked up to the forbidden rooms. One of the doors was cracked open, and by the light of the crystal chandelier, I could just make out a piercing blue eye looking down at me. I looked back to our group leader as she and an older woman disappeared down the stairs toward the back of the house, but she was confiscating the old woman's camera and didn't see me.

I stepped quickly to the foot of the stairs just as an old woman, who might have been some relation to Elvis, ran down the stairs to me.

"Where'd she go?" she asked.

"Who?"

"I thought I saw Priscilla," she said. Then she looked at me, and there was something familiar about her smile. "Maybe I'm just a foolish old woman." Then she turned and walked back up the stairs as the person in the room tossed a carefully folded paper airplane to me.

She turned at the head of the staircase and watched as the airplane see-sawed back and forth then fell at my feet. It had Elvis' TCB and lightning bolt logo embossed on both wings. I scooped it up just as the nasal voice of the tour guide rang out, "Sir, this way! Now!"

I glanced up to the room, and as I watched, the woman I'd spoken to transformed into the old woman from the desert. She smiled at me, made a face at the tour guide, who evidently couldn't see her, and faded from view.

I nodded a furtive "yes" and followed the group downstairs.

Chapter 72

The next circle of hell we visited was the so-called "Jungle Room," named by Lyndon B. Johnson himself, in reaction to the most hideous collection of amateurishly-carved furniture I've never even heard of. Evidently, Elvis thought the name was a compliment, because he took to referring to it as the "Jungle Room" himself and began spending an inordinate amount of time there.

Our tour guide informed us that it took the King only about thirty minutes to pick out the wreckage, pay for it, and arrange for delivery. Given the amount of time it takes to set up, say, a smart phone or a laptop, I figured that Elvis probably took ten minutes in actual selection time and devoted the rest to convincing the salesman he was really serious about wanting that junk.

The paper plane burned like a live coal in my pocket, and it dawned slowly, as I had finally realized ideas are wont to do with me, that apart from its sophisticated, aerodynamic design, linen paper construction, and reasonably cool logo, there might be a message on it. Evidently, the tour guide had decided I was one to watch, and she made it a point to stay close to me. That, added to the surveillance cameras jutting out from behind curtains, through the leaves of plants, and everywhere else, made it next to impossible to do anything without it being documented. I decided I'd have to wait.

J. and Max were, as the rest, unaware of what had transpired between me and the staircase, particularly the reappearance of the old woman from the desert, and maybe that was for the best.

During the visit to the trophy room, I managed to slip out and was in the process of dragging the communiqué out of my pocket when J. and Max caught up with me.

"Hey, hon, wher'd ya go?" Max asked.

"Oh, I needed a little air."

"It is kinda breathtakin', ain't it? I mean, knowin' that Elvis Presley wore them clothes and won them awards and walked around out here. I bet he stood right where I am right now," she straightened her back and smiled down at her feet.

"Maybe he was wearing some of those clothes and holding a gold record or two while he was doing it," I said.

Max laughed and I looked at J.

"What are you doing out here?"

"Well, the trophy room is nice, but I've seen a lot of pictures of it," J. said. "I wanted to look over the grounds. Particularly over there." She motioned to where the graves of Elvis and some of his family had been placed for protection from vandals.

"Your plans don't include that, do they?" I heard myself asking. "I mean, you didn't, you know, bring a shovel or anything?"

"What are you talking about?"

"I'm still trying to figure out your plans. I was worried that maybe you thought of trying to take Elvis back to Arizona, let the drier clime preserve his body. Prop him up at the head of the dining room table." By then they were both looking at me the way they sometimes did.

"Hell, I don't know," I said. "I'm just spit-balling here."

"Huh? No, of course not. I may be crazy for Elvis, but I don't want to dig him up and take him home with me," J. said.

"Good. I think there are rules prohibiting that. By the way, did anybody peg who you're impersonating?"

J. looked a little annoyed.

"No. Hayseeds. You would think that a lemon-colored smock dress with three huge buttons up the front—something you'd never see after 1967—white gloves, cat-eye sunglasses, and the rest would tip them off."

"Yeah," Max said. "Not to mention the heavy eye shadow and that black wig. Who'd wear a beehive hairdo these days?"

"And not have ulterior motives, you mean?" I asked. They gave me the look again. "I'm just kidding . . . geez, you chicks. Anyway, the comb looks nice. Don't let them not noticing drag you down; it's not for them anyway. Did you see anything strange back there at the house? I mean, other than the decor?"

"What's wrong with the . . . uh . . . whatever you said?" Max said defensively.

"Like what?" J. said. "And besides, I bet if your house hadn't been redone since the seventies, it'd show its age also."

"Like about the upstairs."

"We didn't go upstairs. Did you?" J. was suddenly very interested.

"Started to, but Ms. Mussolini stopped me."

"Yeah, did you see her take that old woman's phone away and delete all her pictures?" Max asked sullenly.

"Yeah. Now what about the upstairs?" J. asked.

"I don't know. I thought I saw someone is all."

"Oh no, not you too," Max said. "Julie almost killed that reporter."

J. eyed me speculatively and was about to say something, when suddenly our guide yelled at us that the tour was over and we could wander around near the graves if we liked or we could leave. Judging by the way she looked at us, she preferred the latter.

I started to tell them about the paper airplane and the old woman, but stopped again, though I'm not sure why.

Max said she wanted to go look at the car exhibit, and J. said we'd be over shortly.

We found a bench under a huge oak tree and sat down.

"And did you accomplish what you came to do?" I asked.

"No," J. said. "Not yet. It won't be much longer now."

"What about Max?"

"What about her?" she snapped.

I said nothing. After a moment, J. sighed and slumped a bit.

"I don't know . . . since my wife took off four years ago, I haven't dated much." She paused. "I haven't dated at all." She looked off.

"Your particular manner of dress might have some bearing on that. Wide Ruin doesn't seem like the kind of place where open-minded women abound." I looked at her and suddenly realized just how much I'd come to like—*really* like—her. "You'd do better in Dallas or Houston," I said, wishing I knew what to say, or how to say what I felt. "Phoenix maybe."

"I just started dressing like this a year or so ago."

"Huh?"

"I didn't cross-dress before. And actually, I thought that since there are eight million Elvis impersonators, I'd had a good idea. I showed up at Rosie's one day—as Priscilla—to see what my friends, or who I thought were my friends, would say about my idea to be a Priscilla Presley impersonator."

"And?"

"You'd think I'd have guessed. At first they just laughed and acted like I was some sort of freak show. Later, it was worse. Much worse."

"Why didn't you just give up? That's what I would've done," I said.

"Like the way you've given up on your grandparents? Or are you still going to make that visit?"

"It's not that I've given up, but no, that's not gonna work out," I said.

"I think you should."

"I wish I could; I really do," I said. "I only got to see them three or four times before they died."

J. just looked at me and then nodded her head a little. "What was that about going up there, then? Just another lie?"

"Not a complete lie. Their old house is still out there somewhere, and my mom still owns it. She and Ralph pay an old couple to look after it. My grandparents are buried there too. It wasn't much of a plan, but I figured on trying to find it, though I don't know why or what I expected. As for Ralph, he's really not a bad guy. I just treat him like shit because of who he *isn't*." I'd never really thought of that before.

"Some introspection? So maybe there's more to you after all." She smiled at me. "And as for the yahoos in Wide Ruin? There was no way I was going to let them get away with humiliating me into changing. I decided not to make them that important, so I started dressing like a woman a lot after that." She looked at me for a long moment. "You know, it's not like I expect you or anyone else to understand."

"That's good, because it makes no sense whatsoever," I said.

J. squinted a bit. "Well, you might be surprised to discover that most people would say stealing a car just because you're a spoiled little turd and don't like your stepdad doesn't make a whole lot of sense either," J. said. "Particularly, as you intended to drive it to a place that doesn't exist anymore, for you to visit people you don't know, because you've suddenly decided you want to see some other people who aren't alive."

I looked at her and shrugged. "Yeah. When you put it like that, I guess that doesn't make any sense either."

Then she smiled. "Wrong. It's the only thing you've done that does make any sense," she said.

I just looked at her with that dumb look that I was coming to realize suited me well. Finally, I said, "I don't get it."

"You never do," J. smiled again. "It, your grandparent's home, does still exist, moron, but now it's just a physical place, a house occupied by strangers. But as memory—a good memory—of better times or their home, your dad, and your family, it still does. That's the reason Elvis is so important, not so much because he had a great voice, was handsome, and a groundbreaker . . . it's not that. It's because of what he represented—and still represents—to countless millions of people around the world. For decades."

She was right, of course. She usually was. But I wasn't ready, I guess, so I decided to get back to the topic of her.

"Okay, whatever. Back to you. Now you like dressing like a woman?"

"Yeah, I kind of do."

"Uh-huh . . . let's leave that one alone for now and go back to Max. She's starting to get that nervous tint about her."

"Yeah, I know."

"What are you going to tell her? Anything?"

"Well, of course it depends on what happens tonight. After I finish up here."

I knew better than to ask about that, so I took a different approach.

"Is something going to happen? Do you expect that you, or something else, will change?"

"I don't know what I expect."

I couldn't really fault her for that. Dale and Howard were still at large, and they were close too.

As if she were reading my mind, J. asked, "What about the twins?"

"I guess they're waiting for me on the other side of that wall," I said.

"What are you going to do?"

"Oh, I'll make out, I guess. Maybe shoot both of them. Say I was cleaning my gun."

"You got a gun?"

"Been meaning to get one. Really, I guess my choices are to keep running or just go back with them. They're really not bad guys, any more than Ralph. He likes to act like they're his muscle, even though there's not much need for that kind of help in his industry; he likes the idea of it. Before them, he had the real thing, though. I guess it's the same thing that makes accountants buy attack dogs, thinking it'll offer protection they don't need from something they can't name right up until the day they get bitten. This guy's name was Patrick, of all things. Big Irish guy that Ralph recruited right out of prison. He got so bad that everyone was afraid to go to work. Luckily, he got busted at an underground poker game—parole violation—and got sent back to prison. Ralph still hears from him occasionally. Death threats, that sort of thing, even though Ralph had nothing to do with it."

"Video rentals. That really is what your father does?"

"Yeah, nationwide chain. That and play gangster. Some guys think they're cowboys, some guys think they're—" I looked at J. and thought a course correction was in order, "uh, something else . . . anyway, he wants to turn it into a real stepfather/stepson business."

"What's your mom do?"

"Valium, mostly." J. started to speak, and I cut her off. "Joking. Golf at the country club and church work."

"Not turning back in Oklahoma is going to cause some trouble, huh?"

"Well, I still have an ace-in-the-hole back in Dallas, I guess."

"What?" J. asked.

"A little of Gianfranco's money. It's no fortune, but it'll see me through for four, maybe five months. Surely in five months I'll have some answers."

She looked at me for a long moment. "Let's get Max and finish this," J. said.

Chapter 73

We found Max waiting outside at the car museum, where she immediately pronounced everything inside as junk that she wouldn't steal if she had a gun to her head, which I doubted, but whatever.

J. asked us to follow her across the street and back to the wall around Graceland, where we found untold thousands of names, dates, and messages to Elvis. Other communications were scrawled, scratched, painted, and otherwise recorded on the stones of the retaining wall.

Taking a black Sharpie from her clutch, J. wrote something on the wall and then told Max to read it. Max did, and then looked at J., stood on her tiptoes, and kissed her on the cheek. When she pulled back, Max had a strange look on her face. For that matter, we all did.

J. handed me the disposable camera she'd bought and asked me to photograph them.

After I took the picture, J. motioned me to the wall. She and Max stepped aside.

In neat block letters, J. had written:

Dear Elvis,

We dropped by, but you weren't home. We're sorry and we miss you.

Julie, Max, and Colin

I stepped back. Then I read it again, just to make sure I hadn't missed something. I hadn't.

J. and Max were looking at me expectantly.

"Is that it?" I asked. "We drove 1500 miles for you to write 'Sorry we missed you'?"

"That's it."

Max shook her head. "Don't you understand?"

"I guess I don't," I shot back. "I was kidnapped so that she could deface a wall. That doesn't make a whole lot of sense to me."

"He doesn't get it," J. said. "Maybe someday he will."

They took off walking in the direction of the parking lot, holding hands. As I watched them, I couldn't help but wonder what would happen when they were back in Arizona, beyond the sanctuary of Graceland.

I suddenly remembered the airplane note in my pocket.

I took it out, unfolded it, and read the message that was written in a graceful, cursive-style lettering:

> I'm doin' it my way . . .
>
> E.
>
> P.S. Tell J. she knows how to TCB. That comb was my favorite.

Suddenly, the logic and correctness of what J. had written unfolded and expanded in my mind exponentially, out like ripples in calm water, and up, gaining momentum, wave upon wave, at ever-increasing speed, until it was one undivided, massive wave. A Logic Tsunami.

I ran to catch them.

Chapter 74

They were standing off to one side of the parking lot, using the slender shadow of a light pole for cover and staring at the Cadillac. The twins were sitting in it.

"Now what?" J. asked as I walked up.

"What happened to you?" Max asked me.

I didn't say anything, but led them back to the ticket counter at the main building, pulled out my phone, opened the Uber app, and ordered an "Uber Black" sedan. Pulling a hundred-dollar bill from my hip pocket, I placed it face up on the counter and asked the girl manning it to wait fifteen minutes after we were gone, then page the two guys in the pink Cadillac and tell them they had a message from Colin. I asked her for an envelope and put the car key in it.

"Give this to them."

"All right," she said, looking at the money. "Anything else?"

"Tell them I'm at MEM." Yeah, I googled the Memphis airport code; it's not like I'd just know shit like that. Anyway, I was ready for travel of a different sort and saw no sense making it simple for the twins.

I slid the bill towards her using my pointy finger, but kept it pinned down as she put her own finger right in the middle of Ben Franklin's smirk. She looked up at me. "Fifteen minutes," I repeated.

She smiled. "You got it!"

I released Ben into the wild.

Chapter 75

The Uber driver was named Francine. It'd obviously been over twenty years since she'd turned thirteen, and I damn near abandoned my evolving plan in the nano-second it took for her beauty to register. She had a type of "rain, shine, whatever" perpetual beauty, and she flashed an incandescent, life-proof smile in the rearview mirror every time she spoke to me. But much as I wanted to loiter in the MEM area code and use rideshare, duty beckoned, as I'd placed myself on a timetable. On the ride to the airport, I reserved two airline tickets to DFW (Dallas; that one I knew) and took an earnest vow—as in, one I actually meant—that in the future I'd take more Uber rides.

At the ticket counter, I gave the attendant the record locater code as J. and Max looked on at a complete loss as to what I was doing, but I ignored them and used some points on Gianfranco's American Airlines credit card to upgrade them to first class. Dallas.

"Here. Take these," I said, handing them their boarding passes. "Both of you do have a valid i.d., right?"

Neither spoke, but a slow grin began to seep into Max's face. J. dropped her shoulders a bit, reached out, and lightly slapped my shoulder.

"We'll send you some money for them when—"

"Forget it," I said.

I slipped Max the key to Gianfranco's locker at DFW airport.

"And this. You'll be needing what's in the locker. After you get to Dallas, you can either fly on to Arizona, hitchhike, take the bus, steal a ride, or rent a car. If you opt to rent a car, get unlimited mileage and say you're not leaving Texas," I said. "If you steal a car and it goes sideways, call me; Dad has a battery of lawyers."

"Dad? J. asked.

"Yeah," I said. "I think it's time to start calling him that."

"What are *you* going to do?" Max asked.

"Wait for the twins. Can I have a word?" I gestured to J. with a nod over my shoulder.

We stepped out of earshot of Max.

"I'm just curious. You going to tell her before Arizona or not?"

"She'll figure it out," J. said.

"Particularly if you do that panty key dangling bit for her, like you did for me—"

"No," she said. "She's much more perceptive than you."

I couldn't argue the point.

"Y'all are going back to Arizona, right?"

"For a while, at least. How can we contact you?"

"I gave Max my cell number. If she loses it—or, more likely, tosses it—call Joe at Rosie's. He's got it. When I figure out my next move, I'll try to reach you at that diner in Wide Ruin."

J. just shook her head as if the dog she was backing for "Best of Show" had just hiked a leg at one of the judges. Then she pulled her own cell out—a phone I didn't even know she had—punched in some numbers, and suddenly mine was buzzing to let me know I had a new contact.

"You—"

"Don't we all?"

"How did you get my—"

She just shook her head.

"Stay in touch. Promise?"

"Probably."

"Probably?"

"Maybe?" I said.

"I know I can't trust you," she said.

"Hell no," I said.

"Fair enough. Look, I—-"

"Don't. I had a good time. For the most part. Now, if you'll excuse me, here comes my ride."

About that time, I heard a familiar pair of voices.

"Hey! You!" Gino and Guido shouted as they ran toward us, simultaneously grinning and slapping each other on the back. J. leaned forward into a protective stance, but I caught her arm.

"No," I said. They ran up and stopped. Gino, or maybe it was Guido, said, "We've got you now!"

228

"Shut up," I said. They looked at each other for support. "I think you boys are in for some hard times."

"What'd you mean?" one of them asked.

"Y'all burned Gianfranco's Mercedes," I said grimly. A moment of shocked silence was observed by most. This changed.

"It wasn't us!" they wailed in unison.

"Who then?"

"Somebody else! It got stole—"

Max began inching back in an effort to hide behind J., but I reached back and caught her wrist between my thumb and forefinger.

"What do you think Dad's going to think?" I asked.

"Dad?" I think it was Guido.

"Gianfranco."

"The truth! He knows it was you," Gino (I think) said.

"But I saw y'all do it," I said. I looked over at J., who was smiling sardonically at the twins. I looked back at them. "Pretty sure he'll see it my way," I said. "After all, truth aside, it's easier—and cheaper—to fire two screwups than one stepson."

The twins looked genuinely terrified, and I suddenly felt a little guilty about scaring them. Anyway, I had their attention and lightened up a bit. A good ruler knows when to be generous.

"Go wait for me in the Cadillac. We're gonna run this car over to some guys in Arkansas, then take the Amtrak to Dallas. Try not to attract my attention or otherwise annoy me, and maybe I'll work something out so you don't have to take the blame. Maybe."

They started for the car. "Guido! Gino!" I yelled after them. They stopped and turned around. "Back seat."

J. and Max started laughing.

"You look different," Max said to me.

"Yeah," J. said. "Yeah."

"This is for you," I said, handing the folded note to J. "But wait until I'm gone to read it."

"Okay," she said.

"You really takin' that Caddy back to them boys in Arkansas? How you gonna find 'em?" Max asked.

"Oh, I thought I'd just take it to the barbecue joint, wipe it down really good, and leave it there. That guy's uncle probably has an extra set of keys. If he doesn't, it's high time he got some made."

"Well, it's your car . . ." Max trailed off.

"No," I said. "It isn't. That's the problem. The only thing I really own is that I've been an ass."

J. nodded her head. "I think this trip did you more good than you realize. More than you may ever realize. You're still an ass, but not a complete ass like you were when we met. You're like . . . a half-ass. Or something. Maybe there's hope."

I shrugged my shoulders, and before we said good-bye, I gave them the Valero card.

"Use it in good health and with much abandon," I said. "If it ever gets canceled, you'll know things didn't work out, family-wise, at least not in the way I'm hoping for."

"Thanks," J. said. "We will." Max just shook her head.

I walked away from them then, towards the exit of the Memphis Airport that led to the parking lot where I knew the twins were waiting patiently in the back of the '59 Cadillac Coupe de Ville. The automatic glass doors opened, and I stepped out into the afternoon sunlight, then turned around and looked back.

Hundreds of people were bustling about, trying to catch flights, find loved ones, decipher the flight boards, ferret out which gate was theirs, in short, do any of the thousands of other, lesser things that fill our days and years. Max was taking in the scene, sort of leaning towards the throng with a happy, adventurous smile on her face, and of course there was J., towering square and confident in the middle of it all, as big as a myth.

Then the doors hissed back together, and I was left alone, staring at my reflection.